The Silent
Avenger

James Berry

Copyright © 2015 by Jam
The Silent Avenger
By James Berry

Printed in the United States of America

ISBN 978-0-9850048-4-2

Dedication

To Mark, Greg, and Tim

Author's Note:

Romania was an ally of Nazi Germany from 1940 to 1944 and had a Jewish population of 750,000 before World War II. In four years, one-half of the population had been killed, starved, and robbed in the most horrific, barbaric ways. Romania caused more deaths of Jews than any other country in Europe except Nazi Germany. Unlike other countries in Europe where Nazi military killing squads carried out its genocidal acts, in Romania much of it was done by the indigenous citizenry and gendarmes.

Sixty years following the war, the Romanian governments under communism and post-communist regimes carried the mantra of Holocaust deniers, making it one of the best-kept secrets of the war. It wasn't until 2004 that an official government statement was issued acknowledging there had been a Holocaust. Today, in the country of Romania the core Jewish population is less than 10,000.

In recent years, great concern has risen over attempts to rehabilitate the images of convicted and executed Romanian Nazi war criminals. This speaks to the country's continued systemic anti-Semitism. Knowing these historical facts will help the reader follow the story in book two of the Zionist Series, *The Silent Avenger.*

Contents

Prologue

A man stood alone at the side rail of a darkened ship dressed in a black, heavy coat as gusts of moist, cold air stroked his leather-worn face. His eyes gripped the alluring moon's reflections bouncing from the water's surface, followed by ribbons of vapor floating upward, all showing eerie features of ghost-like intangibility. Nature was giving sparkling stage performances for the waiting man.

The large freighter showed no signs of life. It was idle, silent with engines cut low. Wartime measures were in place—no lights—no radio transmissions. The big vessel, like a lurking predator concealing itself from its prey, lingered in darkness, poised, ready to spring when instinct signaled. The lone man aboard the beast of steel was the invisible master of a ship who held the destinies of many now daring to brave the cold waters of the night. While waiting for his mission to unfold, vivid memory took him back to the events of his life that formed him into what he became. *Remembering the history of his personal holocaust brought a cold, riveting chill over what was left of his soul. The man pulled his coat more snuggly around his tall, rigid frame, forced glove-covered hands inside his warm, wool jacket—and waited while memory gave torment—memory that was paradoxical: it was a long time ago, yet it happened yesterday. His pain had no chronological continuum. It was always current, carried on the back of memory.*

Chapter 1

The Making of Executioners

Whoever sheds the blood of man by man
shall his blood be shed. (Genesis 9:6)

It was noontime in a remote Romanian forest, and the smell of cooked fish permeated a campsite nestled under foliage-filled, low-hanging, tree branches. Around the campfire sat three young men who had the appearance of being older than their years with unshaven beards and unkempt hair. Dusty clothes matching the red, lateritic dirt under their feet made them appear as part of the landscape. Fish being cooked on a hot grill over the campfire had been caught the day before and kept on a stringer in the nearby cool stream. It was rustic, raw nature in its most vivid form.

For seven days, the young men had lived in a rugged forest filled with wildlife, all competing for survival. The three visitors from the outside world had become part of the competition living off the land while on a work assignment.

The father of one of the men owned and operated a lumber mill that produced commercial lumber for housing construction and had an adjunct furniture and cabinet shop. The section of forest they were camping in grew an indigenous tree used in making high-end, finished, wood products. The mill had a long-term lease on this section of forest and made annual harvests to meet the demand market. The assignment given the young men was to count and mark harvestable trees before the loggers arrived with their equipment. This was their fourth year of the annual event, an experience they always welcomed. They were best friends, outdoorsmen, had spent a lot of time together through the years hunting, fishing, and camping. Learning to live off the land with the challenges of competing with nature and wildlife had taught them interdependence, trust and methods of survival. The wilderness had elevated and fine-tuned their senses, something necessary in a place where bears, wild boar, and wolves stalked the landscape. In the wild, survival was the mother of invention and it proved to be so with these three. They developed an enhanced visual acuity, heard sounds that carried messages undetected by the novice ear and found that certain smells moved about by gentle breezes carried hidden meaning. It was another world that optimized survival skills.

Entertainment for the three rugged campers included fishing the fish-filled streams and hunting large and small game. Their down times were spent reading. On their camping and hunting ventures, each would bring a book the other two had not read, and their return home was marked close to the time when each party had read all three books. It was their experience of living in the wild that taught them about unrefined nature in glaring terms of survival. Their intelligence exceeded the brute forces of lurking predators, but smarts without experience would always come up short. Experience had taught them that the forest's Eden-like, floral beauty carried a deceptive dual image. Beyond its subtle alluring picture of peace and tranquility lay lurking dangers roaming over the garden floor. It was like the two natures of man. If one accepted only the beauty he saw and denied the ugly roaming over the garden floor, he would never survive the wild.

The three young men were not related but had been childhood friends for as long as they could remember. They had been in the same shul and together had learned their ancient Hebrew language at a young age in a class taught by their Rabbi. Now, that friendship expressed itself in adult bodies.

All three stood in contrast with unique talents and physical differences. The one called Seth was the shorter. He was barrel-chested with dark, curly hair, quick-witted with a flair for mimicry. His family gave him the name of Seth but somehow picked up the sobriquet of Bub, which seemed to fit his personality. Bub at a young age had gone into archery and had developed his skill to the level of winning wide recognition in that field of sport. However, his interest was more is using his talent in hunting wild game than in competition matches. His family owned and operated a market that sold a little of everything from dry goods to locally grown fruits and vegetables.

Moshe was the quiet one among them. He was thin, angular, athletic, and gifted with cerebral qualities. He carried savant traits but was socially and emotionally well-adjusted. Though Bub and Moshe's physical frames stood in contrast, their hair color and texture matched. He was gifted in math and excelled in the game of chess. Everyone knew him as the chess-player-Jew whose father was a tailor. It was an ancient game championed by a descendant of an ancient people who lived precariously among suspicious and sometimes unfriendly neighbors. There were times when he was tempted to lose a chess match so less attention would be drawn to him, but he could never bring himself to it.

Michael was the third member of the group and was the son of the owner of the mill and natural leader of the three. He broke the typical stereotype mold of what a Jew in this region was supposed to look like. He was taller than Moshe, well-proportioned, exhibiting blond hair and blue eyes. Even the pretty goyim girls in town would show him their eyes with a second glance. He was twenty-one years old, engaged to a beautiful girl in his village, and would be married in three months. His perceptive skills allowed him to quickly arrange complicated situations into simplified, actionable responses. He was known to think fast on his feet and rarely lost an argument. His signal trait was never to act on an issue unless all the facts were known. Another skill he showed that had practical results was his insight for invention. At his father's mill, he had created certain mechanical changes that reduced the manual lifting loads of its workers increasing a greater margin of safety and production. Moshe and Bub had come with Michael to the mountains because they often went camping together, were like brothers, and were being paid for their work.

After living in the forest for seven days, everything was packed and ready to be loaded aboard their two motorbikes. The project of measuring, marking, and counting the trees had been completed on the third day, but they chose to extend their stay for another four days. One bike would carry its driver and equipment; the second bike would carry the other two. They were cleaning up the campsite when the sound of another bike was heard coming in their direction. This was unusual. People never came to this region of the forest—it was too remote, dense, and secluded. The three young men looked at each other. Whoever was coming their way was some distance from them, and the narrow trail leading to where they were would require a few minutes to be reached.

Before saying anything, Michael and Moshe grabbed their rifles.

"Let's check this person out before he reaches our camp," said Michael.

Bub's comedic nature showed its other side. He took his bow and satchel of arrows as if he were competing in a championship match. "I'll follow you out of sight," he said.

All their lives the three had learned to survive together in a community of anti-Semites. When in a mixed group of peers it was always safer to be together, and when Michael was with them, even looks of aspersions rarely occurred because of his blond hair. Their initial reaction today to the sound of the coming motorbike came from two sources: their history of negative experiences of anti-Semitism and survival instincts.

Bub lingered behind staying hidden off the side of the trail. Michael and Moshe moved ahead, and as the motorbike neared, they stopped and waited. Bub saw the man's bike come to a stop. He got off slowly and stood near his two friends. He could tell from his distance that they were talking, then he saw the man give Michael what looked like an envelope. Bub sensed a quiet, eerie feeling settling over the event now happening, and like a dark cloud ripping apart the atmosphere with shattering strobes of lightning, everything came at once. Michael fell on his knees, screaming the name, "Rebecca!...Rebecca!...my Rebecca!" Wails of horror from Michael and Moshe reverberated up the trail where Bub was now running in their direction. He knew tragedy had happened to someone, somewhere. He ran as fast as he could to reach his friends who were now beside themselves. He looked at the man who had come in on the bike—it was the foreman at the mill, a friend of the family. Then he heard the news. It was the end of his world, as he knew it. German and Romanian Nazi soldiers, along with certain townspeople, had killed several hundred Jews in their village and all their families were among them. There were no survivors.

The blackest day of history enclosed the three. The stranger who had come in on the bike was now trying to console them. What the foreman dreaded was now being realized. Three beautiful young men that stood like giant trees in the forest had been cut down and were being ripped apart like logs at the mill. Each wished they had died with their families. A veil of despair smothered them in abject hush. Each found a place of solitude to mourn the day they were born. The man who brought the news of death left his bike where it was and slowly made his way to camp, sat on a log knowing it would take time for them to return. He would stay with them for as long as he was needed.

Hours later, they returned to the campsite. The man still sat on the log. Neither spoke. Even the forest yielded to an eerie silence. The greatest evil ever had pushed three young men over a precipice into a pit of despair and hopelessness. They were prisoners to pain, chained to a memory that would destroy the idealism of what was best and good in man. They were made a wasteland, thrown onto a barren, lifeless desert, hearing only voices calling for revenge and justice.

Throughout the night, words were not spoken nor did any sleep. All four watched the burning campfire embers, and the man who gave support to the grieving looked from time-to-time at Michael whose eyes were never taken from the piece of paper handed him when he drove into camp. It was a letter from his sweetheart explaining why she had to take her own life.

The foreman of the mill stayed another day, and before leaving he handed Michael a small booklet, saying, "I have taken time to gather all the information I could about those who participated in the killings, thefts, and rapes. Not being Jewish, people talked freely with me knowing they would never be held accountable for what they did. They were bragging, like boastful idiots about what they'd done. Everything is written down in detail, and someday it will be used in a court of law as evidence. I made two copies, one for you, and one for me. You will find names of people who did specific acts. Some are locals and others are Romanian Nazi soldiers. I must tell you that much of the information in this booklet is from people who witnessed firsthand what happened and were abhorred by the event. Someday, retribution will be made for this evil."

What he didn't tell Michael but included in the back of the little book he was leaving with him, were the names of the four men who raped the girl he was to marry.

Michael just listened with a riveted stare of hopelessness, numbed and shattered in a lost world. Words coming to him from his family friend sounded like they were far away. Like a lifeless zombie, the foreman saw Michael's hands reach for the booklet being handed to him. Their eyes met. What the man saw were eyes that didn't belong to the young man he knew as a child. Even his face had changed into a cold, frozen image. What he'd been in life was being morphed into something yet to be realized.

"Mr. Popescu, I assure you that as long as I have breath there will be retribution, not in a court of law where Jews have no standing—but in a court of my justice."

The foreman would remember those words in the days, months, and years that followed, the times when mysterious deaths would occur among the names written down in that book. It would also be his legacy of not informing the authorities upon hearing news of their deaths.

"Michael, the three of you should not return to your village. It's not safe, and if certain people see you, they'll inform the authorities."

"What happened to our home, the mill, the properties belonging to Bub and Moshe's families?"

Mr. Popescu dropped his head, closed his eyes, and gave a deep, anguished sigh. "I am sorry to say that all your properties, including your sister's and her husband's have been taken over by those who were part of the massacre.

"Where can the three of you hide and be safe? If I knew, I could bring you food supplies from time-to-time."

"For now," said Moshe, "we'll remain where we are. We know how to live off the land, and from here we will wreak havoc and revenge on the names you left with Michael."

"I want you to know you will be in my thoughts, and I'll do my best to help you any way I can. Before I depart, I'll leave with you two large bags of rice and beans that are on my bike. They'll help for a while."

"Don't worry about us," said Bub, "we have experience living up here in the wild."

They watched the harbinger of horrifying news slowly mount his bike. The pain of the man's completed mission hung over him like a dark, somber cloud as he disappeared on the trail he took to reach them. Now, the forest they had loved to camp, fish, and hunt in would become a place of permanence, a friend that would teach them how to survive as predators in their cause of justice. They would learn brutal lessons acted out on the forest floor among living organisms, a place where a snippet of another kind of Darwinism was in play, the kind where predatory violence was successful only when coupled with instinct, nature's transcendent form of intelligence. On the attack side, it was sometimes size, speed, or strength as demonstrated in the brutal bears, wild boars, and wolves, all carnivorous creatures seeking to be the fittest and most dominant. But the three lost souls left on an island of survival would also learn the strengths of the smaller, weaker species that kept them hidden and out of the paths of the violent aggressive ones, like the horned viper that carried an arsenal of poison, and even smaller creatures that could camouflage themselves to live another day. The forest that would be their teacher would be a wonderland of mystery shrouded with violence. They would learn to mimic the sounds of the wild and use those sounds to develop a primitive, cryptic, messaging system, that when used, it would go undetected as a sound being made by a human voice. The violent laws of survival in nature would be their silent partner and teacher in their pursuit of justice. *For the young man with blond hair and blue eyes, the forest would be a womb that would give birth to a respectable Dr. Jekyll, fully prepared and equipped to release avengement in the dark figure of a Mr. Hyde.*

Chapter 2

Mr. Hyde's Courtroom Justice

The painful memories of the man dressed in black at the side rail of the darkened ship were interrupted by someone looking down from the ship's bridge with night-vision glasses. A message was being sent by the first mate over a headset worn by the lone man watching and waiting. It was information he wanted to hear: everything was go—there was nothing big moving in their direction on the water for a distance of ten miles. The man knew the radar and technology aboard the ship was the most advanced in the world.

The message coming from the first mate created a calm confidence in the man dressed in dark clothes. Even his silhouette on the deck floor from the bright moonlight showed a certain sturdy and robust outline. The man carried a history he couldn't escape. His musings returned while he waited.

He and his two friends had survived living in the wild carrying out acts of justice against those who were guilty of the deaths of their families and seizure of their properties. Of the executions they had done, one stood out above all the others. Quiet, cold, night air knifed its way across deck of the silent, still ship. It served to sharpen the man's memory.

The year was 1942. A Nazi Romanian Iron Guard military jeep had pulled out from its camp on its way to another military post. Inside were its driver and the driver's senior officer. The vehicle was small, an open military transport used primarily to carry officers to and from different command posts. To reach their scheduled destination, the route would take them over a remote, winding, dirt road that narrowed as it entered a stretch of heavy forest growth with low-hanging branches. In the backseat sat the officer holding a briefcase closely guarded.

When the jeep slowed to make a sharp bend on the road, the officer heard a loud thud followed by an agonizing gurgling scream. His eyes turned to the driver, who was now slumped over the steering wheel veering off the road with a hunter's arrow embedded in his neck, followed by another arrow penetrating his chest. By the time the vehicle had hit the trunk of a tree, two men were pulling the officer from the Jeep at gunpoint, and another had removed the dead driver taking his wallet and identification.

Everything happened so fast it left the officer dazed. He was now being pushed away from the wreckage where his hands were tied. Stunned and disheveled, the officer saw just three men who had pulled this off. He heard someone say, "Bub, check what's in the vehicle, there may be something we can use."

A young man whose face carried age and experience beyond his years walked over and took from the disabled jeep two rifles and a briefcase. The three captors noticed when the briefcase was lifted and removed the Nazi officer's eyes followed the man carrying the case. He let it be known that what was inside the case had significant value. Leaving the dead driver by the jeep, they faded into the forest.

After walking thirty minutes over dense, rugged terrain, the officer was told to stop. He could tell the area was their campsite. His frightened eyes studied his captors. They all carried side arms and a rifle, and it was apparent they were experienced in what they were doing. One of the three was armed with a large competition bow and a satchel of arrows, the kind used for hunting big game. Among the three, one had striking features that stood in contrast to the other two: he was tall with blue eyes and blond hair and seemed to be the leader of the group.

He knew they were Jews, except for the tall blond—he looked German, and he had seen him somewhere before. "Look, I know what you want," said the Nazi Romanian officer, "and I have plenty of it on my person. Inside my pockets are several thousand Lei banknotes—take them, they will buy you anything you want."

The three said nothing—just stared into the eyes of the man they held captive. The officer saw the blond man sit and take something from his pocket while the others went through what was seemingly a ritual, something they had done before.

"So you have a lot of money on you?" said one of his captors. "Where did you get all this money? This is money of wealth, not the kind earned by an army officer. Answer me!" demanded his interrogator.

"From dead people, people who no longer had use for it. It came from Russians killed in battle."

"How many Jews did you kill to acquire this much money?" said his inquisitor.

"The truth is it is money I took as bribes so certain Jews

13

wouldn't be killed." The officer knew now his life was in danger. If they wanted his money, they would've taken it before now, and for him to tell half-truths would go down better than blatant lies. His eyes darted from interrogator to the young blond man sitting holding a piece of paper.

Sudden quietness blanketed the campsite. All eyes turned toward the Bowman, who was now walking over where he'd placed the briefcase after arriving at camp. He opened it and dumped its contents out on the ground. Bub, a man who could place an arrow through the heart of a victim at a great distance, ran his hands through the pile of Lei banknotes, gold, and diamond rings, all stolen from Jews before they were killed. On top lay an envelope on which was written: Accounting Record of Jewish Property. The three captors showed no response upon seeing the money and valuables taken from Jews.

Moshe, his interrogator was first to speak. "So you helped yourself to the money? What is the name of your senior officer who was to receive this delivery?"

"His name and other names are in a little book among the contents on the ground...please, believe me, I had nothing to do with any of this!"

His inquisitor's eyes became intense. "I asked you a question. Who is the big man who was to receive this briefcase?"

The Nazi officer showed reluctance in revealing the identity of his superior knowing that the mention of his infamous name would not bode well in his circumstances here with these Jews. But he had nothing with which to bargain. Raising his head slowly and avoiding the eyes of his interrogator, he said, "His name is Colonel Funar."

When the name Funar was heard, a cold wave of doom

rippled through the campsite. The three young men froze momentarily. The captured officer feared the worst. The blond man holding the piece of paper in his hand gave a piercing look at the officer whose head now hung down with eyes closed. He quickly stood to his feet, saying in Yiddish, a language the Romanian officer couldn't understand, "Moshe, bakumen gants der informatsye`du kenen bay der polkovnik." The spoken Yiddish gave instructions to the interrogator to get what information he could about Colonel Funar.

The Nazi officer opened his eyes, saw the blond man walk away into the forest. It was the name Funar that disturbed the man now removing himself, a name that interfered with the business at hand. Colonel Funar would be summoned at a later time, but for now, he would attend to the court in session and let Moshe be the caretaker of information derived from their captive.

The Aryan-looking man had lived in the wild long enough to know how to be invisible and subordinate his feelings to lower, unrefined, survival instincts. His success hinged on keeping emotion in tow, freeing up his predatory skills that marked his actions. He was free to be wild. He had no family, they had all been killed, and others had taken over everything his father owned. He felt like a slave gladiator inside a Roman Coliseum to entertain others in the sport of violence. However, he had altered the course of events. He had trained to do battle for his own cause and not for the amusement of the audience. His sword reserved for those who organized and promoted violent exhibitions, those who sat in special front-row seats. It was these who had fallen by his hands, and instead of the bodies of defeated gladiators being dragged out of the Coliseum in public view, it was those in the spectator seats in charge of the entertainment carnage who had fallen by his sword.

Colonel Funar was one of the chief organizers who sat on the front row alongside the Emperor and raised his fist with a thumbs-down for thousands of his people to be slaughtered in open pits, starved, and brutalized in unspeakable ways. This was the man who would someday enter Mr. Hyde's court and be judged for his crimes. Wheels of justice sometimes moved slowly, but they could grind very fine. This man, Funar, was on his list and next in line. But for now, another court session was calling Mr. Hyde to the arena for battle.

At the campsite, Moshe was showing his skills as an interrogator, skills he'd learned surviving in the forest. Successful tracking of live food in the wild depended on properly interpreting signs one found on the ground. Moshe followed the trail he created with questions posed to the officer, sometimes leading the subject in a circuitous route to make him trip over something he was hiding. For thirty minutes, he badgered the man until he broke revealing the intelligence they needed about the infamous Colonel Funar: where he was from, his family, and field operations. The man had become a victim of the interrogator's raw talent.

Movement came from the shadows of the dense forest at the edge of the camp, then, a figure emerged into the open. The tall blond man had returned still holding a piece of paper in his hand.

"Finish with it Moshe!" said the blond man, interrupting the inquisitor. The impatient, brusque sound of the man's voice carried authority. The figure from the shadows stepped closer. Eyes that matched the verbal command riveted the officer now registering intensified fear.

Everything had the elements of a primitive court scene. It was designed that way. There would be no defense, no appeal, and no audience. The man would have the same trial he gave others, the difference being they were innocent.

It was a courtroom scene showing order, discipline, and experience. The Bowman walked over and cut the rope that bound the man's hands, turned, and walked back where he had stood, leaving the interrogator to finish his part.

"Strip off your clothes," demanded Moshe. Nervously, the officer took off everything except his undershirt, underwear, and socks.

"I said, 'strip off everything.'"

Standing naked with his clothes piled to one side, the German-looking man watched as his two compatriots tied the officer's hands together and forced him to kneel where he stood.

The man was being tried where nature provided a heightened acoustical and visual reality. Even those who brought him here were part of the habitat. It was a place without a jury box or a defense attorney—only a judge and he was the injured party.

The man holding the piece of paper walked slowly over and stood in front of the naked, kneeling officer, now begging for his life. The energy of emotion was expressing itself differently with the two now looking at each other face-to-face: one was hysterical; the other was calm, deliberate, and calculating.

"Moshe, you and Seth can leave now," said the blond man. Even this was an intended, calculated verbal statement in the hearing of the man now kneeling. He

17

wanted the Romanian officer to know that he was in the audience of one for a reason. It was what the blond man said to him that cleared the officer's memory.

"I am a Jew and pose as a traveling merchant. I can move among Romanian civilian society and go unnoticed. I even visit your churches to learn your religious culture to be more efficient in what I do. Inside those churches on Sunday, I listen to your priests slander and berate my people and teach anti-Semitism, then on Monday morning they lead the mass killers to the sites where Jews are hiding. My friends here with me move at night, I move in the daylight. You have seen me around different army posts plying my trade. This was why we knew you were coming this way at this hour of the day. Everyone has a price for information, and you of all people should know that. The man who put the arrow through the neck and heart of your driver is a champion archer. This becomes useful when silence is needed, and people like you give him the opportunity to keep his skill up.

The man stopped begging for his life and was now silent. He knew these were not Jews cowering in fear, running for their lives. They were methodical, smart with jungle-like survival instincts and had forced him to grovel in humiliation—acts he had forced on helpless Jews and their families before they were killed. The officer saw the Aryan-looking man take a picture out of his pocket, then held it in front of his eyes, saying, "This is the lady I was engaged to marry...look at her real good!"

The Romanian officer saw something akin to a ritual being played out, something he had done before with everything well rehearsed. His voice deepened, and his eyes turned into cold steel as he opened the piece of paper he'd been holding, held it in front of his face, demanding, "Read this aloud!"

The man was shaking. He knew what this was about. He stammered, reading line-by-line the last letter written by the love of his captor's life. It was the letter given him by the foreman who brought the tragic news to his camp that day:

My Dearest Michael:

You have and will always be the love of my life. You will hear my story when you return. I cannot live with the memory of what's happened, and my body that was saved for you in marriage is no longer sacred and honorable. I would never want you to have this as a memory in our marriage, and I would never want to carry the memory of that burden, so when you return, I hope your sadness will not linger because of me. I am forever yours.

Love, Rebecca

Silence was deafening as the letter was slowly and carefully folded and put away. The rapid pounding of the kneeling man's heart could almost be heard. Then the young, tall, blond-looking Jew took a step forward and spoke.

"Under your command and by your orders, my people have been made to strip off their clothes and stand naked before open pits and shot. However, you are not here today for that. You have been brought to my court because you were one of the four men who raped my Rebecca. She chose to die by cutting her wrists, rather than live with the memory of ignominy. You killed her and will be the third to die at my hands. Today, I'm your executioner to bring justice without mercy, and your naked body will be left here in the open field for wild animals to tear and rip apart and be eaten as carrion. You will now join others of your own kind with Colonel Funar soon to follow."

In the distance, the sound of a single gunshot brought the blond man's friends back to the campsite. Before leaving the execution scene, they gathered the officer's clothing and all the money taken from Jews, money that would now be used to move the hand of justice, the kind of justice that showed no mercy. The three had a strict protocol when one was marked for execution: it was always up close and personal. Those who were not chosen were casualties of war. Each member of the trio maintained a personal list of names scheduled for execution and was acted upon after consultation and careful strategic planning. Though some women showed complicity in some of the slayings, their names were not on any list.

Chapter 3

The Colonel

The man dressed in dark clothing on board the idle freighter now leaned against the outer rail watching the vaporous movement of energy drifting and swirling about. It gave invitation to entertain the memory of his personal history as an Avenger—that integral part of him that carried out justice in the name of Mr. Hyde.

Patience was always the predator's virtue. He remembered his patience while searching for Colonel Funar on a cold December night in 1943. It was a time when the people of Romania were watching their dead soldiers come home from the Russian front in boxes—if they were fortunate to be brought home. Frenetic energy pulsated throughout the country.

The forested mountains had provided a safe haven for three young men who were growing old fast. Their base of operation was in the mountains where a natural covering concealed them from their enemies. Michael, the leader of the group with his blond hair and Aryan-looking traits, was unrestricted in his movements. The other two, because of their physical features, were confined to night activities. It was after the capture of a Romanian officer carrying a briefcase full of money taken from Jews that their mission expanded to using the wealth they found to assist Jews in hiding and those brave Romanians who were lending help and protection. They maintained two motorcycles, always kept them hidden, and out of sight, unless the German-looking member of the party needed to use one for reconnoitering or shop for the group.

The three had moved down from the mountains close to a military encampment in search of an officer directly responsible for the death of Moshe's mother and father. Moshe and Bub remained hidden while Michael moved about the area gathering intelligence. Up to this point, they had failed in their search for the infamous Colonel Funar, but knowing he was a field commander would put him around army encampments.

One of the most effective methods of obtaining information was in the use of money. The payment of money always loosened the tongue, and they were in good supply of it. Michael carried the image of a respectable middle-class Romanian. He rode a late-model motorcycle, dressed in nice clothes, and appeared to be anything but a Jew. He often visited bars and entertainment centers where lips were always loose, and if they weren't, he would buy the drinks until they were. Subterfuge was not part of Michael's nature, but he learned to perfect it in order to carry out his mission.

It was his lucky day when he parked his bike in front of a well-patronized bar frequented by soldiers. When entering, typical bar room music was playing and two soldiers in uniform were seated at the bar. Other patrons were scattered about the large room drinking and engaging in loud conversation. He seated himself alongside one of the soldiers at the bar. They were low ranking, probably living from paycheck to paycheck. He noticed they were drinking very slowly as if to savor each sip to make what they were enjoying last as long as they could. Michael was good at conversation.

"You fellows from around here? I'm on a business trip just passing through, and I notice there are a lot of servicemen in the area. Let me buy you some drinks just to show my appreciation of your patriotism."

"Hey, thanks," said one of the soldiers. "It's not often we meet people like you who offer to buy drinks."

Michael didn't pursue questions until they had been drinking for 30 minutes. Both tongues were getting loose while he held his drinks at bay. The blond man sitting at the bar always knew when to strike. He was clever, instinctual, and disciplined—skills he'd survived with in the wild, and were now being applied to gain information about a man who murdered Moshe's mother and father.

The path Michael led the two soldiers down with loosened tongues gave evidence of their vulnerability to alcohol and smooth talk. The man they were looking for turned out to be their commanding officer, and they did everything but draw a map where the officer stayed. The Army encampment lived in tents; however, officers were provided housing units inside the town.

Michael stayed at the bar until the two soldiers chose to leave. Unsteady on their feet, they managed to swagger through the front door followed by Michael. As they stepped onto the sidewalk, he noticed them standing at attention saluting an officer being driven in an open military vehicle.

Michael quickly moved up behind the two soldiers, asking, "He must be an important person?" Their tongues were still loose.

"Oh, that's Colonel Funar!" said one of the soldiers.

"His family lives in that large mansion-looking home just outside town. He's probably home visiting."

Michael froze. The inebriation of the two young men gave him time to collect himself without anything registering. They parted ways, and Michael resisted the temptation to scope out the Funar residence during daylight. His move would be at night.

Back at a secluded campsite, three Avengers went into discussions drawing up a two-pronged plan. First, they would spend three nights together staking out the Funar mansion on the outskirts of town to determine its occupants and their movements to and from the home. On the fourth night they would split up, Michael would stay at the mansion, Bub and Moshe would attend to their mission in town. They always worked as a unit, but in view that the two operations were in the same area they chose this action so continuity wouldn't be lost in the surveillance at the mansion.

The arrangement for the fourth evening was that if everything went as planned, Bub and Moshe would return to the mansion and meet up with Michael. If circumstances didn't warrant that eventuality, they were to return to their base of operation.

All three carried side arms, wore dark clothes, and were strategically positioned on the perimeter of the compound. For three nights, they saw a lot of activity in and around the home but saw no evidence of the colonel. However, being predators they never wearied in waiting. Time was always on their side.

On the fourth evening, they separated, Michael to the mansion, Bub and Moshe to town to carry out their plan. Before reaching the town, Moshe took from his pocket a written description of an eyewitness' account of the officer's role of leading his squadron in pulling men, women, and children from homes, forcing them into the streets, then shooting the victims as they begged for mercy. It would be read again before the night was out—but in the hearing of the man designated for execution.

Moshe remembered the survival instinct a large python snake exercised after killing a wild goat or pig. Before swallowing its kill, it would scout the area to be sure there were no driver army ants nearby. They were carnivorous creatures that marched like a disciplined military and would eat anything in their pathway. The snake knew its vulnerability was after its satiation. The principle the python snake applied to its own preservation would be reversed tonight in their predatory operation—they would scour the area first before the kill, and then allow the act of justice be their satiation. The regimentation of army life required early to bed, early to rise. However, in this officer's case, there would be no rising.

Michael was now by himself at the large Funar mansion compound and had positioned himself where he could observe most of the outside area. Unlike the previous three evenings, there was no activity of people coming and going. Darkness had settled in at five, and it was nearing nine o'clock when three vehicles drove up and parked near the front door. The drivers entered the home and began carrying out boxes loading them in the vehicles. It appeared they were moving out. Then someone came out the back door carrying what looked like a luggage case, entered a tool shed, and shut the door. He waited for the person to return. Ten minutes later a figure was seen moving away from the shed going toward the back porch without the luggage piece. With his field glasses, he could tell the person was a woman when she stepped under the porch light at the back entrance. Then all the lights were turned off, except the front porch and outside security. The sound of vehicles starting up could be heard as dark figures emerged from the home. Taillights from three cars were seen driving from the compound.

Michael moved through the darkness, avoided the security lights in search of the electrical breaker box. It was important that he work in darkness. After disconnecting the power supply, he waited to see if someone were still inside, knowing if that were the case, someone would soon light a candle or show a flashlight. What was important to him was the luggage case the woman had taken to the equipment shed. Michael always came well supplied with tools. Within half-a-minute, the lock was broken, and he was inside the shed. The building had no window so the light from his flashlight would never be seen from outside.

He saw nothing but what a maintenance person would require for keeping up a large compound. The case had to be in this building somewhere. It wasn't until he examined the concrete floor that he saw clues that might be telling. The grass outside was heavy with dew, and the floor showed footprints that stopped at a certain point in front of a large work bench. Nearby on the floor were marks and scratches indicating something had been pulled across the floor. Now he understood what the party had done. He grabbed the workbench, pulled it away from the wall. On the floor was a hidden storage compartment covered with a locked, metal door. After breaking the lock and lifting the cover, two luggage cases came into view.

In a short time, Michael had both luggage pieces open

on top of the workbench. His suspicions of the sudden departure from the mansion and the need to hide luggage in the dark of the night proved to be right. The two cases in front of him contained a fortune: cloth bags showing Hebrew script filled with Romanian Lei notes, diamonds, gold, and other forms of jewelry, a fortune taken from Jews killed in the Holocaust. Colonel Funar had a network of collecting stolen property and it all ended up in his hands. It was wealth he didn't share with his superiors, and to avoid a paper trail, banks were not used. Hence, it was now thought to be hidden, safe until it could be retrieved or accessed when needed.

He closed the cases reflecting on the execution of the officer who abused his beloved. It was on that mission they intercepted one of the colonel's deliveries, money and valuables that had been stolen from Jews after brutally killing them. The wealth they intercepted that day had been put to good use toward those in hiding. What he now had in his possession would guarantee continued help.

With both cases in his grasp, he pushed the shed door open with his shoulder. Everything around the compound was dark making the lights in the city look like a Christmas tree. Then suddenly, sirens sounded, and everything went black—it was an air alert. He wondered how Bub and Moshe were. What was going on might lend itself to their advantage. A quick look at his watch told him it was nearing midnight.

It was at a time when Romania was allied with Nazi Germany and both were fighting the Russians. News of the Americans bombing the Ploesti oil refinery had created further consternation. Something was going down and it was reflected by the residents in the mansion moving out.

Up to this point, Colonel Funar had eluded Michael, but he took consolation in knowing that had it been otherwise the stolen fortune taken from Jews might not have been found. The home itself awaited his inspection. He was about to break the lock on the back door when he heard the piercing sound of a Nighthawk. He stopped what he was doing and listened further. The sound came again. Bub and Moshe were on the compound somewhere. He moved to the corner of the home so his birdcall response would apprise them of his location.

Moshe and Bub were soon at Michael's side showing signs of heavy breathing from having evaded crowds gathering in streets from sirens and the blackout. After breaking the door open, each turned on his flashlight. Michael sent Bub upstairs to clear the top floor. He and Moshe would check out the bottom area. Michael saw Moshe going to the kitchen sink to wash his hands and knife. They never discussed executions. Each considered it personal, and questions would be an invasion of privacy. Tonight, the execution required silence and the use of a knife.

When Michael and Moshe moved to the front door near the living room, they found packed boxes.

"They were in a hurry to leave," said Moshe.

"These are probably boxes they didn't have room to carry," said Michael.

Bub had returned from upstairs and was concerned that the electrical power might come back on.

"I'm going outside to find the electrical control box," said Bub. "We don't want any surprises with the power returning."

"That's been taken care of," said Michael. "Perhaps you

could close any open window shade on this floor."

"Let's see what's in these boxes they left behind," said Moshe.

Three men who had become hardened by the violence of war, loss of family and executions, began opening the boxes left behind. In a darkened room with only flashlights showing what was being pulled from the boxes, a strange, vacuous atmosphere settled about them. They couldn't believe what they saw: boxes filled with horrifying graphic photos of Holocaust victims, some showing Colonel Funar directing and participating in the genocide. Three men who knew violence firsthand were compelled to look away from the gruesome scenes. Included among the photos were reels of film and documents Colonel Funar had drawn up as orders to be carried out in the mass executions of Jews. The three were left speechless and numb.

The first to speak was Bub. "Why would a person guilty of these crimes attempt to keep the evidence?"

Michael, the strong, bold leader of the group, in a subdued, almost trance-like state, gave a succinct incisive response. "Genocidal war criminals only live in the present and are blinded to the consequences of actions. This person enjoyed a morbid kind of voyeurism of Jewish dead. He needed what's here in these boxes to feed his evil, sick nature."

Bub and Moshe saw Michael look away from the boxes of horror to a darkened corner of the room. It was the contrast of light and darkness, good and evil that gave birth to Michael's words spoken in soliloquy. *"We may be just three small voices screaming for justice in the dark, but instead of shedding tears we will renew our commitment to the cause of justice by making others weep, and let God be the judge of our actions."*

"We have to move fast," said Bub. "They could be back anytime."

"Let's put the boxes we want to take with us at the back door alongside those two luggage cases," responded Michael. "What we can't carry with us, we'll hide in the woods and return at a convenient time."

"And let's not forget," said Moshe, "to turn the electrical supply back on before we leave."

"I know where it's located, and will take care of it when we leave," said Michael.

The party of three carried to the edge of the compound the colonel's fortune taken from Jews killed in the Holocaust along with the boxes containing war-crime documents, photos, and film. Moshe and Bub waited while Michael went to turn on the security lights which would give the area the look it had when everyone vacated the home earlier in the evening. Soon the figure of Michael emerged and was first to speak.

"When they return, everything will appear as they left it, except for what we've removed."

"And it may be several days before they come back," said Moshe.

They had taken sheets, tied ends together, and with the use of a pole created a hauling apparatus much like a hammock where two people could bear the weight of each end of the pole on a shoulder. The simple carrying device allowed them to take everything, leaving one person free to carry the fortune contained in the two luggage pieces.

Moshe and Michael each shared the weight of the pole holding the vital boxes of evidence, while Bub carried the cases. After trudging the distance of a mile, they sat down

30

to rest on a distant knoll and watched for the city lights to come on. Though the sirens weren't blaring, the city was still nestled in the cradle of darkness.

Up to this point, Michael had said nothing about the two luggage pieces, and with much of the tension now over, he said, "I want to show you what I found in the shed behind the home."

He took one of the cases, opened it, saying, "I found these two luggage pieces in the back shed stored underground in a hidden compartment." Bub and Moshe saw him shine his flashlight on the contents inside the case.

"The other case contains pretty much what this one has," said Michael.

"It's a fortune, all taken from our people," said Bub. "I'd like to be a fly on the wall when they return and find it missing. It would be an entertaining spectacle, and if I'm the one to continue carrying these pieces, knowing what I now know, the physical load will be lighter."

There's another kind of weight we have to carry," added Michael. "It's the weight of responsibility to use wisely what we've found to help those still in this wicked country."

An hour later, the countryside and city were still in darkness, and they were making their way where their bikes were hidden deep in the forest. They loaded the two cases on their bikes, hid what they couldn't take with them under water-repellant canvas, and made their way over trails that kept them concealed until they reached camp.

That night Michael listened to the large water globules splattering the top of his tent accompanied with arrhythmic, staccato sounds. Though it wasn't raining, the dense, overhead foliage had collected water droplets from the moist-ridden air and was giving its own welcome. He pulled his heavy covers up over his shoulders and reflected on how elusive the colonel was. He had temporarily escaped his net, but the man was left dispossessed of Jewish stolen wealth. Michael would let history measure the weight of the war-crime evidence taken from his home.

Chapter 4

The Reunion

The large freighter was still dark and idle. The man dressed in clothes matching the night clung to his memories. They had taken him on a journey never to be revisited, and before he sealed his past for the new life in front of him, he had the need to walk through the last year of his life.

Gentle nature swayed the large ship with rhythmic, calming movements while twinkling stars continued to punctuate the night sky with orbs of light. The man standing and waiting knew all about nature but unlike most who were observers of its scenic beauty from afar, he had seen it up close in its varied forms of vicious cruelty—the other side of the face of gentleness and calm. It was from the cruel side of nature that he had learned to be a predator and survivor.

It was after the war that time seemed compressed together as one unit of interlocking events, a continuum, a flow of actions without stops and starts. He had survived the Holocaust in Romania under Nazism, and when the Communist came to power, the totalitarian rulers still refused to acknowledge the country's mass genocide and took measures to imposed restrictions on Jews leaving the country. Anti-Semitism was still pervasive regardless of what government was in power.

Bub and Moshe moved to Bucharest and opened a small market together, and after store hours one taught archery and the other tutored advanced students in algebra and calculus. Michael had changed his name, passed himself off as non-Jewish and was hired by a shipping company where he soon held the rank of first mate. In time, he earned his captain's license, and with his affable nature, he quickly ingratiated himself among those whom he worked as well as his superiors.

City life became part of the Avengers' new normal. They had moved from the mountains to the city, but living under city lights and walking on concrete sidewalks had not changed what they were. He was away for weeks at a time sailing around the world on ships delivering and picking up freight, and when he came home, he stayed with Bub and Moshe. It was then they would leave their store in charge of a trusted friend and conference together for the next execution. This time, he had been at sea for several weeks and had returned. Bub and Moshe were expecting him when they heard his knock on their door.

"That must be Michael," said Moshe. "Why don't you put on some coffee for us, I'll get the door."

The door swung wide, and two men embraced like brothers, followed by Bub. He always brought them something special that wasn't available in Bucharest. Tonight it was two large boxes of dried dates from the Middle East.

"Mind if I open my box now," said Bub. "They'll go well with a fresh pot of coffee."

"Any news since I've been gone?"

"First, we'll speak of the news you're interested in," said Moshe.

"Yeah," said Bub, "we've done a lot of research on a certain party of interest, even traveled to the sight mapping out a plan of action."

"And which party is this?"

"It's a man who took the authorities to the site where my brother, his wife, and child were hiding," said Moshe. "They were then summarily shot in the presence of the informant. My brother had a home, but it was confiscated and given to the man as a reward. It was their policy to offer money to those informing on Jews in hiding—in this case, it was the home."

The memory of the lone man aboard the idle ship recalled the heat of anger rising among them that night. It was measured by the look in their eyes and the stark blanket of hush covering them. They were dangerous when they were quiet. The effacement of evil people who killed their families was their reason for living. Moshe's eyes showed the never-ending story of pain. Their lives had become dichotomous—they lived in two realities: the present and the past.

"When do you want to deal with this matter?" he remembered asking.

He and Bub saw Moshe pause in considerable thought before he spoke. "I'm glad you're here, Michael. It's been difficult dealing with this without your presence, and since you are now here, the sooner we act on this, the better."

Conversation among them moved from morbidity to subjects of relationships.

"Michael, do you have social interactions with women in your ports of call?" asked Bub.

"I visit bars, women are always there, but they never interest me. Besides, they aren't Jewish, and if they were, it would be a reason not to be interested. No one will ever come up to the level of Rebecca. What about you two?"

"The Jewish community in Bucharest has diminished in number reducing opportunity for socialization," said Moshe. "Perhaps, we aren't intended for marriage after what we've done and continue to do."

"You may be onto something," Michael said. "We were cursed having not died with our families, and now we're cursed by what we have to do to live with ourselves. Marriage may not be part of our existence, but there's one thing sure, we could never be married and do what we do."

"David couldn't build the temple because of the blood he shed," said Bub. "Is there something there that applies to us when it comes to marriage?"

A strange aura moved about the room among three men who never took time to question what they were. Then Michael spoke up. "Yet, look at David and what he became because of his violence. Samuel, the great Prophet, was a violent man when circumstances warranted it. He used a sword to execute Agag, the king of Amalek, who ripped up pregnant women."

"How will history judge us?" asked Moshe.

Another cold blanket wafted itself over the three. No one said anything until Michael spoke. "History written by European ideologues will never give the Jew doing what we do a fair and objective review. Their paradigm of classroom idealism never fits into the human experience of a Holocaust survivor, someone who has no rights to his property or even his life. They've never seen their families killed in front of their eyes, women taken and raped, and property seized. They've never lived in a country where they are an illegal entity, a country without legal recourse."

When Michael finished speaking, something was left hanging in the air. Silence continued until he resumed his defense.

"The evil forces that brought about the Holocaust created what we are. Justice demanded response. If those who killed our people sleep well at night, how much more pleasurable should the night's sleep be for us who extinguish life among those guilty of murder, rape, and plunder?"

Two days later in the middle of the night, three Avengers, now in their forties, were on their motorcycles going to a city where Moshe's brother and family had once lived. They would arrive before daylight, drive into the woods and sleep during the day, then prepare for a nighttime operation without the light of a moon. Bub and Moshe had already made careful surveillance of the area. The man who turned in Moshe's brother now lived in the home alone.

Like ghosts in the night, they were invisible. They came in the night and would leave in the dark. They wore dark clothing and avoided walking close together. Once engaged, everything became instinctual. They walked a hundred feet apart, two on one side of the street and one on the other. Michael waited until Bub and Moshe reach the backside of the home before stepping closer to the front yard. Only the darkness of the night was his cover.

Bub and Moshe entered the home through the back door while he watched and waited. Ten minutes later, they joined him, and with a casual retreat, they moved through the night as they returned the way they came. No one was on the streets at one-thirty in the morning, and the darkened house still appeared as it did when they arrived. They had been predators once again doing what others failed to do in a court of law: bring justice to the guilty.

No one spoke as the three made their way to their bikes in the woods. They had been Avengers of the night using the skills learned when surviving during the Holocaust. It was a repeat performance, and when they pulled out onto the main highway, they saw in the distance Moshe's brother's home in flames. They knew in the morning, only a charred body that had been hanged would be found. However, Moshe wasn't looking at the burning building— all he saw was his brother's family riddled with bullets. With hands clutching the handlebars of his bike and tears coursing from his eyes, he remembered his little six-year-old nephew he used to teach how to compete in the game of chess. The brisk wind from the speed of the bike wiped clean the tears on his face, nature's way of removing the visual sign of pain. Oh, that he could have that wind inside his soul to brush away the curse that had metastasized itself to his memory—then he would be truly free!

The man with a mission on the darkened ship forced his memory away from his former life, a place never to be revisited. With hands grasped firmly to the ship's rail, he watched the moon cast its sparkles through the gossamer vapors rising from the water's surface. Moonlight sparkles illuminated the rippling waves as if they were musical fingers flitting across the strings of a harp giving life to the listener. Tonight, he was the listener. *For the first time since he was a young man, he saw a particle of beauty in the moonlight's performance. It was the other face of nature he had avoided—the kinder, gentler side. He was a dead man coming back to life a day at a time, made dead by a Holocaust from hell but given a spark of life when he heard the news that he had one surviving family member of the Holocaust, a nephew, the son of his beautiful sister.*

The man's memory pulsated with the events that led to the miracle of finding his only surviving family member. It was an experience that would change his life forever. It all happened after he boarded a freighter as the first mate to deliver freight to Western Europe. Though he held a captain's license and sometimes sailed his own ship, he attempted to keep a low profile, and on this voyage had signed on as first mate.

The first night at a port in West Germany, his leisure time was spent watching TV in his private cabin. He found a local TV station carrying a documentary on the Romanian Holocaust and was mesmerized by what he saw and heard. It was a program beamed to the world exposing what had been kept hidden—a Holocaust beyond anyone's imagination, a Holocaust few people knew anything about. Survivors were giving testimonials of what they'd been through, stories he'd heard and seen a thousand times. Personal memory pain gripped him.

When it was time for the last person to speak, he couldn't believe what he heard. The speaker was a young doctor from his village and was describing how his German adoptive mother found him as an orphaned infant hidden in a wagon of hay. His mother and father, along with other Jews in the village, had been massacred. She had been visiting her German husband who was a general in Hitler's Army. The woman took him to her country and reared him as her son.

The intent of the documentary was to inform the world

of a hidden Holocaust in a country that refused to acknowledge it. At the end of the telecast, the announcer gave a phone number inviting viewers to write or call if they were survivors of the Romanian Holocaust. The Katharina Foundation had sponsored the documentary.

He sat shocked and overwhelmed at what he saw and heard. After dialing the phone number shown on the screen, he reached one of the operators and found that the young doctor who had been adopted by a German woman was the chairman of a global enterprise. His world was spinning. Here was someone leading the fight for his people, one in a position of wealth who could help his cause of bringing justice to those guilty of war crimes, and the man was from his village. That night he abdicated his responsibilities as first mate, went onshore, and never returned to the ship. He had the need to present his case before the young doctor who could further his cause in a land void of any pathway to adjudicate the evils inflicted upon his people.

Once off the ship, he attempted to contact the doctor but to no avail. He called repeatedly, but those in charge refused to give him an appointment nor would they connect him by phone. He could understand. The man ran a global enterprise, and the people beneath him were protecting his valuable time from someone who was off the street. Then he began to make visits to the site itself attempting to get through security to see someone who would give him an appointment. Then one day he was told to write a letter and give it to the chief of security, and he would see that it reached the chairman. That was the turning point.

It was early in the morning when he delivered his letter to the security desk. The man called his superior, followed by the appearance of a large man showing a shiny baldhead. He looked at the sealed letter, then at him, saying, "Please be seated." Turning to another security officer, the burly man said, "Run this up to Dr. Hans' executive secretary."

He remembered the look of suspicion the chief of security had when he was told, "Be prepared to wait a long time, and you may not get a response today, but you're free to stay here in our waiting room."

He sat thinking that he may never get in to talk to the man. Then he saw the large, bald man returning with gusto in his steps.

"Today's your lucky day," said the man, "come with me, Dr. Hans will see you in the boardroom, but you have to be cleared by security."

Security frisked him, then he was taken by the big man along with another security person to a large boardroom. Upon entering, the room's elegance and decor spoke of a level of affluence he'd never seen before. Two additional security personnel were stationed outside the boardroom. He sat at the large conference table between the chief of security and the accompanying officer.

They had just sat when the door to the boardroom opened. All three rose to their feet. A casually dressed man stood in the doorway staring at him. He was tall, blond-haired, and carried a troubled, somber look. He recognized him to be the young doctor he saw on the Romanian Holocaust documentary. The chairman stared at him with laser-like eyes, then moved slowly toward where he was now waiting to be introduced. Without looking at the two security people, the chairman was heard saying, "Max, leave us alone—wait outside the boardroom." When the closing door gave the sound of a click, the chairman and stranger were left looking at each other face-to-face.

"I'm Hans Baughman, and you are a Romanian Holocaust survivor?"

"Yes, my name Michael Pencovich."

"Please be seated, Mr. Pencovich."

The chairman walked away and stood in front of a beautiful painting hanging on the wall. With his back facing him, he heard the chairman say, "Yes, I know your name from your letter. You say you have no surviving family members?"

"Yes, that's correct."

The whole conversation was spent with him seated at the conference table while the chairman looked at the painting with his back turned toward him. When the young doctor turned to face him, he thought he saw moistened eyes.

That was the day when his life began to change. Subsequent meetings brought them closer together when the doctor invited him to inspect a couple of freighters that would be used to smuggle Jews into Israel. It was that day on a freighter he met an old man, a prophet, and a Romanian Holocaust survivor. The old man spoke words of power and persuasion in describing the person in Isaiah fifty-three. That was the day he walked through a portal of light and found himself changed.

Then came the climactic event of being told that the young doctor was Jacob, the son of his sister, Rachel, the little one-year-old he had pulled around in his wagon, and who was now one of the wealthiest men in Europe.

The rush of memory was interrupted. The man at the side rail of the ship heard a voice coming through his headphone. It was the first mate speaking.

"Captain Pencovich, our high tech equipment tells us that something small is closing in on us."

"Everything is in place and we're ready for them," responded the waiting man. The gentle rocking and swaying of the huge ship pulled his mind back into the tangible world where he was now making a new life.

Under the moonlight in the vast empty ocean came the sounds of swishing, sounds gladly welcomed. He took from his pocket a flashlight, beamed its torch across the rippling, rolling waters in the direction of the sound of oars struggling to reach the hidden sleeping giant. Through the mist of shifting fog came a flashing light announcing the arrival of visitors. His heart leaped. He once had a mission bent on justice, tonight it was one of opening prison doors so the captives could go free.

The whooshing noise of oars increased, then abrupt, dead silence. Once more, he flashed his light, not across the open sea but sixty feet below the deck where he stood. A small, hardly seaworthy boat rested in the swells of moving water alongside a wall of steel. Inside, were crowded together forty men, women, and children waiting to be taken to a land of their ancestors. Under the cover of darkness, a special operation was being finalized.

At the signal of the man dressed in black, what had seemed like a ghost ship took on vibrant life. From all quarters of the vessel came a crew of men with special training to assist those who had risked their lives to return to the land of their ancestors. The last two men who stepped onto the deck of the ship embraced the leader of the operation. Darkness concealed identities, but the moonlight gave vivid reflections of tears trickling down cheeks. They were a team rejoined, not for the cause of taking life but saving it by delivering a people to their ancient shores.

"Did you bring the Funar documents?" asked the captain.

"They're inside the boat now being lifted to the deck of the ship," responded one of them. To make this a stealth operation, the small boat that precariously carried forty passengers would later be dropped overboard.

The members of the group had been instructed on how to conduct themselves once on board the ship. They saw the man in charge flash a signal to the first mate and then came the whine of engines and grinding of the propeller. They huddled together, only whispering in conversation. The ship had to navigate without lights until they reached international waters. Once they crossed that point lights came on, followed by yells of jubilation. Some wept, others fell to their knees to thank God they were free. They formed a single line, and the man in charge led the group to their quarters down below.

This was the maiden pickup on the Black Sea for a people returning to the land of their ancestry with another coming two hours later down the coastline. The captain of the ship made his way to the radio room with his two life-long friends to send a message to his only living relative who was responsible for everything that went down.

Chapter 5

A New Name

A wealthy young doctor sat at his desk in his plush office holding a memo from his executive secretary while reminiscing on his life. Two years earlier, he was a struggling intern at a hospital not knowing that his adoptive mother was one of the wealthiest women in Europe. She had kept this from him during his entire life, and it was only when she passed that the truth of her wealth was revealed. Being the sole heir of all her wealth, he now carried the burden of managing it for a land and a people for the coming Messiah. God had been good to him—someone was sent to help carry the heavy load, and he was privileged to give her his newly changed name.

Names were important to the young doctor. Since the passing of his mother, he had come to despise his surname, as did the one who found him orphaned in a wagon of hay in Romania. All his life he carried the name Baughman, a common German name bestowed upon honorable people. However, two years ago it became a name of infamy because of what he discovered: the man who gave him his name was a Nazi general who collaborated during the war with the central government. He would never allow the name Baughman to be passed on to the woman he would marry, and upon finding his birth name, he legally changed his surname. By changing his name, he gave honor to the three women of his life: to the woman whom he married, his birth mother that died in the Holocaust and the noble lady who reared him for a mission he was now fulfilling. Jacob Isler was his new legal name, and though Jacob was his legal given name, he still went by the name Hans, the name his German mother gave him. The name Baughman was forbidden to be used by any who addressed him.

The young doctor was still holding the memo from his executive secretary in his hand when her voice came over the intercom.

"Doctor, did you get my memo? Security wants to know what to do with the man they have downstairs by the name of Albescu showing a document that the package he has for you must be delivered by him personally. What do you want me to tell them?"

"Tell them, 'If he can produce documentation that he is employed by the West German Embassy in Bucharest, then send him up?'"

The man coming to see him was a Romanian who worked for the West German Embassy in Bucharest. Hans had hired him through a team of intermediary people to research existing family records of births, marriages, and deaths. He wanted documentation to support the action he'd already taken for his new legal name.

In Romania, one could get about anything he wanted through bribery. The country was ruled by a dictator who himself was the chief example of corruption. Without the knowledge of the public, he sold Jews like slaves to be awarded exit visas to emigrate to Israel. Millions of dollars were given to him under the table for a few Jews to be allowed to leave the country. The only time bribery was frowned upon, was when someone was left out of the loop.

Hence, the Romanian doing Hans bidding found everything that was available on record for a price.

The flashing light on the intercom showed the secretary calling.

"Yes, what is it, Miss Shuster?"

"Doctor Hans, my secretary has informed me that the gentleman security has cleared is in her office waiting to deliver the package you ordered."

"Thank you. Please have your secretary bring in the gentleman."

Instead of calling her secretary on the phone, the one who wielded the power of second-in-command without the title left her upscale office. She wanted to see the man who received payments from intermediaries who acted on behalf of her company, payments that went through her office. The chairman had ordered this arrangement with her requesting it be held at the highest level of secrecy.

When entering her secretary's office, she saw a man seated with a briefcase resting on his lap showing a tense, stiff posture. His articulate dress didn't match the signals his body language projected with darting eyes, shifting feet, and clenched fists. Without addressing her secretary, Sonje Schuster walked to where the man sat, extended her hand, saying, "You're Mr. Albescu?"

The gentleman stood to his feet. "Yes, I'm here to leave Dr. Hans something he assigned me to do, and it must be delivered to him personally.

Turning to her secretary still seated at her desk, the man heard the one who had taken charge, say, "Freda, would you please take our visitor to the chairman's office?"

"Sir, my secretary will take you to the chairman of the board of Katharina Enterprises."

Chairman, he thought, this was something he didn't expect. The Romanian entering Hans' office had never seen or dealt with him personally. Intermediaries had been used to communicate and make payment from time-to-time, and only after finishing his project was he told to deliver the results to a Dr. Hans at the main corporate office building.

In his country, dealing with people who had power, position, and money were often unpredictable and sometimes dangerous. He had second thoughts about following through with this, and when entering the office and seeing the elegance and affluence, he was sure he'd done the wrong thing. This had the makings of something that could come back to bite him.

His mission had a mystery attached to it from the beginning. He rarely saw those who gave him instructions and payment for his work. It was over the phone and the use of mail that everything came together. His awkward shuffle across the room revealed his tension—body language was telling his story. His eyes were drawn to a framed picture of a beautiful woman on the desktop. The chairman spoke first.

"Good morning, I'm Jacob Isler, the party that ordered the work you say you've completed. Please be seated."

This person is Jewish, the man thought. Then he was troubled all the more—he remembered that name, Jacob Isler, in his research—but how did he survive the Holocaust? He was born in a community where most of the Jews were killed or shipped out to camps.

The Romanian had taken on and completed a project that he now regretted. If certain people in his country ever found out what he'd done, he could be in serious trouble. Romania had covered up its own genocide that exceeded

48

what happened in Western Europe in its barbaric slaughter and widespread civilian participation. The crimes and atrocities committed by civilians showed the extent of how systemic anti-Semitism was. What he'd done for this man might be interpreted as aiding and abetting that element of the global community attempting to force from the Romanian government an official admission to the Nazi Holocaust. He did the polite thing—he responded to the chairman.

"Good morning, Sir. I'm Marku Albescu and have finished the project your people assigned me to do. It took longer than I expected because of the number of government bureaucracies I had to go through."

Up to this point, the man had so much churning going on inside about his own vulnerability over what he'd done that he failed to focus on the person behind the desk. Now that dialogue was engaged, he was surprised to see that the chairman was very young and wondered how someone of his age could be in charge of this global company. He was also shocked when Hans pulled out of the drawer a file containing his personal history.

"Mr. Albescu, I am one who researchers everything about a person before I do business with him, especially when it comes to personal matters. Inside this file is the complete record of your life. My people did not contact you until you were fully vetted. I know more about you than your employer, and I want to assure you that you'll have no exposure in fulfilling my request for the information you have brought me."

"Mr. Isler, if your file is as extensive as you say it is, you have quite undressed me this morning." The Romanian knew that if he had a complete file it would include his activities beyond the border of Romania. This seemed to be tending badly for him.

"In reviewing your file before assigning you the project you just completed, for which you were paid very handsomely, I noticed some very interesting facts that came to us from outside the country of Romania."

The man saw the finger on the guillotine tightening. Racing through his mind was the thought of being set up for something he had no control over. The man behind the desk may be young, but he wasn't a novice.

"Mr. Albescu, what I have here in my possession is known only between you and me. I used multiple parties to create puzzle pieces of information, and I took the individual pieces and put them together to find out who you are."

"And what is your ulterior motive in telling me all of this?" *All the man could see were blinking neon lights saying blackmail.*

"Mr. Albescu, your late father was Romanian and your mother was Jewish. You were four-years-old when she died in the Spanish flu epidemic in 1918, and I happen to know that you have secretly helped Jews in your position at the West German Embassy."

"You have further undressed me, Mr. Isler. I detect that your inquisition carries either honor or blackmail."

"It is intended to be the former," said Hans. "Money will buy almost anything except loyalty. Loyalty can never be bought. One can pay money for an act that may appear to be loyalty, and one may reward loyalty with the payment of money, but money alone will never motivate loyalty.

"Mr. Albescu, how loyal are you to your Jewish heritage? To what extent would loyalty to your Jewish heritage motivate you to help Romanian Jews get to Israel?"

The Romanian couldn't believe what he was hearing. The man behind the desk knew more about him than his children. Only his wife knew his mother was Jewish, and he alone was privy to his helping certain Jews.

"People in my position," said the Romanian, "have limitations on the extent of their loyalty. I have a wife, a son, and college-age daughter."

"What would your loyalties be if you had no concerns over your wife and children?"

"That would put me in a different position altogether."

"And what would be the conditions that would guarantee security for your family?"

There was long silence. Hans saw the man's face register an uncomfortable reluctance in his reply: "My children and wife would have to remain outside the country with funds available to be with them every other week."

"Presently, you work for the West German Embassy and seem to handle the German language very well. If you made me your silent partner in a business that would require frequent travel to Europe, you could live as a family here and operate the business in your country as cover."

"And may I ask what my portfolio would be in these clandestine operations?"

"The overview would be the creation of a tourism business consisting mainly of coastal recreational deep-sea fishing and the renting out of seaside condos near sandy beaches. Your patrons would be Europeans. Along with this would be your responsibility of creating a network through which information would be passed to key operatives. The business would act as a front to smuggle

Jews to waiting freighters. The business must be successful with a strong bottom line to avoid suspicion.

"You have the experience of public relations on an international level having worked in our Embassy, and we will bring in professional people with expertise in this field to help you get it off the ground. To make everything look authentic, the record will show you having taken out a large bank note as your vested interest.

"Now, Mr. Albescu, it is for you to evaluate your loyalty. If you choose to act on this proposition, it must be for no other reason than your mother's people who have suffered beyond belief."

Hans saw tears come to his eyes. His vision was fixed like he was looking at something in memory. A cold, stone image settled over him.

"Many of my mother's family died in the Holocaust," the man said. "Even today, when in bed at night, I sometimes weep thinking of those terrible times. My wife is very generous and always gives positive support."

"If you want to further this discussion," said Hans, "my executive administrator, Miss Shuster, who does much of my bidding, will give you her number, and you can contact her to reach me. Please be assured that what we have discussed will be held in the highest confidence. And it goes without saying, I appreciate the packet you have delivered today."

"I must admit, Dr. Hans, I'm leaving today feeling better than when I entered your office. Earlier, I questioned that being a possibility."

Both stood to their feet and shook Hands. As the man left the office, he heard the chairman say, "Feel free to call Miss Shuster at any time." Hans looked at the beautiful lady in the framed picture on his desk, saying out loud, "Sheena, because of you and the strength you give me, I can take chances on clandestine operations."

No sooner had the office door closed that he saw the intercom light.

"What is it, Miss Shuster?"

"A Mr. Pencovich is on your private line."

Hans had been waiting for the report on the initial launch of Operation Henry, a secret undercover project of smuggling Jews out of Soviet Bloc countries that refused travel visas to Jews. The mission was under the direction of his uncle, Michael, the only survivor of his Jewish family in Romania.

"Hello Michael, How'd things go?"

"Good news! Everything went as planned. Our first pickup included forty, the second group held forty-five. Of the two rescues, there were fifteen children accompanied by parents. Also, I am pleased to inform you that Bub and Moshe boarded with the first group and will prove to be invaluable assets as we develop and fine-tune Project Henry operations.

"Moshe and Bub will have opportunities for life-changing experiences as I have had in previous weeks and months. You and Mr. Reznik have brought light and life to me in a way never thought possible, and I hope my dear friends will come into that realm of faith."

"We'll pray for that end, Michael. I would like you to train them well because I have need of your services in other matters, and they need to know your job. In fact, try to get a few days open so we can take a flight to Israel and inspect land sites for a parts factory that will help with the employment of the new arrivals."

When they hung up, Michael reflected on how his world had changed. *Who would ever think his beautiful sister's little one-year-old he pulled around in a small wagon would someday run a global enterprise and that he would work for him with such extensive responsibilities? Purpose in life was growing in Michael a day-at-a-time.*

When Hans went home after his day's work at the office, the lovely lady in the picture on his desk met him at the front door with an embraced welcome. Waiting in line behind her to extend their greetings were Mr. and Mrs. Reznik, his new bride's mother and father. It was an evening for celebration.

Chapter 6

Abandoning Life's Dream

The dining table carried the graceful look of the lady who had directed everything for the occasion. The centerpiece included six scented flaming decorative candles surrounded by a wreath of woven, fresh flowers, all effusing fragrance that spoke of a special event. Each candle represented each month of marriage.

Matching the table's elegance was the beautiful Dr. Sheena dressed in clothes purchased by her husband with her approval. She came into his life when she wore plain, simple outfits, and even now would continue that tradition, but her husband wanted her wardrobe to match her beauty and grace, and wanting to please him, she yielded to his wishes.

The six months of marriage she was celebrating tonight had been the happiest days of her life, and for this special occasion, she had brought in Hans' favorite chef and his assistant to prepare and serve a lavish epicurean dinner.

Before the four gathered around the dining table, Hans said to his father-in-law, "Pop, you're the priest of our family, and we want you to give a Jewish blessing over our marriage."

Both parents went and stood behind the couple, and

placing their hands on them, they heard the elderly father give the blessing from memory:

The Lord bless you and keep you; the Lord make His face shine upon you and be gracious to you; the Lord turn His face toward you and give you peace. Many waters cannot quench love, neither can floods drown it. If a man offered for love all the wealth of his house, it would be utterly scorned. I am my beloved's and my beloved is mine.

Sheena took her husband's hand, saying, "I want my husband to know that he has made me the happiest wife in the world."

"That's the way it's supposed to be," responded her father. He leaned over and kissed her on the cheek.

"Papa, you've always been a wonderful Papa, and it's because of you I can be the wife I should be to Hans."

Hans turned and kissed Sheena, then said, "Pop, let's all sit down and eat before it gets cold. We want to talk to you about something."

"Hans, it's not going to be about my husband's housing project in Israel, Is it? He lives that assignment day and night! Especially, now that it has new immigrants occupying the newly finished units. Now don't get me wrong, I want him involved in what you've assigned him because it gives him something to live for, but Hans, it's too much when he talks to me about it in his sleep."

Hans and Sheena looked at each other showing subdued smiles that gave affirmation that her mother was in her normal crotchety mode expecting a response from her husband that would further energize conversational banter.

Normally, the old man would engage her knowing everything was contrived for teasing. But tonight was different. He was a skilled diamond cutter, knew where to place his cutting tool to produce the best results. In life, he'd done this with his beautiful daughter and was admiring her charm and elegance. He knew what the evening was about. He looked across the sumptuous table at the most beautiful stone he'd ever seen. He knew she was God's gift of beauty, but beyond her outer mortal frame, there was inner transcendent splendor, the quality of character and fineness that only God could create, and his hands as a father had been part of that shaping and polishing. He knew table talk would later move away from the celebratory atmosphere of this beautiful event, and that it should be savored and made meaningful. The diamond cutter's skill morphed itself into another kind of tool using soft, meaningful words as the hammer made the cut.

"Mr. and Mrs. Isler, Momma and I would like to make a toast to you on this very special occasion of your six-month wedding celebration. First, our lovely daughter brought us life and joy, then she gave us a son in her marriage to Hans."

The old man stopped, looked across the table at Hans with an intended frown on his craggy face. "Hans, I didn't like you when Sheena brought you to our home to meet us. Moreover, when she told us you had proposed marriage, I went through a death experience. You were taking my little girl from me. Momma was ecstatic about the engagement but not me."

The father paused speaking, reached across the table and took hold of Hans' hand and pulled it toward him, saying, "However, you grew on me when I saw how you made my daughter happy and fulfilled, and now you're like my own son."

The old man's wrinkled hand was still clasping Hans' when he heard the man who took his daughter from him say, "Pop, I never had a father. A beautiful and honorable lady adopted me, and now that she's gone, God has given me parents to take her place."

Upon hearing these words, Hans felt the grip of the old man tighten. Like a closing drama being performed, it was the tight squeeze of the aged hand used to make people as beautiful as the stones it cut and polished, that gave silent applause to those watching the act. Both had affirmed to each other their newly established roles, a time when touching and feeling spoke louder than words. It was an act that would seal memory forever.

The atmosphere created in conversation and body language morphed into a mystifying force, an energy spreading itself throughout the dining room creating solemn quietness that gave honor and respect to the decorated table holding six glowing candles and a colorful wreath of flowers. Together, they punctuated a festive event with opulent fragrance, leaving an unscripted mysterious oneness. After a long pause of voluntary silence, Hans was first to speak.

"I would like to announce that Michael, my uncle, has made another pickup off the coast of Romania. Pop, these are Jewish immigrants who will fill those units you're putting up there in Israel."

Does this mean that my husband will be spending more or less time in Israel with the arrival of new immigrants?" asked the mother.

"Our responsibility is providing funds, engineering, and

construction of the units. Management is handled by the department of immigration and housing."

"I'd like to go on one of Michael's pickup voyages," said the old man."

"I'm sure that can be arranged," said Hans. How do you handle motion sickness and rough waters?

"That'll be no problem," said the father.

"Do I get to go along too?" asked the mother. I prefer being with my husband than staying alone."

"I'm glad you suggested it," said Hans. On board, there are extra staterooms with private baths and three meals a day. Both of you will have a lot to contribute to the new arrivals making their way to the land of their ancestors."

"We should. We've been there and done that," said the father.

They had finished dinner and were waiting for coffee and dessert to be served when the mother and father took special note that their daughter had become quiet and detached. Hans knew what this was about. She had an announcement to make that would devastate her parents and chose tonight's special occasion to tell them. Hans glanced at Sheena conveying a message that now was as good a time as any to announce her recent decision.

"Mama and Papa, I have something to tell you that I have struggled long and hard over after giving serious consideration to your investment in my life and education. You have dreamed of me becoming a doctor, and with your help and encouragement, that goal has been achieved. However, I need another year of internship to qualify for private practice. Your goal for me was to become a physician, have a profession that would make me independent and self-sustaining. It has always been my goal as well.

"I will forever be grateful to you for your encouragement and support. It was because I went into the medical field that I met my wonderful husband. Now that we're happily married, I look at life differently.

"As you know, all of us are forced to live in fortresses because of Hans' wealth and his support of Israel. Our lives are always under scrutiny. We have to be micromanaged when we go out, others are always watching over us. Hans once told me that I would never be a doctor in private practice because of his wealth. He has allowed me to see this for myself, and because of his vast wealth, this is the way it will always be.

"Therefore, I alone have made the decision that I'll not finish my internship at the hospital my husband owns but will become a partner, not only in our marriage but also in the work God has called him to do for Israel. I know you may be disappointed in my decision, but my choice was made after much thought and prayer."

Sheena's eyes were now focused away from her parents. She had dreaded this moment. Her hands were under the table on her lap—she was the little girl now telling her mother and father something they didn't want to hear. Her spirit lifted when she felt her husband's hand take one of hers. It gave her courage to first look at her father. He had a grin on his face that was as wide as the one he carried when she graduated from medical school. Her mother didn't speak with a smile, she used words.

"My dear, your father and I have already discussed this matter knowing it would happen at some point, and we think it is the best thing to do under the circumstances. Besides, you'll always be a doctor."

"Well," said the father, "I think we should celebrate this along with the special occasion that brings us here tonight, your six months of marriage. And if my olfactory is correctly registering what I smell, it can be done with my favorite hot apple pie served with good strong Middle Eastern coffee."

Chapter 7

The Executive Secretary

It was a normal workday for Sonje Shuster when she stopped at the entrance of the underground parking garage to be cleared by security. Everyone in security knew her and was always surprised when she acknowledged them by name.

"Good morning, Miss Shuster."

"Morning, Joe, how's the family?"

"Fine ma'am, thank you for asking."

"Has my boss arrived?"

"His driver hasn't pulled in yet, but that doesn't mean anything, he's sometimes dropped off in the front—he's never predictable—says that's the way it's supposed to be."

The lady who just arrived was the administrative assistant to the chairman and the second most powerful person in the company. He never tired of the wonderment of her gracious persona. She was in her early forties, a lovely lady who looked ten years younger. Security officers who saw and spoke to her daily as she came and went knew her better than those who entered her sealed chamber where corporate power brokers waited to see the chairman. She knew everything inside-and-out about the global enterprising corporation of which she was an integral part because of positions held through the years before becoming the chairman's executive officer. Her role was administrative secretary, one who acted as a gatekeeper and advisor to the chairman. At her disposal was a well-maintained staff of clerks for the perfunctory clerical duties. *The security team frequently wondered why she had never married. She was a beautiful lady.*

The gate lifted permitting her to drive pass the security station into an underground parking garage where only approved administrative personnel were allowed to park. She pulled into her designated parking site, marked: Executive Secretary. To her left was the reserved spot for the CEO, and on her right was where her boss's driver always parked the armored vehicle that drove him wherever he went. Both spots were empty. She had arrived earlier than usual.

She turned off the engine, but memory froze her momentarily. She carried secrets of personal history the chairman knew nothing about, history before he inherited his mother's wealth, and it was all about him and his late mother. Someday, she would have to tell him the whole story. It was a promise he'd made to his late mother. But when...and how? It was a weight carried to work every day, and today it seemed heavier than ever before.

Life flowed back into Sonje's limbs. She pulled the keys from the ignition, gathered her attaché case, and forced her svelte frame out of her upscale vehicle. Without locking the door, she walked in her normal, elegant manner to the private elevator waiting to take her to the office that carried out decisions affecting people around the world. Her private life was solitary, but that side of her changed once she stepped onto the property of Katharina Enterprises, a global company she had helped develop over the last twenty years. Employees, who approached her in hallways and offices, would almost bow in her presence. She not only possessed power from her position and experience, she commanded respect because of her quality of character and warmth. Her eyes were beautiful pools of blue for a woman of her age, but it was what they spoke that people remembered most.

She had been asked by the chairman himself when he took over his late mother's vast wealth to be his administrative secretary because he needed someone to work closely with him who knew the inner workings of the company. What was unknown to her boss was that she was more than an experienced advisor in financial matters. She had been his late mother's best friend and confidant and had it not been for her, his life might have turned out differently. She was a hidden part of his life.

Sonje had come to work early and found that the front office receptionist had not arrived. Turning to go to her plush office down the hall, she heard the door open. Thinking it was the receptionist, she turned to greet her but saw a tall, rugged-looking man with dominant facial features standing and looking about the room, mesmerized by the affluence it effused. A voice broke through his stupefaction.

"May I help you, Sir?"

The man paid no attention to the person speaking but continued looking at the elegance of the office décor. Still taking in the aesthetic atmosphere of the room, he responded without looking at the lady.

"Is Jacob in?"

"You must be in the wrong office, Sir."

He looked in her direction where she was standing.

Their eyes met. Neither said anything for a moment. Eyes were doing the talking. The man thought hers were beautiful but carried a look of mystery. Each had stepped into the other's private domain. Without words, eyes were measuring something common to both: the mystery of hidden pain.

Who was this man, she thought, who carried a look of purpose with an energy that spoke of rustic valor and confidence? Without speaking, a strange aura emanated itself between the two. Common experiences of two strangers were serving to awaken an uncommon world.

Words failed them. Their prolonged fixed stare was broken when the man spoke. "Is Dr. Hans in? He's my nephew, and I'm to meet with him this morning."

She had already lost her typical poise and self-confidence. *Now she was being told that the man who stood in her presence was her boss's uncle. How could this be? The chairman had no living relative.* The lady who knew as much as the chairman about the inner workings of the giant corporation was at a loss for words. He had come to discuss Operation Henry with Hans, a secret mission known only to a select few, and Miss Shuster was not one of them.

"Oh my, now I recognize you! You were Dr. Hans' best man at his wedding!"

"Yes, I was honored when he asked me to serve in that role, an honor indeed."

"I'm glad to formally meet you Mr....?"

"The name is Michael, Michael Pencovich. Just call me Michael."

Another bomb hit her. This was the mystery man who called the chairman on his personal line, and she remembered handling the call.

"Please come to my office, and I'll see if the chairman has arrived."

She was thinking that a lot of class ran in that family. The man radiated confidence and persuasion, and it was all mingled together with the pain she knew he carried. Now her initial intuition about him was confirmed: he had lived through the Holocaust in Romania, much like herself in Nazi Germany, but she wasn't Jewish. A strange feeling came over her: she knew something that even Hans' mother never knew.

By the time they reached her office, the intercom light from the chairman was blinking.

"Yes, Dr. Hans?"

"When Michael Pencovich arrives, send him to my office."

"He's here now!"

What a strange day, the secretary thought. Perhaps, the man she just met could be helpful in disclosing what his nephew needed to know. She knew Hans' office had a separate, private entrance, and his uncle could easily be whisked out that way. She wished otherwise.

The CEO and CFO were both waiting for their appointment with the chairman when Michael came from the chairman's office.

"Mr. Pencovich, may I speak to you for a minute before you leave?" She waited until they were alone in her office, then called her personal secretary.

"Please come to my office, Freda, I need you to stand in for me for a bit." Turning to Michael, she asked, "Where are you parked, Michael? You did say, 'I should call you Michael.' Is that all right with you?"

"Oh, please do. My driver is waiting for me in the

visitors' parking lot."

"I would like to walk part of the way with you and ask you some questions."

By this time, her personal secretary had arrived and found Miss Shuster standing near a tall man she didn't recognize. *She thought it strange—most people who came in to see the chairman she knew, and he was dressed quite commonly. Surely, he's not Miss Shuster's friend. This would be uncharacteristic of her. She never knew of her having male friends, and he didn't fit her class.*

"Freda, if the chairman calls, tell him I'll be back shortly and that you're filling in for me. Oh yes, allow me to introduce Dr. Hans' uncle, Mr. Pencovich."

The secretary's face froze. Standing in her presence was a close relative of the chairman, known to be one of the wealthiest men in Europe. She did her best to maintain her composure. *Sonje Shuster took note of her secretary's response to what she was just told about the stranger standing among them. She had the same reaction earlier.*

"It is my honor to meet you, Mr. Pencovich."

"It is a greater honor to meet you, Freda. I hope I shall have the pleasure of meeting you again."

"Thank you, Sir."

"Please don't call me sir, Michael will do very well.

When Michael and Sonje left the office, the secretary had to steady herself. *She wasn't a gossipmonger, but if she were, she'd have a lot to say. He's suave, she thought. If he were German, he'd be a good politician. However, his dress didn't match the status of his nephew's wealth.*

The door closed to her office and everything went quiet between Michael and Miss Shuster as they began a slow walk toward the elevator. The strange aura that filled the room when they first met returned leaving a foreboding, somber silence. Michael said nothing—he didn't ask for the walk. Now they were alone in the elevator descending to the bottom floor.

"Michael, I must meet with you to discuss a matter that doesn't concern you but someone near and dear to your nephew. It must be in a private location, and before we meet, I must receive assurance from you that everything you hear will be kept confidential."

"Do you have family, Miss Shuster, a husband, children?"

Why was he asking me this? she thought. Sonje said nothing, and Michael didn't pursue the question. Finally, she said, "I usually don't talk about myself, Mr. Pencovich." She suddenly became formal and distant, then inquired, "Why do you ask?"

"You're the one who requested to meet with me, and I'm trying to practice propriety by knowing your marital status before I ask you out for dinner where we can discuss your matter, and I will assure you that what I'm told will be held in confidence."

"I'm not married Mr. Pencovich. The young man I wanted to marry was killed in the war."

The secretary saw Michael look away. Mutual pain was showing itself again. He'd now bonded with her experience of losing someone intended for marriage. Still looking away, he responded saying, "If you accept my offer, I'll pick you up at seven tonight."

The people who saw the two walking together were startled seeing the executive secretary out of her element, walking with a stranger whose dress stood in contrast to her elegance. She was usually friendly and observant, but today she was neither. By the time Michael and Sonje reached the entrance to the office building, he had her address and phone number in hand.

"I'll pick you up at seven," said Michael. "Jacob provides me a vehicle and a driver, so I shouldn't have a problem finding your place."

"Are you staying at his place?"

"Yes. They insisted, especially Jacob's lovely wife, Sheena. Jacob persuaded her to hire household help. Had they not done that, I'd not stay with them. I'm quite self-sufficient, you know, having lived...well, I'll not tell you about that."

Sonje lived in a dichotomous world, one side showing itself in her open, self-confident, professional role in the corporate world. In this part of her life, she was secure, respected and admired. However, her private life was one of mystery, a place where she had made a masterful science out of protecting herself with a walled fortress of silence to the exclusion of others, especially men.

Something happened inside her today from the moment she looked into the eyes of Michael. It was the magnet of pain he carried that was luring her to invite a stranger inside her walled fortress. Her professional corporate side of using him to fulfill the promise made to Han's mother was her rationale for unlocking the steel gate people were forbidden to enter. She also knew something bizarre was going on inside with her feelings of intrigue and excitement.

On her way back to her office, curious looks came from those she had walked by reaching the front entrance. She had passed them speaking to a stranger who stood in contrast to her elegant form. Moreover, the stranger

69

appeared to be the one in charge of the conversation, something uncharacteristic for the lady known as the second most powerful person in the corporation.

Chapter 8

Common Ground

Michael was waiting inside Hans' walled residence when his driver pulled through the gate. The vehicle came to a stop. The driver got out and opened the rear door for his passenger. He noticed he had a different driver now assigned to him. Both were standing outside the vehicle when Michael asked, "How is it I have you as a driver instead of the gentleman who drove this morning?"

"It's a change of shift, Sir."

"My name is Michael, and what name do you go by?"

The driver didn't know who his passenger was but knew he was important to the chairman—he was staying with him in his home.

"My name is Luis."

"Have you been with the company long?"

"Five years, Sir."

"I believe I said my name was Michael, and it would be respectful if you addressed me by that name."

"That would be against protocol. We have a rulebook we're required to go by if you know what I mean. We address our passengers formally, and only answer questions posed to us."

"My, they have you in a straight jacket, don't they? Just between us, when we're alone it'll be a first-name basis. That way no one gets in trouble."

The driver was taken aback. He'd never driven a passenger who commanded so forcefully his space like this person. He wondered if he were a high-ranking military officer. His self-confidence and plain talk gave a magnetism that demanded respect.

"Before we leave, Luis, I must confide in you. I'm in need of an upscale place where dinner is served and there is maximum privacy in secluded booths. Business matters will be discussed that no one should hear."

"Michael, you're in luck in that I do the evening driving schedule and take executives in the company to such places as you are requesting. How many are in your party?"

"There'll only be two of us, and the other party will be picked up at this address."

The driver took the piece of paper handed him and looked closely at it—then broke protocol in a moment of unguarded dialogue.

"This is a swanky part of town,"

After initiating an opinion to his passenger about the area of town they'd be visiting, the driver caught himself. *This man he was picking up, thought the driver, had such an openness and unconventional manner that he forgot protocol—commentary was not part of his job and warranted being written up.*

"I'll call the establishment and reserve a table for two." Michael saw the driver reach into the vehicle, pull out a small book, thumb through it until he found what he wanted. After dialing the number, he said to the person at the other end of the line, "Please make reservations for two in the quietest and most secluded area of your establishment. The name is Michael." When they requested a surname from the driver, he looked over at Michael.

"They need a surname, Michael!"

"Tell him it's Smith, Michael Smith."

"Sir, the name is Michael Smith."

After the driver left the compound and was on the public roadway, he broke protocol again.

"Is Michael Smith your real name?"

"Of course not!"

I did it again, thought the driver! This man possessed such informal, magnetic appeal that one could easily forget the code of behavior required of a driver. From the back seat, he heard his passenger say, "Leave the privacy window between us open, it's less claustrophobic, and I hope you don't smoke."

"It's against the rules," answered the driver.

"Well, I agree with that rule!"

It was ten minutes to seven, and Sonje Shuster was on pins-and-needles. She always dressed upscale with the most in-vogue styles, always modest but very debonair. She could not explain to herself why the envelope had been pushed by wearing exquisite costly jewelry, and if they ended up going to a place that matched Michael's dress, it would be a night of horror. More attention was given to what she looked like than the reason for meeting with her boss's uncle.

The address took Michael to an exclusive, high-end, suburban-gated development with large, rolling lots covered with park-like features. The vehicle stopped at its entrance where a security guard stood in front of a closed, daunting, iron gate. Michael saw that the lady had acquired money somewhere in her journey through life.

"Your name please," asked the guard.

"Luis, don't give him the Smith name, that won't do.

Give me your phone."

Using the phone number given him by Miss Shuster, he dialed her.

"Miss Shuster, this is Michael. Would you please tell this security officer here at the front gate that I'm Michael Smith, and am here at your invitation?"

He handed the phone to the guard. Approval was confirmed, and the driver proceeded to the guest parking lot.

The name, surely it couldn't be, thought the driver, it couldn't be the lady known as the second most powerful figure in the company! It was rumored she had money and was self-made.

The driver jumped out and opened the rear door for Michael. "Well, Luis, you're in for a boring night this evening."

"Oh, I'm used to it, it's my job."

"We'll be back soon, and by the way, with two in the back seat, I lose my claustrophobia so you can close the centerpiece."

The exquisite layout of the development inside the ten-foot wall was a city within itself. It had all the markings of having been built for the rich and famous. It was apparent his lady was rich and the famous part remained to be seen. It was a long stroll to her cloistered home inside a well-designed, park-like setting. Foliage-filled greenery with gorgeous aromatic flowers lined the pathway leading to her site. After walking over a small bridge, under which flowed a narrow, man-made stream, he saw her home nestled alongside large ponderous oak trees. The scene wrestled from Michael all the levity created with the driver. Its calm beauty pushed him back into his history before the sordid events of the war. He knew part of his healing included remembering the better days. He stopped, held his head high and breathed in the fresh air of freedom, then walked slowly to the front door. The route he'd taken to reach her home was for visitors. She had a private driveway for her own use in the back of her home.

The administrative secretary, whose wealth and position gave her everything needed to boost her image and self-confidence, couldn't understand why she was anxious and was concerned she'd show it when Michael arrived. To avoid looking fretful, she stood at the door and waited for Michael to ring the bell a second time. She controlled even the opening of the door, allowing it to move slow but lost control of the event when she saw the way Michael was dressed. The slow-moving door rapidly opened full-bore showing her guest attired in the suit he had worn at his nephew's wedding. This was unexpected, almost knocking her off her feet.

She hardly recognized the man at her door. He had a commanding presence and what she saw was competing with the purpose of the occasion. Now she felt calmer about over-dressing for the evening. Michael, still reeling from flashback memories, had lost his zest for comedic commentary about anything. The serious look showing on his face made Sonje wonder if he regretted having made this engagement. Neither said anything until they crossed the small wooden bridge. Michael was first to speak.

"You have a lovely place here. It reminds me of the time of my life when I lived in the mountains amongst rugged trees like these just to stay alive."

Sonje saw a flash of pain that was more like a gust of air wafting itself onto a beach where someone had been washed ashore, alive but weak and in need of help. The breeze she felt carried vague signals of what lay beneath a surface of hurt. Only people who had his experience of shoreline rescue could see another's darkness. This was what she saw in his eyes in her office earlier today and was the reason she allowed herself to be with him tonight.

"Mr. Pencovich, we all have symbols we carry around that point to events of rescue."

By this time, they had reached the visitors' parking lot where the driver stood waiting alongside an open door with thoughts swarming inside about his new passenger. For Sonje, something historical happened tonight inside her walled world: for the first time she allowed a man to enter her gated community to pick her up for dinner. The high, gated walls she lived behind symbolized other kinds of walls she had built to keep people out. Her corporate world was an open book, but outside that world, she was a mystery. Tonight, she allowed those walls to be breached.

From a distance, the driver could tell that the lady walking with his passenger who called himself Mr. Smith, was none other than the powerful Miss Shuster. *What a night, he thought; this was grist for the old millhouse of talk and gossip. Everyone knew her as the dresser, but tonight she had diamonds galore, and he was sure it wasn't for the benefit of a business meeting. He wished happiness for her because of the person she was and what she'd done for his little boy.*

The driver's rigid protocol of formality returned when the executive secretary approached the vehicle alongside his male passenger.

"Good evening, Luis," said Miss Shuster. "Is your little Joel in school yet?"

"Good evening, Ma'am. Oh yes, he just started this year."

Michael knew there were several hundred employees at the central office building, yet she knew the name of the driver's son!

Miss Shuster was first to speak after boarding the vehicle and it came in the form of a question.

"Mr. Pencovich, why are you going incognito by the name of Smith?"

"Miss Shuster, you may think you know everything there is about your company because you're the chairman's executive secretary and part of the administrative team, but it appears there are hidden agendas you know nothing about. My expertise is used in one of these operations, and it's best that I leave no paper trail."

For the first time, the lady who held the position of power and respect felt insecure and awkward being told something she knew nothing about. She had achieved where she was in the company because of the chairman's mother, and her focus must not be sidetracked—she would get on with her purpose of meeting with this man and avoid being drawn into his influence.

When seated at their table, Miss Shuster instructed the waiter to bring them water and not return until summoned. It was a booth appropriately secluded so conversation could be made in privacy. She had requested this meeting, and Michael saw in their cloistered booth a self-confident lady struggling to pull together enough strength to deal with the matter on her mind. Her folded tense hands held over the white, linen-covered table registered what was showing on her strained face.

"Mr. Pencovich, before I begin to tell my story, I want

reassurance that what you hear will be held in confidence. Can that be agreed upon?"

"I have already given you my word in that matter."

"Mr. Pencovich, I know you are a very intelligent man with certain innocent cunning skills that make you a leader among men. My deduction comes from the fact that I fit into that category myself. Like people say, 'It takes one to know one.'" Michael interrupted to set the record straight.

"Miss Shuster, if there is innocence, it lies only with you. I am not innocent but will affirm that I'm here today because of my survival prowess."

The lady who had a grip on power knew how to quickly evaluate someone with limited information by interpreting body language: it might be a key word, facial expression, a twitch, glance, or sudden silence. Though body language carried the stronger weight, it was her intuition and experience that found the light switch in the dark of night. When Michael denied his innocent cunning, she saw contradiction, and had it not been the urgency of her own need, she would've followed up on his statement.

"I have requested this meeting tonight because I'm obligated to take action on a promise I made to Hans' adoptive mother, my closest and dearest friend in life. I have chosen to ask you to help in this matter."

"Miss Shuster, I don't see myself as an important figure, but in whatever way I can help, I am more than willing to do so."

"Thank you," said Miss Shuster, whose face was now showing a look of trepidation. Michael saw the sparkle in her blue eyes lose luster as she prepared to step into the throes of a dark memory.

"It is to my regret that for you to help me I must tell

you something that concerns a painful part of my life. I have struggled with great difficulty bringing myself to this point of revealing something so personal. Intuition tells me that you may have been through my similar experience, and for this reason, I'm going to be brave because of what someone did for me.

"I am German but a survivor of a concentration camp where Jews, gypsies, and others were kept for slave labor and extermination. The only person who knew the story I'm telling you was Katharina.

"My father was a doctor, and when the SS were rounding up Jews to be taken off to death camps, he hid a Jewish family on our premises. Late one night the Gestapo was heard pounding on our door. Even to this day, I wake up at night and hear those pounding sounds. They took us all, the Jewish family, my mother, father, and me. Without a hearing, without legal recourse, we were sent off to a concentration camp. Though we were German, we were treated as Jews, separated from each other, and conscripted to forced labor. The brutality, torture, and hunger ravaged our minds and bodies. We became frail and weak. Some welcomed death. My mother and father broke in health, disappeared, and I never saw or heard from them again. I was abused by the guards, and in my emaciated state, I became undesirable. I thanked God every night that I had reached that state and wanted to die. Then one day Americans came to our camp and freed us. I had lost my will to live, as did others in the camp. Those who could walk and fend for themselves were taken to a resettlement facility where a proper diet and sleeping quarters were provided. Others were put in hospital facilities and given medical treatment."

The secretary's detailed account of her tortuous, brutal life in the camp had been told with her eyes fixed on her hands. She paused for a glance at Michael. His eyes had the look of seeing something in his own past. Tears were coursing down his smooth, rugged face, leaving the message that he knew about her pain. This encouraged her to continue.

"I had no family to claim me, no place to go. I was in the same state as the Jews I lived among. After several weeks, a modicum of health returned, and we were visited by two people who would change my life forever. A beautiful German woman and an older Jewish man came to our camp to assist those who wanted to emigrate to another country. When they came to me, found that I was German and heard my story, the beautiful lady took me home with her that day and gave me a life. She had a little boy whose name was Hans. In those early days, I helped her in her home with chores and with the small lad she smothered with love and care. The little fellow had been orphaned when his parents were massacred in a village in Romania. The lady was very wealthy but chose to live a modest life for the sake of her son. I was sent away to the university, trained in finance, and when I returned, the lady who rescued me taught me everything about investment and business. I learned everything she knew and became her voice in official business decisions when she was unavailable. Mr. Klein, her long-time friend, welcomed me as a silent working entity on her behalf.

"It was Katharina's design that Hans would never know about me as long as she was alive, fearful that it would bring to light the matter of her wealth. Her intent was to raise him without the affluence of wealth believing that he was saved from the Holocaust to be used by God to help his people. I became her best friend and over the years have become wealthy following her investment advice. She made me promise that after she was gone, I would give her son an envelope with an enclosed letter telling him about me. She said, 'It was needful for him to know that her best friend helped her to be a good mother at home.' I now carry the burden of that letter and it is the reason I have requested this meeting with you. Do you have any advice for me?"

By now, Michael had pulled himself together to respond. "First, may I ask how you became his executive secretary?"

"I served on the administrative team in different capacities and knew everything about the inner workings of the company. Hans is a brilliant administrator, conceptually fast, understands people, and is a forward thinker. But being thrust into running this massive operation, he needed someone to lean on, and he asked me to come on board. Between Mr. Klein and me, we helped him get his footing, and now he's off and running on his own. And I take pride that he chose me to be at his side."

"You know, Miss Shuster, when he reads that letter he may request another advisor because you will always remind him of his mother."

"My, you're insightful, Mr. Pencovich, just like your nephew. He even looks like you now that you're all spiffed-up."

"Speaking of being spiffed-up, what makes you so aggressive with your mode of dress?"

Michael saw Miss Shuster recoil with controlled umbrage. Being a self-made, independent woman who could handle conflict in the workplace, she found it unsettling when it was about her person. He had stepped over the line into her space. Yet, she was the one who made herself vulnerable by opening the iron gate to her bastion. Now, after exposing something so personal that she had carried around for years, he had the temerity to criticize her person. She registered resentment in a subtle way: "Mr. Pencovich, shall we place our order?"

"Definitely, it's that time," said Michael. He left the table to find their waiter, and when he returned, his guest was gone. A note had been left on the table where he sat. It read: "Went to the ladies room, will be right back."

When the secretary returned, Michael could see that her eyes were red and swollen from crying. He knew she was a fortress of indomitable strength, but he had touched her most vulnerable part. They had the menu on the table in front of them, and they quickly placed their order. She said nothing.

"Miss Shuster, you'll have to pardon me for lacking tact. I don't know how to be tactful. I lost it when the Nazis killed my family, and the girl I was to marry in three months was taken, raped, and later committed suicide because she couldn't live with that memory. I still have the farewell note she left me.

"Miss Shuster, I used to have tact. My parents taught me well, but after these events, I died. For years, I was a dead man until God sent an orphaned nephew, adopted by a German woman, the same woman who saved you. He led me to a prophet, his father-in-law, who introduced me to the Giver of Life. Now, I'm coming back to life a day-at-a-time."

While Michael spoke, he never looked up. When he finished, he felt a hand touching one of his and heard the words: "Thank you, Michael, for what you said. Your words have made me a better person. What you said gives me the courage to answer your question." *Sonje Schuster was taken aback when she realized she was touching Michael's hand. She had never touched a man's hand like this before to offer solace, but it felt so natural.*

"I don't really need an answer to my impudent question," was Michael's response. He welcomed the lady's touch on his hand. Then looking up, he saw she had tears in her eyes. Something inside him wanted her to keep her hand over his. It felt like a warm embrace, a rope dropped into the well of his dark world, a lifeline trying to rescue what was left of his soul. She slowly slipped it away, saying, "I'm like you, Michael, I've been damaged, and I'm smart enough to know that the reason I dress like I do is that I'm trying to compensate for what's lacking inside."

"I suppose we all do this in one form or another," said Michael.

The waiter arrived at their table to take orders suspending the crucible in which they found themselves. Underneath their small talk and chatty dialogue throughout the evening, they both knew they were a pathway for each other's personal growth. They were two people who stood on common ground, and that by combining their strengths they could find their way out of their own wastelands.

For the rest of the evening, only the safe ground of social interaction was visited. They steered themselves closely to the center avoiding any precipitous and awkward engagements. Upon nearing her fashionable estate, Michael asked, "Do you wish to be taken on the roadway to your home or be escorted by foot through the parkway?"

"If you're my escort, I would prefer nature's path."

Michael had never been around many women, and of those his life crossed, interest was short-lived. The phantom ghost of the girl he was to marry always hung over him. His mind kept her alive, and tonight he was with a woman who suffered the same painful abasement. The driver pulled into the visitors' parking lot, opened the door on Michael side. She felt his hand take hers giving assistance in stepping out of the vehicle. After standing, he still held her hand under the streetlight while he spoke to Luis.

"Luis, give me ten minutes and we'll be ready to roll."

Sonje offered no resistance to the clasp of Michael's hand intertwined with hers even in plain view of the driver. She took time to welcome guilt from wishing he would continue his touch until she reached her home, but he slowly released his hand, leaving her a memory of someone who, after hearing her story, could show unfeigned feeling. This simple gesture of touch gave her a sense of inner self-worth.

The sounds of the night were out in full force as they made their way up the well-lighted pathway, leaving the driver saying to himself: *Tonight, I didn't have to go to a movie to be entertained, and even though a lowly driver and not part of the star cast, I saw the action up close. It's not every day one gets to see big stars moving in the circles of a commoner—this was human-interest over-the-top.*

Walking side-by-side, nature was serenading two people who had divulged to each other the secrets of their tragic histories. The overhead cooler stratified air was lending itself, like a canopy preventing the escape of nature's aromatic wonders, enhancing Sonje's mental preoccupation with the touch of Michael's hand. It was nature's nighttime sounds piercing the darkness that filled Michael's brain, sounds that brought back memories of surviving in the wild by learning to mimic the voices of an untamed world.

"Miss Shuster, do you hear the sounds out there in the darkness?" My friends and I developed a language using those sounds to survive in our struggles in Romania. Listen to the crickets...."

In the silent moments that followed, Michael gave the sound of a cricket near Sonje's ear, then turned his face away and gave the squawk of a Nighthawk. The darkness that shrouded them didn't permit him to see the face of the woman whose life had been awakened, now showing a dropped jaw with a look of wonderment. He continued his own form of entertainment in the dark by giving another Nighthawk call with certain sound-pitch variations, saying to the lady standing beside him, "I just gave a message to my colleagues telling them a patrol of five Iron Guard soldiers were coming in their direction."

"This is incredible," said Sonje. "How am I to believe this is possible?"

"This was why it was successful. People couldn't believe humans could do such a thing. This was only one of our methods of surviving."

Michael avoided the subject of being an executioner, and when they reached the front door, he said, "My advice about the letter you are to give Jacob from Katharina is that it should be done right away. Life is short and prolonging the event will not make it easier. I will take it to him myself if you so wish, but it should be done soon."

"If I give it to you tonight, when will you deliver it?"

"Either tonight or tomorrow morning," said Michael.

"That being the case, please tell the chairman that I'll be away from the office for a week, and Freda will fill in for me. Come in please, and I'll get the letter for you."

The interior of her home looked as Michael expected—upscale and equal to the level of her dress code. She soon returned with a brown envelope marked, confidential.

"Michael, inside this large envelope is another envelope containing Katharina's letter to Hans. When this is delivered, I will have fulfilled my vow to my best friend. Tell Hans that I'm the mystery person who once-a-month puts flowers on her grave."

"We'll hope and pray for the best," said Michael. "I enjoyed being with you tonight. It turned out differently than I expected."

"The same can be said for me, and before you leave, I have a request that I hope you will keep. Please call me Sonje from now on!"

"I will remember to do that, Sonje. Goodnight!"

She stood on the porch and watched him walk down the pathway until he was out of sight, then paused to listen to the sounds of the night.

Chapter 9

Invitation to Pharaoh's Palace

Sonje was lying in her bed the next morning knowing the chairman had already received the letter Michael had delivered either last night or this morning. It was a great help for Michael to do what she had avoided. It was now his choice to decide her fate. He was the one who chose her to be his administrative executive secretary when he came into ownership of the massive enterprise his mother had built, and it would be up to him to choose another if he so desired.

She had made everything at the central office her life. It was like a living organism, and she had helped make it run like a smooth machine. Her future rested in the hands of her best friend's son, who was now the captain at the helm of the corporate ship. She was left to ponder what his decision would be. She wished she were on a cruise, visiting America or Canada, just away from here.

Then what she didn't want to happen, happened: the telephone rang. She let it ring and ring until finally the receiver was lifted from its cradle. The voice that came through was what she didn't want to hear. He sounded angry.

"Sonje, why didn't you sit with me in the family pew at my mother's funeral?"

She was speechless. She didn't know where he was

going with this. What she didn't know was that he was reliving his trauma of not having any relative to sit with him at the funeral, and she was her best friend in life and should have been in that pew.

"I wasn't a family member, Hans, and according to your mother's wishes, you were not supposed to know at that time."

"Well, you're a member now, and I want you over here tonight for dinner at seven o'clock. And I want you back at work tomorrow because I need you for some special events coming up, which I will explain later."

She lay still on the bed. Her thoughts were on Joseph in an Egyptian prison managing for the warden the complex state prison system. Information reaching the king demanded the skills he possessed. He not only had answers to the king's dream, he had advice in managing Egypt's economic future. Now, like Joseph who had served behind walls of anonymity, she was being summoned to the palace after years of servitude, all part of the brilliant plan devised by the woman who used wealth to promote Israel for the return of the Messiah.

The site where the chairman and his wife lived contained a large spacious compound garnished with exotic plants and colorful flowers. It had a driveway leading to the entrance allowing disembarkation of passengers, after which the car would be parked either in a garage or in a parking lot away from the residence. Sonje had been given the instructions by the gate attendant that she should proceed to the parking lot where company vehicles were parked.

Sonje was nervous when she pulled further into Hans' compound and saw four company cars parked and the drivers surrounding someone holding court in their midst. As she slid out of her vehicle and stood to her feet, a burst of loud laughter came from where the drivers had gathered. *Surely, they aren't laughing at me, thought Sonje.*

They hadn't noticed her arrival, even though an attendant had opened and closed the large metal gate. Someone's eyes in the group caught Sonje moving closer. Total silence followed. From the center of the group, Michael stepped forward, and the others stood at attention and gave a slight nod toward her as she walked by.

"Welcome, Sonje," said Michael. I've been assigned to be your official escort."

"This is becoming a common occurrence. I'm honored."

"I'm sorry there'll be fewer opportunities for me to serve as your escort. I'm leaving in a few days on my mission."

"I hope it's not dangerous," said Sonje.

"It's a calm storm considering the rough waters I've been over."

"I will miss you. You will promise to write me, won't you?"

The longer they walked, the slower their strides became. After last evening's event with Michael, it was easy for Sonje to create dialogue.

"I see you hold court and mix well with the common folk," said Sonje with intended sarcasm.

"I'm a common person."

"That's what you want people to think, but you're anything but common. Your kind is rare to come by."

"Is that supposed to be a compliment?" said Michael.

"Perhaps, it would be better said that you are a common

person with uncommon traits."

"I see you're not only a smart lady but a diplomat too."

"Michael, it's amazing how creative we can be when small talk is needed to fill empty space."

"Well, as they say, 'Necessity is the mother of invention.'"

Sonje lowered her voice and asked, "What was Hans' initial reaction to Katharina's letter?"

"I gave the letter to him last night, he read it, took it and Sheena to another room. Thirty-minutes later, he came out and said, 'Thank you for the letter.' Your experience tonight will tell the rest of the story."

By this time, they were at the front door. Instead of Michael opening the door, he turned to Sonje, saying, "Are you ready for this?" Then he pushed the doorbell. The door swung open wide. In front of her stood a reception of four: Hans, Sheena, her mother, and father. The large front room had been decorated with balloons, flowers, and a large sign that read: You're One of Us.

Sonje had worn her best for the evening, but it didn't match what she felt on the inside. However, when she saw Hans' acceptance and recognition of the service she'd given to his mother, her internal personhood grew to match what she wore. Her best friend, though gone from this life, was now giving back part of herself through her son's recognition of her service through the years.

Dr. Sheena was an artist with both sides of her brain fully equipped for any occasion. Tonight creativity was showing itself with the decorations and arrangements at the dining table with the flowers, candles, and a delectable gourmet spread. Most of it was prepared under her direction and supervision.

It was the old Prophet, now called Pop, by his new son-in-law, who queried the new family member about her faith. He soon found that she was as articulate enunciating her faith beliefs as she was in defining her dress code.

Sheena directed the seating arrangement around the table. Michael and Sonje were placed side-by-side, the prophet and his wife across from them with the master and mistress of the home at each end of the table. Hans stood to his feet so his speech would generate a greater somber and meaningful tone.

"Yesterday, I was given a letter from the lady who took an orphaned Jewish child and reared him as her own. I was told in that letter about another person who was sent to a concentration camp, along with her parents and a Jewish family they were hiding in their home. This person was the only surviving member of that group by the time the Americans arrived. She was taken into my mother's home and made an invisible family member where she worked with Gustov Klein, who is no longer with us. Together, they ran her vast enterprise while she was at home caring for me. This was all done so that my life could be prepared for supporting Israel for the return of the Messiah.

Sonje, from now on you will not only be my Executive Administrative Secretary but my older sister—the way my mother, your best friend, would want it."

When Hans sat, a veil of quiet settled over the dining table. Sonje's hands were folded on her lap. Her heart leaped when the man next to her covered them with one of his with the gesture of a tight squeeze, then withdrew it in quiet repose. It was the common man giving an uncommon expression of approval and congratulation for her adoption into Hans' family. She responded to Hans by standing.

"Tonight," said Sonje, "I feel like Joseph who managed the warden's prison until his hour came to appear in the court of the king. My service to Katharina was out of my love for her and the challenge of the responsibility. When I see some of the results of my commitment to her, it makes my servitude, if one is to call it that, even more rewarding. I am overwhelmed with your acceptance of me."

Across the table from her sat the old prophet with tears in his eyes. He was a man who measured everything in terms of quality and it was in full force tonight. She concluded by saying, "Some in life choose to bring death and destruction. I was a victim of those kinds of people, but others yield to the providence of giving and saving life. Hans and I had the mutual experience of knowing such a person—he as a son, and myself as a friend."

Hans brought closure by adding, "Now before we dine, I've asked Pop to give us a Scripture reading."

The elderly man whose energy far outweighed his craggy, aged look, calmly said: "We have two special guests among us, one has already spoken, and the other will share in the reading with me. You will be surprised to know that Michael has kept up on his Hebrew and will inspire us by reading it in the original language"

"I am reading from Isaiah fifty-three," said Michael. "Mr. Reznik led me to see that the Suffering-One in this narrative was the historical Jesus who died and rose again and who will return and take his rightful place in Zion. The dead spirit inside me was given life in its completeness but other intangible parts of me that I carry about in my mortality patiently wait for renewal. Only God can give life in a wasteland of ruin and despair."

When Michael finished reading the text in Hebrew, the

old man read it in German, and in conclusion, said, "God gave us a beautiful daughter. With her marriage to Hans, we gained a son, a son from the birth of a marriage. And as we have heard tonight, I have acquired a second son by a spiritual birth."

Up to this point, Sheena had said little and to soften the atmosphere, she made jest out of the subject at hand: "Papa, you're becoming prolific with sons tonight; perhaps that's a sign of great expectations." She leaned over into the face of her mother seated next to her, squinted her eyes, saying, "Mother are you holding out on us?"

"My dear, I'm not Sarah and your father isn't Abraham, but there will be a great expectation from me all bundled up for you at Christmastime, a special complimentary gift from Charles Dickens.

"Oh, you're fast on your feet tonight, Mother!" said Hans." Michael thought the stroke of genius was in Sheena setting the stage for the clever response, while Sonje was tempted to believe the histrionics were rehearsed beforehand. It was left for the old man to know the truth: his wife was just plain smart and witty.

Chapter 10

The Flight

Sheena was now no longer in the internship program at the hospital and was free to work with her husband in moving smuggled Jews from Soviet-aligned countries to Israel. Her contribution would be in overseeing the staffing of medical personnel on board the ships carrying the arrivals. She was a medical doctor, and though not licensed for private practice, could serve as an administrator in this new effort of moving the ancient people back to their land. Her new schedule also allowed her to be free to travel with her husband at will.

Sonje was back at her desk serving Hans as his administrative secretary being addressed as Sonje, and serving as chairlady in his absence.

Michael had returned to his post somewhere on a mystery ship in the Black Sea. He and Sonje were in correspondence, each taking time to write twice a week using teletype machines. Hans had given Michael a mission to train his life-long friends, Bub and Moshe, to take over his role when he was called to serve elsewhere. Hans knew his technical and inventive skills would soon be in demand. They needed to move a factory from South America into Israel for the creation of new jobs for arriving immigrants.

It was at the break of dawn when Hans, Sheena, and her parents arrived at the hangar where the company plane was already outside warming its engines for a flight to Israel. Sonje, their new family member, was among the group and had joined them for a trip to Israel to inspect the housing development under construction for new immigrants. The trip would also afford them the opportunity to search out industrial sites for a new factory soon to be moved into the country. A week earlier, Hans had wired Michael suggesting that if he could break free, he should fly into Israel from a foreign port, that his advice would be helpful in the early-stage planning. Fritz, the radioman, and one of the two pilots were waiting to assist with the transfer of luggage.

"Fritz, has the food-catering truck already serviced the plane?" asked Hans.

"Yes, Sir, and I had them drop off the special order as well."

"What special order is that?"

"Mr. Reznik's apple pie."

The old man was standing nearby and was full of early morning jest. "Now Hans, just don't you plan on getting my apple pie. You already got the apple of my eye, and now you want it all, even my specially ordered apple pie."

Fritz was laughing along with the pilot, and Sonje was making a mental note of how different life was outside Hans' austere, formal office where everything involved business and tough negotiations.

Unlike others of great wealth who would have brought along stewards and flight attendants to serve everyone on board the plane, it was Hans' simple, utilitarian approach to wealth that created cohesion and family-like atmosphere. As soon as the plane lifted off, the ladies heated and served breakfast, and the men made and served three different types of coffee.

Fritz managed the radio room, an extension of Hans' flying office. Sonje's assistant was standing in for her back at central headquarters, which kept her close to the radio throughout the flight. She had just settled in her first-class seat inside the captain's quarters with the rest of the party when someone knocked on the door. Hans opened the door. Standing in front of him was Fritz holding several folders. The radio operator took notice that those inside the Captain's quarters were either reading, looking out the windows, or sleeping.

"Sir, here's something that just came in for Miss Shuster…the sender says it's important!"

It was customary for a transcript to be delivered in a folder cataloged by topic with the transmission time. Hans took the folder, saw it bore a significant name that concerned him but gave deference to the one who was the gatekeeper to his office. Sonje took the envelope, read the transcript, and handed it to Hans, saying, "This is for your response."

The transcript read:

Sonje, a gentleman by the name of Albescu called your private line saying he wanted to talk to Mr. Isler about a proposition he had made to him. He left his number for a return call. I await your directive regarding this matter…Freda

Hans closed the folder and returned the transmission to its envelope. "Sonje, this is a response to a proposal I made to someone who possesses the skill to help us fulfill our mission of moving Jews back to their homeland, a vision that you and I share together. If he chooses to come onboard, I want you to be the liaison between him and our legal team in drawing up the details for my suggested clandestine business venture in Romania."

"And what will the business venture entail?" asked Sonje.

"The creation of a tourism enterprise consisting of coastal recreational deep-sea fishing and ocean-side rentals on beautiful sandy beaches. The patrons will be European. Everything will serve as a front to smuggle out Jews who are refused emigration papers."

Hans could see Sonje's wheels turning. Up to this point, her relationship with him had been on a professional level, and she had felt safe, but now everything had changed, and it was difficult to adjust to this new role as a family member. *When Michael was around, it was different. He understood who she was underneath her professional surface. They shared common pain. She would test Hans and see the extent of his acceptance of her in this new role.*

"Hans, Michael left abruptly, hardly saying goodbye. Does he have a secret mission?"

"He's in charge of our Prince Henry project. He organizes and arranges nighttime smuggling pickups in coastal waters helping Jews who are not allowed to emigrate out of their countries to Israel. He is a born leader and is demonstrating those qualities by his proven successes."

Sonje saw that Hans didn't fall over the tripwire she pulled up in front of him. He was open with her—a good sign.

Nearby were Sheena and her mother who appeared to

be asleep in their oversized, first-class seats. He continued his conversation with Sonje.

"You seem comfortable around Michael," said Hans.

"That's because of two things," said Sonje. "First, we both carry similar pain from the wartime years; and second, he challenges me by his impertinence—he tends to say what he thinks. Our mutual pain has a way of ameliorating this latter issue. No one has ever talked to me like he has about my manner of dress. I resented it deeply...I thought it none of his business. But later, when he apologized for it, it broke my spirit and it was like a mirror being held up in front of me where I viewed things about myself I never saw before. He is so smart and clever that I now wonder if his apology was all part of a design."

Sonje was so absorbed talking about Michael that Hans' smile went unnoticed after glancing at Mrs. Reznik who was showing signs of pretending to be asleep.

"We'll all soon be seeing more of Michael," said Hans. "I'm adding to his responsibilities, which will require him to be close to my office. He'll have to find a secure place to stay when that time comes."

From underneath the mask of pretended sleep, his mother-in-law, without cracking an eyelid, said, "He can stay in that vacant house in our walled compound. That arrangement would allow my husband to have one of his sons next door." Up to this point, Hans thought it was only his mother-in-law listening-in, but when his wife gave a controlled smile at her mother's suggestion, he knew there was an audience of two. *Human nature being what it was, thought Hans, didn't require a visit to a theater to be entertained.*

Chapter 11

The Surprise

Hans' arranged trip to Israel was intended for business and a brief hiatus. The business would include the housing project for new immigrants and industrial site inspections for a factory. He would meet with Israeli officials responsible for land-lease programs for outside investors while the old man checked in on his housing project for new arrivals. The downtime would be their vacation.

The plane was scheduled to touch down in Tel Aviv within the hour. The women hurriedly prepared the catered brunch for everyone except the pilots—they were on their own for that event after landing.

"Pop, are you going to share your apple pie?" asked Hans.

"Nope, if I give you an inch, you'll take the whole pie, but what I will do is give you my coffee cake that comes with our catered meal."

His wife couldn't stay out of the fray. "Dear, I bake apple pies for you all the time. Why is this one so important—is it better than mine?"

"Pop," said Hans, "You just stepped on a landmine."

"And thank you, Mr. Chairman, for setting it!"

For Sonje, the tease and banter served to congeal her sense of acceptance and position in her new family. But she would feel more comfortable if one of them knew the pain she carried beneath her glamorous exterior. Where was Michael when he was needed? Suddenly, Hans invaded her thoughts pushing her away from self-focus.

"Sonje, we need to conference with Albescu. He apparently wants to go with the offer I extended to him. If this is the case, we will work with our legal department on creating a dummy corporation that will act as the legal entity in partnership with Albescu. When our legal team finalizes the straw man corporation it will be the only face the Romanian government sees. After we land, stay with Fritz, our radio person who staffs the teletype and confirm with Albescu a viable appointment time for the three of us. If this turns out as I hope it will, we will then turn our legal team loose for them to do their thing so we can get this operation rolling. Because of the corruption in that country, a lot of money will be thrown around, so be prepared for an awkward situation that doesn't fit into our Western standards.

"When you finish your project with Fritz after we land, there'll be a special driver here to take you to the villa where we're all staying. Fritz sleeps on board the plane and takes care of the radio."

Sonje felt infused with new zest being given something important to do. She was inching herself closer to the inner circle and would be part of the interviewing process with Mr. Albescue. She now felt better than at any point of the trip.

Hans and his group left for the villa where they were booked, and Fritz made coffee and went to work with Sonje in the teletype room. The back and forth communications extended beyond an hour. Moving information between three countries among three parties using phones and radio systems was a slow, tedious effort. Finally, an appointment date and time were confirmed. Sonje gathered her stack of communication papers on the radio table and prepared to leave for the captain's quarters to pick up her carry-on satchel.

"Thank you, Fritz, for your work. You certainly know the management and operation of this room."

"Thank you, Miss Shuster."

"Fritz, you can call me Sonje."

"Oh, you honor me, Miss Sonje."

Sonje smiled, left the room for the captain's quarters. She saw the door was open and knew she was the last person to leave and distinctly remembered closing it. Upon entering, she was startled to see a figure reclining in one of the first-class seats reading a book that shielded his face. She thought it was one of the pilots, and after collecting her purse and carry-on bag, she turned to leave and was about to exit the door, when she heard the words: "Am I allowed to call you, Sonje, too?"

She knew that voice. Could it actually be the person she wished it were? Are her senses playing tricks on her? She stopped and turned around. The man had lowered the book, and Michael's face was as big as life itself.

Unprepared for what she was experiencing, she froze like a statue staring at the man who had engaged her thoughts on this flight. Men considered her a beautiful person, and many attempted to court her, some of great wealth and power, but she never opened that door to any through the years. Now at forty-two, she was looking at a man three years her senior, the first man who had occupied her thoughts since leaving the death camp. Her emotions and feelings flashed in front of her. Like a flag waving in the breeze, they were telling her something she already knew. She couldn't hold it back. Now, she understood why she felt calm and secure around this person. He knew her pain because he suffered the same way. Her faith leaped out at her. Pain wasn't confined to the drama of human life, even God knew pain through His Son's suffering, and that's why people chose to be near Him. He made them feel calm and secure. Being emotionally charged, something foreign to her nature, she became weak and had the need to sit. Michael thought she was ill, got up, closed the door, and sat in the chair next to her. "Can I get you something to drink?" said Michael. "You're not acting well."

"I'll be fine in a moment, just give me time. Seeing you here so startled me that it was like seeing an apparition from another dimension. How in the world did you arrive here with everything being the way it was—you on a secret mission and the rest of us whisked off on a sudden trip to Israel?"

Michael pushed his memory back to the bright moments of younger years, something he had avoided. "I'm proud of my nephew, Jacob," said Michael. "He carries all the qualities of my beautiful sister. She had bright, golden blond hair and would dress her firstborn up like a little doll before I came by to give him a ride around the village in his small wagon. She was my only sister, and when we were younger, she took care of me like she was my mother. Jacob is intelligent like her too. God sent Katharina to save his life for the mission he now has for Israel's future."

Michael stopped speaking, turned, and faced Sonje with teary eyes. Neither spoke. What seemed like a suspension in time was broken when Michael added, "Sonje, as Katharina saved Jacob for his mission in life, she rescued you for the mission of saving me."

Sonje's universe stopped. She felt like she was a patient in an open hospital emergency room with a life-threatening injury in need of a curtain to be pulled around her for privacy. Now, it was her pain that was strength for Michael as his had been for her. They were symbiotically connected. Each gave strength to the other. Sonje broke with deep sobbing, tears were blurring her vision with dark mascara streaks marking her face. Then the wonder of all wonders, she felt Michael's arms around her pulling her into his embrace. She closed her eyes yielding to what her emotions were telling her: his arms were the curtain, the covering she needed around her hospital bed to prevent others from seeing her vulnerable pain and hurt. A man who carried his own injuries and scars was now accepting hers.

Chapter 12

The Little Book

Michael and Sonje sat at a beachside dining table overlooking the beautiful blue Mediterranean. He couldn't take his eyes off her lovely face, her hair ruffled by nature's salt air with gusts of calm, cool, coastal breezes. Sonje's memory was still pulsating over the way Michael treated her before and after leaving the captain's quarters aboard the plane. First, he reminded her that her eyeshade should be taken care of, then they went to the radio room and said farewell to Fritz while holding hands. Leading her to his waiting vehicle, he treated her like they were a young couple on a date.

"A penny for your thoughts, Miss Beautiful," said Michael, interrupting her flow of memory. Had she not known better, she would think her experience was from being high on something. Now, being addressed as Miss Beautiful intensified her feelings.

"You have turned my world upside down. Are you for real?"

"I am as real as you are beautiful."

"You certainly know how to tantalize my emotions."

"Do you enjoy your emotions being tantalized?" asked Michael.

"My emotions have never been tantalized until you came along. Yes, I welcome the experience. This is the world I spoke of that's been turned upside down. But what about you, Michael?"

She saw Michael turn his eyes away from her. She was held in suspense not knowing how he would answer.

"I dream about you at night and think of you during the day. You are always in my thoughts. However, since Jacob has brought me to Israel on business, I have chosen this opportunity to disclose something about myself you need to know that may impair our relationship."

Sonje saw in Michael something she'd never seen before—a force of energy surfacing from another life that had made him what he was.

"Sonje, I have a hidden life that few people know about. Some would call it my dark side, others would use the term, justice. If I were to write a book, it would be on the best-seller list. Before we go any further in our relationship, you need to know who I am and what I have done, and when you have heard everything, you will be free to change your mind about me."

Michael had carried with him a small bag containing personal effects. She saw him reach into the satchel and take from it a small diary-looking book that appeared well worn. He held it in his hand as he began his story.

"Sonje, I was away in the forest on a project for my father along with my two close friends when all our families were killed and our properties confiscated. My friends and I knew how to survive in the mountains and we pledged together to be the arm of justice on behalf of our families. A Gentile family friend left me this book I hold in my hands. It contains the names of people who killed, stole, and raped our people. We came from good families who were pillars in the community, were educated and smart.

But the Nazis turned us into efficient killers. We took this book and it became our execution list. The guilty were soldiers and locals. In this book are four names of army officers who raped the girl I was to marry. I have already executed three of them by my own hands, and the fourth has evaded capture. This is the overview of the person I became because of the Holocaust. I leave the story and this book with you so you can re-evaluate your relationship with me. This has been difficult for me to share."

Michael handed the small book to Sonje. For the first time, she saw weakness in this stalwart man—his hands were trembling.

Michael, who was never at a loss for words, was silent, his eyes fixed on the hands that now held the little book. Had he watched other body-language movements of the lady in front of him, he would have seen Sonje's own story rising from her caldron of hurt.

"Michael, look at me! I need your strength to tell my story."

He moved his eyes from her hands to her face. She appeared unmoved by the story she just heard. Was she listening? Perhaps, she doesn't want to believe what she was told.

"Does Hans know what you told me?"

"He was the first person to hear my story."

"What was his response to you?"

"He's a doctor and treated me as he would a patient."

"Michael, I need to tell you something that is difficult to do. When I was in the concentration camp, I was abused by two guards, and after the war, I vowed to get even. That opportunity came when I gained my wealth. Wealth gives one control and power. No one knew what I contrived against those who ran that camp and those who abused me. My best friend, Katharina, was never told what I'm about to tell you. You're the first to hear this part of my life.

"With the acquisition of money, I hired private investigators to find the whereabouts of those two guards. Extensive research was done on old military records, some requiring a court order. In the meantime, I was considering what measures I would take to see justice carried out. You see, Michael, I was seeking justice, not for others but for myself. They had ruined my life and had it not been for Katharina's intervention, I could've ended up like the young lady you were going to marry."

Sonje saw life beginning to flow back into Michael when she connected her experience to the girl he was engaged to marry.

"At the time, I was so energized for justice and revenge that I was willing to do anything. At one point, I considered hiring an underworld hit man.

"After all the research and reports were in, I found that one of the guards had been killed when the American force took the camp. The other guard had been taken prisoner and after the war was released into society. My investigators continued to compile information on this subject. I knew everything about him, where he lived and worked, the name of the woman he married, and the names of his children. I took it on myself one day to stake out his home. I saw his wife, his little children running about. It was then I realized if something happened to the father, those little kids would be without a father. As much as I wanted justice and revenge for myself, it couldn't rise above the level of those children's needs.

"Had it not been for those children, I could have easily

carried out justice against my offender.

"You had more noble character than I, said Michael."

"No, that's not true, Michael. You had more pain and greater loss. Never in a lifetime would I think less of you because of what you shared with me today."

Michael grabbed Sonje's hand, saying, "Come, let's take a walk on the beach, and I don't want you to say anything until I ask you a question."

She thought it strange for Michael wanting to leave so abruptly for a walk on the beach, but she welcomed the tight squeeze on her hand. As soon as they reached the water's edge, he stopped, took her in his arms and she heard words from his lips she never expected.

"Sonje, will you marry me, though I'm poor and have nothing?"

He felt her frame stiffen and pull away.

"Marriage...you want to marry me...after everything I've told you?"

"Have you ever thought about us together in marriage, Sonje?

"Michael, I dream about it every night, but I don't see myself worthy."

He softly brushed her hair from in front of her face, then slowly ran his fingers through it, saying, "When you become my wife, our union together will be as pristine and innocent as a newborn babe."

"Oh, Michael, your words are life-giving, like water poured out on dry, parched lips. Whisper those words once again softly in my ear."

"I'll whisper more than that in both of your ears if you promise to marry me."

Michael felt her stiffened frame relax, followed by the

words, "Michael, I want to marry you more than anything in the world. I would even marry you today if you insisted. I don't want a large, ostentatious wedding, just a private one with our family and friends."

"It'll be as you wish," said Michael.

By this time, they had slipped off their shoes and were walking barefoot, holding hands, enjoying the feel of squishy, moist sand under their feet.

"When shall we announce the wedding?" asked Michael.

"I'll leave that up to you but the-sooner-the-better, as far as I'm concerned."

Sonje couldn't believe what was happening. First, she was whisked off to a flight to Israel, given a proposal of marriage, and now talking about making it public.

"Next to the wedding itself," said Michael, "the announcement will be the biggest event of our lives. Tonight at the dining table, we will put everyone in shocked disbelief."

"Michael, I'm not sure everyone will be that shocked. Sometimes women have extrasensory perception. My concerns are that everyone will approve."

"It doesn't matter as long as we're the ones who approve."

Sonje stopped, looked at Michael, and pulled him close. "I told you that I would marry you, now hold me tight, and whisper into my ears those life-giving words once more."

Chapter 13

The Announcement

When Michael and Sonje arrived at the villa and checked in, they found their luggage waiting for them in a holding room near the front office. It was an upscale coastal resort, providing all the modern amenities of a luxurious cruise ship, including private access to the ocean-side beach.

Unknown to Sonje, Hans had controlled the events on the plane before landing so she would have to stay over to complete her assignment, which required a special driver to pick her up. He wanted Michael in Israel for two reasons: use his technical knowledge for site locations for a factory and help Sonje adjust to her new role in the family. He knew there was warm chemistry between the two, and with Michael nearby, the adjustment to her new role would be easier.

Michael and Sonje followed the attendants carrying their five pieces of luggage—four of which belonged to Sonje. She remembered how he chided her about her spiffed-up dress, and looking at his single case bouncing along with her four in the hands of the bellhops, she took Michael's arm, leaned close to his ear, and whispered, "Women need more luggage than men. Besides, I want to be beautiful for you."

To her surprise, he put his arm around her in public

view, saying, "You can bring along all the cases you want, but they'll never make you more beautiful than what you are inside."

"You know how to make me cry!"

"I know how to tell the truth," responded Michael. And speaking of telling, tonight is our big announcement—about three hours away."

"Yes, and I am so excited! Perhaps we should spend the time resting before the event so we'll be more at ease."

"A splendid suggestion, I'll drop by at seven-thirty and pick you up."

"I'll be waiting on pins-and-needles for the knock on my door."

He opened her door using her key. Both entered, followed by the luggage carriers. The room matched the upscale coastal setting. Michael left carrying his single piece of luggage, saying, "My room is adjacent yours. Whoever booked reservations made it convenient for us."

While Michael and Sonje were resting for the big event of the evening, the rest of the family was swimming in warm coastal waters, walking the sandy beach adjoining the villa and picking up shells from an ancient coastline, a coastline that had been marked in history with the footprints of those who changed the world.

That night at the villa, a party of four sat at their reserved table under the clear, evening sky waiting for Sonje to arrive. Nature was giving a prelude performance to an important event with on-shore breezes and sounds of swishing waves falling on ancient sand, all accompanied by the distant, stage-performing twinkling stars. Quietness, like a blanket, covered them with aesthetic awe.

Silence was broken when Mrs. Reznik asked, "Hans,

where's Sonje?" She saw Hans and Sheena look at each other. Nothing slipped by her and she knew that look.

"What's going on here?" she asked. "I thought we were going to be together as a family!"

"Sonje is with Michael, Mom."

"With Michael! What do you mean with Michael?"

"Michael was in the country when we arrived, and he picked her up, and they're out-and-about somewhere."

The old prophet's wife, whose business was to know other people's business, mulled over Hans statement and wouldn't leave it alone.

"This is interesting...very interesting. I noticed they were becoming chummy—Hans, are you trying to be a matchmaker?"

"Mother," said Hans, "I've brought Michael here to help Pop and me locate industrial property for a new factory, and it was convenient for them to spend the day together—let's leave it at that." She didn't see Hans' facial expression when he turned and faced his wife, giving her a wink and a smile.

The secluded outdoor dining room where the four waited had been reserved for Hans' party of six, and it was nearing eight o'clock. Sonje was waiting in her room reminiscing about how her life was so suddenly changed by Michael—it was breathtaking. The force of energy between them had made her stronger as a person.

Unlike the evening when he first came to her home and had to ring the doorbell twice, tonight she swung her door open at the first rap. Michael thought she looked beautiful. Up to this point in their relationship, he had been the affectionate one. That was reversed tonight. Michael's acceptance of her painful abuse empowered her to feel like a complete person. While still standing in the doorway, she pulled Michael to herself embracing him with the words, "God has sent you into my life, and I will be proud to be your wife and stand by you in life."

"Even though I'm poor and have nothing?"

"Don't be silly! Your nephew, one of the wealthiest men in Europe, married a poor girl, and if he can do that, then I can marry someone you call poor. Besides, you are rich in many ways that I'm not."

On their walk to the dining room, they agreed to set the stage so when the announcement was made it would have its greatest effect. They wouldn't hold hands, show affection, or engage in unnecessary conversation, and it would be toward the end of the dining session they would break the news. Michael had dressed casually, and Sonje, in spite of Michael's remarks about her dress, looked well dressed.

Michael and Sonje were the last to arrive, and because Michael had been gone for several weeks and Sonje for the day, they were greeted with gusto. They all sat at the table with Sonje seated alongside Michael. The old man's inquisitive wife began her probe.

"Where've you two been all day. I must say you look quite rested, unlike us who've been on the beach swimming and looking for treasures in the sand."

"Did you find any treasures in those ancient sands?" asked Michael.

"Oh, we found some nice shells," said Mrs. Reznik. What treasures did you two find today?"

It was her beautiful daughter, Sheena, who attempted to dilute, and divert where the conversation was going. "Mother, can you identify any of the shells you found?"

"I'm not a marine biologist, dear, so I have to answer your question with a simple no. It doesn't require a scientific mind to see the color, beauty, and the uniqueness of God's creation."

"How right you are," said Michael. "And probably the greatest treasures ever found have had to do with the discovery of quality and goodness inside other people."

"You're waxing eloquent tonight, Michael, like a philosopher," said Mrs. Reznik. *Sonje thought otherwise. He was giving her a personal steganographic message that passed over the heads of those present. This man she was marrying was clever.*

By this time the waiter was taking orders, and those at the table lost interest in Mrs. Reznik's probing. Halfway through dinner, Sonje kept glancing at Michael expecting him at any time to give a statement leading to a formal announcement. However, Mrs. Reznik wasn't finished with her probe into their activities of the day.

"Michael, what was the highlight of your experience today in Israel?" Everything turned quiet except the sounds coming from the movement of spoons, forks, and the crashing of coastal waves in the distance. The question was innocent and unobtrusive, and he chose to answer it.

He took Sonje's hand and held it so each could see the stage he was setting. They all knew the two had a certain affinity—it couldn't be missed—but were unprepared for what followed.

"In answer to your question, Mrs. Reznik, I take great delight to tell you and everyone here at this table that the highlight of my experience today was when I took Sonje to the beach for a walk and asked her to marry me, and it got even better when she replied in the affirmative."

114

Everything stopped around the table. Jaws froze like they were permanently fixed, and the clatter of silverware went unheard. Eyes used to enhance gourmet taste buds were showing disloyalty to their epicurean dishes. They were now laser-riveted toward a couple who had used the element of surprise to immobilize everyone.

"We haven't decided on a date," said Michael, "Sonje has requested a small wedding. Each of you can be sure that we will enlist your help to make it an event to remember and a time to honor God in the institution of marriage."

Sheena had tears come to her eyes and was first to respond. "Congratulations from Hans and me! How wonderful it is to see two people having suffered such hardships in life find love and comfort in each other. We must look at the bigger providential picture of how we all arrived where we are today. Because of one noble lady, I have Hans, and Michael has Sonje."

The drama was too much for the talkative, inquisitive Mrs. Reznik, and she did what many do under sudden change: the predictable was reversed. She became quiet and reflective. Her husband beamed with a grin from ear-to-ear, then slowly and quietly began to applaud, followed by the others.

Mrs. Reznik's silence was short-lived. She looked at Hans, saying, "Hans, you knew this all the time, didn't you? Don't say you didn't, because I can see it in your eyes. My, my, my...what a wonderful thing has happened." Then turning to her husband, she said, "Papa, your new son is getting a wife, which means you're getting a daughter too! Our family is growing—maybe they'll live next door to us in that empty home where Sheena lived."

"Momma, wherever they live, they'll still be our son and daughter." The two elderly Rezniks were in their own world while the others smiled and silently waited for Sonje to speak.

Sonje's thoughts centered on how her life had been compartmentalized into two worlds, the corporate world of business and her need for privacy behind a walled fortress. The former, created by her mentor, the late Katharina, was what everyone saw. Her memories of the camp were carefully hidden from public view. Katharina had piloted her through the waters of every facet of her vast enterprise equipping her with the tools and skills equal to any in the organization, but every day she struggled with the memory of her camp experience. Now a new day was dawning— there was someone in her life that understood what she'd been through and accepted her and the world she tried to forget. Because of Michael, she was developing into a complete and fulfilled person.

Everyone looked at Sonje expecting a response. She did something that had not been done by Michael: she stood to her feet. "You will have to pardon me if I tear-up. Today has been an emotionally charged event for me, and I want to go on record that I have never been as happy and fulfilled as I am tonight. We are all here because of a lady who found an orphaned infant in Romania. From that act, amazing things have happened. What Katharina was to Hans, Michael has been to me. He found me orphaned and gave me the courage to accept his marriage proposal."

She turned to Michael, placed his face between the palms of her hands, saying, "I love you more than anything in the world." To the surprise of everyone present, she planted an impassioned kiss while the others gave handclapping plaudits.

Mrs. Reznik couldn't contain her enthusiasm, and her need to know launched a series of questions: "Michael, you said, 'no date's been set.' Does this mean one month, two months, or six months? Will the wedding be in a church or a synagogue, like our daughter's?"

"That will all be up to Sonje," said Michael.

Sonje fielded the question. "I'm sure it'll be on the order of Hans and Sheena's, I thought it was beautiful and carried all the spiritual significance of Christ and His espoused."

"Well, who'll give you away," said Mrs. Reznik. "Perhaps I shouldn't have asked that question."

"I'd be glad to answer your question," responded Sonje. "Hans would honor me if he were the one giving me away at the altar. He's the son of my best friend."

"Since we're all planning your wedding here tonight, shall I bring in your two friends, Moshe and Bub?" asked Hans.

"Definitely," answered Michael, "but I want you, Jacob, to serve as my best man."

"There seems to be a conflict here," replied Mrs. Reznik.

Sheena joined the planning by adding, "Mother, there'll be no conflict. Hans can walk Sonje down the aisle, and after giving her away, step over alongside Michael's attendants."

"Where will you be living after you're married?" queried Mrs. Reznik.

"That will be up to Michael, He loves the rugged outdoors, and we just might find ourselves a cabin in the woods."

Hans chuckled at the suggestion knowing how Sonje leaned into the cool breezes of exquisite clothing and finery.

Then something came to Hans like a bombshell. He always wondered why the architect finished off his office with such elegance, and now he knew: it was Sonje's influence, and if the truth were known, it was probably her design. He wouldn't bring up the office issue, that was a matter of history, but there was something both parties should understand.

"There is one imposition about where you live after marriage," said Hans. "Our Chief of Security sent me a memo recently emphasizing that we are still considered targets by the Nazi and anti-Semitic elements because of what we do for Israel. Other security sources confirm this recent news release. Therefore all my family members must reside in tight security compounds and be driven by security people."

"Does my place qualify?" asked Sonje.

"Not unless it has a security wall and security personnel around the clock."

The old man spoke up. "It puts a crimp in your lifestyle and this is why I enjoy coming to Israel. There's none of that here, but one learns to live with it."

"I can learn to live anywhere," Sonje said, "as long as Michael is with me." She paused, looked at Michael with a smile. "Even if it's a tree house!"

"Well, since that's settled," said the old man, "I'm going to bed and let you young people work out the details.

"Papa," said Mrs. Reznik, "why are we leaving now, it's just getting interesting."

Chapter 14

Meeting New Immigrants

Michael and Sonje had become celebrities among the other family members. Each felt they were party to their coming together and were anxious to be with them at the scheduled early breakfast before beginning their heavy workday of visiting and inspecting the housing units for new immigrants. The latter part of the day would not require the presence of Sheena and her mother, leaving them free to browse the local shops. Everyone was at the dining table waiting for Michael and Sonje.

Mrs. Reznik would never fit the role of a traditional bluestocking connoisseur of classical literature, but she knew how to punctuate and fill a room with witty commentary about anything from politics to the latest fashions. When she wasn't reading a book, she was talking and probing about other people and their business. However, sometimes she was reflective.

"Last night was a beautiful experience," said Mrs. Reznik. "It reminded me of the time when my husband asked me to marry him." Up to this point, the old man was thinking about the bed he had to leave for this early breakfast and his face showed the need of strong coffee. But upon hearing what his wife was about to say, would be better than coffee to bring him to life.

"Dear, perhaps that occasion should be left for

history...let's savor last night's event and forget my embarrassing, clumsy show of affection." It was then Michael and Sonje walked into the room. Relief showed on the face of the old man. Attention was now on someone else.

As was expected, Michael was dressed in casual form, but they were surprised to see that Sonje chose to dress without stylish flair. Unlike her typical appearance, she was dressed in a simple, smart-looking pantsuit. Both acted in a professional way and were ready for a long, busy day.

Michael pulled a chair out and assisted Sonje at the table. They were polite to each other, but neither showed the emotional display of last evening.

Two hours later the six stood in front of a large housing development under construction. The first phase consisted of two-hundred units that had already been completed with roads, streets, sidewalks, and landscaping. The streets had children running about and even adults taking walks, but vehicles were not to be seen. Immigrants arriving here brought nothing but what they could carry in their arms. On the far side of the large housing complex could be seen more new homes under construction for expected new arrivals.

The old man spoke first. "These 200 finished units we're looking at represent ten percent of the total housing project."

"Pop," Hans said, "I want to congratulate you on your work here. This is beyond belief."

"It's your vision, Hans, that created this. If you're going to credit anyone, it should go to Michael. Look at those kids! Michael brought them and their parents back to the land of their ancestors." The old man wept knowing how the tragedy of the Holocaust affected every family now living in this development.

Sonje saw Michael place his arm around the old prophet, then heard him say, "Mr. Reznik, because of the message you gave me of the suffering Savior, I found life, and I'm glad to give myself in the service of getting others to Israel." Sonje closed her eyes and thanked God for the man she was going to marry.

At this point Michael took charge. "Follow me, I want us to meet some of the new immigrants who have been here only a few weeks. The group noticed Michael taking Sonje's hand as everyone followed him down the sidewalk. It was the first show of affection since last evening, and it pushed Mrs. Reznik into saying aloud in the hearing of her daughter, "Well, it's about time for them to show some of the sparks from last night." A visual reminder her mother often got from her daughter was noticed by others walking behind Michael—a finger over her lips showing a shush sign.

Michael led the group into the development for several blocks, stopped in front of a home occupied by one of the new arrivals, turned around and addressed his family: "I have arranged for a group of the new immigrants to meet with us here in this home. The people you will see and meet in this home are typical of those who risk their lives to board our freighters."

Michael knocked on the front door with Sonje at his side. Others stepped closely behind. The door opened showing a front room bustling with standing people. He moved inside with his family following, then spoke to those in the crowded room. "I want everyone who is here today to meet some very special people who have stopped by to say hello."

After Hans and his group found standing room inside, Michael continued leading the group. "I may have been responsible for picking you up at sea, but we have among us the two people who made it possible for you to be here today: my nephew, Jacob, who provided the funds for this project, and my special spiritual father, Mr. Reznik, who has overseen the construction up to this point."

A man among the new-immigrant group stepped forward in response to Michael. He spoke in Romanian, and Sheena quickly pulled Hans and Sonje close to her so they could hear the interpretation she gave.

"We have come home to the land of our fathers after unspeakable tragedy and pain. To those who were called to save us, we thank you. But I want those who are visiting us to know that the man who picked us up at sea in the dark of the night, not only saved us, he saved many of us years before in the heat of the Holocaust when we were in hiding and running for our lives. Food and money were delivered to many Jews who were destitute and hungry. He also gave money to righteous Romanians who hid Jews from those who would turn them over to the Nazis."

Hans remembered Michael telling him about the fortune he'd found that was taken from Jews and using it to help those in hiding.

Tears were wiped from the guests' faces as they stood and listened to the accounts of brave and noble acts of one of their own.

However, Michael stared straight ahead without showing tears or emotion. He had been pushed back to a time when tears belonged to others, never a part of his world, a time when his mission was to cause pain on those who destroyed his family. Though he plied dark corners of violence for his form of justice, those he helped with the fortune he took from Colonel Funar's home would someday be a footnote in the pages of history.

The new immigrant called his wife alongside where he stood, then continued speaking. "My wife and I along with our two small sons were hidden by Romanians, and this man would bring either money or food every week so we could be maintained in seclusion. When the Communist took over they wouldn't grant exit visas, and today my two sons are still in the country. What Mr. Pencovich did for my family, he did for many others. Some are in this room today!"

Hans was never told the full story of Michael's life. He always knew there was hidden valor in this man and his modesty had kept the whole story from surfacing—until today!

Michael had recovered and was moving among the new arrivals, greeting each of them. Hans turned to Sheena and Sonje next to him and saw that both were moved to tears. "I never knew this about Michael—what nobility of character!"

"I'm left speechless," said Sheena.

Sonje said nothing until she was asked by Hans, "Did you know any of this, Sonje?" She was slow to respond and appeared she didn't want to answer his question.

"Last night we went to his room and talked for several hours. He thought I should know everything about his life experience and what the man told us was part of his story. He is a remarkable person, and I'm so very fortunate he asked me to marry him."

They never noticed that the old man's wife had inched

herself close enough to listen-in to what Sonje was saying, and when the conversation was over and she had relaxed her stretched-out stance, her husband leaned close to her ear.

"Mother, let's get you a special hearing aid so you won't have to be a contortionist next time." Instead of scowling at him, she took his hand, saying, "Dear, did you tell me everything about yourself prior to our marriage?"

Before leaving, all the family went through the crowded building greeting each new immigrant, wishing them well. Sheena was alongside her husband acting as an interpreter, and Michael did the same for Sonje.

Freedom was always in the air when the family went to Israel. Special armored cars were not required to move them about; bodyguards and security people were left at home. In Israel, they used taxis for their transportation allowing them to go and come at will. When the family of six reached the front of the housing development, they found waiting for them the two taxis that brought them to the site. Sheena and her mother took one to browse the local stores, and the other would serve Hans and his team in visiting prospective building sites for a factory his company would be moving into the country.

Hans led his group of four into a small front government office where there sat a secretary who handled traffic coming to see different department heads.

"We have an appointment with Mr. Levi in the Land Lease Division."

"And your name is..."

"Hans Isler."

"Sir, are you the Mr. Isler we all hear so much about here in Israel?"

"Would you kindly tell Mr. Levi we are here?"

"Oh, certainly, Sir, I was distracted by hearing your name."

She quickly rang the office of the man in charge of overseeing the government's land-lease program for industrial commercial development.

"Mr. Levi, Mr. Isler and his party are here for their appointment." She looked over at Hans who was still standing. "Mr. Levi will be right out."

Coming toward them was a man that matched the size of the room used as a front office: small, slightly overweight with glasses hanging down near the end of his nose. Standing next to Hans and Michael only made him match the tightness of the waiting room. However, what he lacked in physical stature was made up by his warm, generous nature.

"Dr. Isler, I'm honored to meet you! Everyone in this country knows what you do for Israel. Come to my office and we'll talk."

After entering his office, Hans introduced his party, one-by-one. After being seated, they watched him take a file folder from his cabinet and lay it on his desk. He stood as he spoke.

"Mr. Isler, just to recap where we are with your application and paperwork, your request for a hundred-year industrial land lease from the state of Israel for the purpose of building a manufacturing plant has been approved and we are at the point of you making a decision on a site location. This folder on my desk contains maps of three different industrial sites, each suitable in size to accommodate your proposed plant."

The government official walked around to the front of

his desk, took the folder, and handed it to Hans, saying, "Dr. Isler, I admire your hands-on approach in helping Israel. Most people in your position would have others doing all the gopher work. Perhaps this is the reason everyone knows who you are. Israelis are known to be gopher workers, they aren't afraid to get their hands dirty."

Thank you for the complimentary remarks," said Hans, "but I do have my Gophers, three of them are with me today." Everyone chuckled and was about to leave when Sonje spoke up.

"Mr. Levi, what is the time frame for us to get back to you on our final decision for the site location?"

"Oh, that's a good question. Thirty days is a rule of thumb; however, if you need longer because of an unplanned eventuality, let me know ahead of time."

When they reached the parking lot outside the government building, the taxi was still waiting. At this point, Michael took over. He opened the folder containing the lease maps and laid them on top of the taxi's hood.

"Driver, there are three maps here. We want you to take us to each one, but first determine the closest and take us there first. Can you do this?"

"Certainly," said the driver. "Let me look at those maps!" He scanned the maps quickly, turned to Michael, saying, "The closest is twenty minutes from here, the next in line is about ten after the first stop, and from there we drive to Haifa. The drive from the second to the last site is near forty-five miles."

"Well, let's be on our way," said Hans.

After three hours, the four were on their way back to the villa where they were staying. They had walked, photographed, and inspected three large parcels of land, one of which would be selected as the site for the new plant. Part of their review included contiguous properties, proximity to transportation, and housing availability.

The vigor showing on the four at the early hour of breakfast in the morning when they started out was nowhere to be seen, except for Michael. It was a strenuous effort for those having worked in plush offices to traverse rugged open land with steep inclines. They were tired, weary, and looking forward to a fresh bath at the Villa.

The hum of the taxi and gentle swaying of the vehicle put Hans to sleep in the front seat. In the back, the old man punctuated the silence with his oft-complained-about snore while Sonje rested her head on Michael's shoulder with eyes closed pondering the new world she'd entered.

Chapter 15

The Coded Message

Hans was at the head of the dining table with Sheena at his side looking fresh and invigorated after his long, arduous day. Soon, Mr. and Mrs. Reznik arrived with the old man holding his wife's hand.

"Papa," said Sheena, "I see you've gotten some inspiration from Michael and Sonje."

"Yes, sometimes it takes the younger to lead the way. Your mother and I came from the era when affection wasn't shown in public as it is today."

"Why didn't Hans and I inspire you, we've always shown our affection around you?"

The old man was slow answering his daughter's question. He would have preferred the silence he created to linger but chose to respond. "Probably it was because you were my daughter. Sometimes, one has to see something from afar to get the bigger picture of life."

"Well Papa, more inspiration is coming your way because Sonje and Michael just entered the dining room."

"My dear, I welcome more of that kind of inspiration."

"Mother, why are you so sedate and quiet?"

"It's your father's inspiration, that's what it is—his inspiration!"

Hans broke into the conversation. "Inspiration is a much-used word tonight, and I hope it stays with us throughout the evening in other matters. I've invited Fritz to be with us for dinner and bring what's come over the teletype, and I don't know why he's late!"

By this time, Sonje and Michael had arrived at the dining table, and after seating Sonje, he remained standing, saying, "I want to announce tonight that our wedding date will be six months from today. It will be a small wedding attended only by family and close friends, and the religious format will follow Jacob and Sheena's beautiful wedding."

Mrs. Reznik, who had been unusually quiet, came to life. "Now that's what I call real inspiration." No one saw Fritz enter the dining room where he stopped and observed the celebration happening around the dining table. He carried a folder containing copies of the day's messages from the home office. Not wanting to interfere with the festivity, he remained standing, waiting for the appropriate time to join them. From the table, Hans caught a glimpse of Fritz and motioned him over to a vacant seat.

"Good evening everyone," said Fritz, "I'm sorry I'm tardy, but a late message came through and I wanted it to be part of the file, so I waited and got out a bit late."

Fritz handed Hans the file and sat where he was bidden. "You overheard our celebration, did you not?" asked Hans.

"Oh, yes, Sir, and I extend my congratulations to Miss Sonje and Michael. Thanks to Dr. Hans, I came to know the joy and happiness a marriage can bring. All through the Bible, marriage is a celebrated event. Even our Lord and his disciples chose to attend one, and it was there He performed His first miracle of turning water into wine."

"I see that you've not only become a married man but a student of the Scriptures."

"That's my wife's influence on me, Sir.

When the waiter arrived to take their orders, it put on hold the subject under discussion, which allowed Fritz to lean closer to Han's hearing with a message he thought only he should hear.

"Dr. Hans, in the folder is an urgent message to Michael from Bub and Moshe. This is why I'm late getting here. It appears to have nothing to do with Operation Henry but is in code form about someone in his past. I hope you don't see my action being impertinent. It carries a sense of urgency."

"Thank you, Fritz, I'll see that he gets it after dinner, but for now let's enjoy ourselves as a family, and let me go on record and say that tonight you are part of my family."

When Fritz heard Hans' words, he couldn't believe it. *This man who has wealth beyond belief is telling him, a lowly serf, someone lower than a commoner who has nothing, is part of his family! Miracles never cease to happen, he thought.*

Communication over the teletype held no privacy rights and was the property of the corporation. Though private and personal information were often sent, the sender always knew it was subject to others' purview. In most cases, people who used the teletype were aware of this, and though something may be personal in nature, it was always presented in a formal manner. Hans kept mulling the matter over in his mind, then said to those around him at the table, "If you'll pardon me, I'm going to the men's room." He quietly took the folder that lay on the dining table with him.

When he returned, he knew no more than what Fritz told him. The message came in code form using phrases and idioms known only by sender and recipient. He would

130

deal with it later tonight. Tomorrow was a free day for relaxation, and he didn't want it to interfere with their down time. He requested Pop to offer a prayer of thanksgiving.

The kosher diet was kept by only three of the party of seven. Those who chose non-kosher orders were Michael, Sonje, Hans, and Fritz. After a hard day of being out-and-about, voracious appetites were exhibited. Hans saw Sheena looking at his lobster and milk-filled coffee, all of which created whispering conversation between them.

"Dear, you're welcome to drink my white coffee and snitch lobster from my plate if you like."

"I would but there are eagle eyes across the table and they don't miss anything."

"I really think they're waiting for you to break the ice," said Hans.

"I may be at the edge of the dining table, but your analogy puts me on the ice in the middle of the pond. Breaking it there may not be a wise decision. You could've used another idiom to fit the occasion."

Nothing passed the eyes of Mrs. Reznik. "What are you two lovebirds talking about now? Whispering isn't polite in a family gathering."

"Mom, don't you and pop whisper to each other at times when you have private love messages."

"Hans, at our age we whisper love messages in the privacy of our home."

"If you're in the privacy of your home, why do you need to whisper?"

A broad facetious grin came across her face. "Hans, you know how to cut a person's legs from underneath her, don't you."

"Well mother, you shouldn't meddle!" said Sheena.

"Dear, that's what mothers are for. Besides, mothers have intuition. I know what you two were talking about. Reading lips helps with intuition. You were discussing our dietary laws. I think that since you are married and in your own home, you should choose what is best for you according to your own conscience."

From the other end of the table, they heard Michael say, "Mrs. Reznik, you have spoken from the fountain of wisdom."

Everyone saw Sheena take her fork, lift Hans' steaming-hot lobster from his plate, and place it on hers. "Now Hans order a fresh one for you and have the waiter bring me a hot cup of coffee with cream."

Everyone roared in laughter, including Mr. and Mrs. Reznik. Levity followed family time around the table until it reached the hour to break up. Hans put closure on the evening.

"Tomorrow is down time. We can do whatever we wish, but we all have to be ready to fly out early the following morning." Then Hans moved close to Michael, saying, "Michael I want you to look at something that came over the teletype addressed to you." He handed Michael the file containing the teletype. Looking at the printout, he quickly read the coded message. A haunting facial expression came over Michael. Something from his former life gripped his present reality.

"Jacob, I will discuss this with you only with Sonje at my side."

"Sheena and I will call on you in your room in fifteen minutes."

When Hans rapped on Michael's door, it was opened by

Sonje, but Michael was nowhere to be seen.

"Michael is outside on the patio listening to the sounds of the breakers," said Sonje. They seem to do a lot to calm him when he's under stress."

Moving to the open door that led to an outside private patio, she called Michael. "Michael, we're all here!"

When he came into the room, he carried the coded teletype message sent earlier by Bub and Moshe. He sat next to Sonje on a loveseat sofa. Hans said nothing, giving him the freedom to take the conversation wherever he needed to go.

"First, let me say that Sonje knows everything about my past. If there is any good, I have left it for her to discover. However, I have told her everything about the bad and ugly, even the teletype that came through today.

"I was good at what I did, and if one were to call it a success, the credit would have to go to my physical features of being tall and blond. Your mother and I carried the same genes—we were both tall and blond. The physical characteristics people saw in me allowed me to move about freely, making those who had killed my family and raped the girl I was to marry vulnerable to what I was capable of doing. Moshe, Bub, and I operated at night in and around our old village because people could recognize us. After our mission was completed there, we moved on to tracking down Iron Guard members in other parts of the country. I have intentionally withheld a piece of information from you that bears telling. The store you visited in our village when you went to Romania belonged to your mother and father. Her husband was one of the ringleaders that incited the havoc and mayhem that led to the confiscation of their property. Four weeks later, he was found executed in the woods.

"Four Romanian Army officers raped the girl I was to marry. This was when my blond hair served me well. I could move freely without restrictions, gather intelligence, and choose the opportune time to act. By my own hands, I have executed three of the men who raped and caused the death of an innocent girl.

"It was my pursuit of the fourth party, a Colonel Funar, that led to the report you heard this morning among the new immigrants. We eventually found where this colonel lived and staked out his premises. It was at the time of the war when the allies were making strategic bombing raids, and military families were being moved out of the area. On the night Colonel Funar's family moved out, I observed a woman carrying a large case to an outside storage shed. After their departure, I found hidden inside that storage shed a concealed underground compartment with two large suitcases full of stolen money, diamonds, gold, and jewelry, all from Jews that had been robbed and killed. Some of the bags containing the bank notes had Hebrew writing. It was a fortune, and we used most of it to aid Jews in hiding. Some of it served to bribe people to get information on our execution list. It was that night inside Colonel Funar's house that we found a treasure trove of evidence of unspeakable horrors of the Holocaust. There were written documents, films, and photographs. Some of them showed Funar himself. Bub and Moshe have them stored at a secret site, and we are the only people who have knowledge of the evidence and the location where they're stored.

"Colonel Funar dropped off the radar and was never heard of again—until tonight, and this leads to the coded, teletype message that arrived today."

Hans and Sheena were stupefied from what they heard and were left speechless. They sat motionless with eyes staring at steady hands holding a document about to shake the ground beneath them. Michael read the coded message:

Michael,

Urgent news has circulated to us from our old underground connections. They tell us that your fourth party of interest, the colonel, is living and working in West Germany under an alias. Though he wore a beard, he was recognized by someone who had seen him personally in Romania. Let us know how you want to respond in this matter.

Bub and Moshe

Hans collected himself enough to give a statement and ask a question. "I wish those documents you found in Funar's residence had been available to me when I made the Romanian Holocaust documentary. Can you make copies of everything you took from his home? If he is in photographs and we can find live witnesses, he can be prosecuted as a war criminal in this country."

Hans and Sheena saw Sonje take Michael's hand. It was a message that spoke of something they had already discussed.

"In the old days, this information would compel me to take action on a despicable piece of humanity, and I would relish doing it. However, I now have a higher and better life with God and the person He has given me. I have already gone on record with Sonje that if anything ever came up

135

where I acquired information of his whereabouts, I would let the judicial system prosecute him. To answer your question, Jacob, I will see to it that all the materials taken from his house that night are delivered to you for legal action."

Sheena stood to her feet. Her tall cylindrical form moved to where Hans was seated, and placing her arm around her husband, said, "Michael, Hans and I believe you have proven yourself a champion among all of us. Your noble character and valor came to us from the immigrants this morning, and now upon hearing what you are going to do for yourself and Sonje, it moves us to tears. How beautiful it is to see Sonje as the centerpiece of your life."

That night before dropping off to sleep, Hans held his wife in his arms thinking how she had made him a better person, and from what he saw tonight, Sonje was doing the same for Michael. Overriding these thoughts was how a Romanian Nazi war criminal could lose his identity and end up in West Germany with a job and a changed name. It could happen only with the help of underground Nazis, and because he was a Romanian, he could move about without suspicion.

Chapter 16

The Pain of Memory

The next morning Sonje was lying on her bed welcoming the flow of energy pulsating through her from yesterday's events. She realized Michael had changed her life in every way possible. She was a wealthy woman, even wealthier than others could even imagine, and up to this point in her life, it was important to her. But this morning it didn't seem to matter that much. If it were a choice between wealth and Michael, she could easily throw it all into the wind. She offered no resistance to her memories now tantalizing her emotions, memories of his touches, words, and embraces, which left her belonging to a world she never knew, could exist. She had never experienced such calm and serenity. Now she understood it was this force of love that compelled men and women of history to give up fortune and fame to follow the Messiah. The man in the Scriptures who sold all that he had to buy the Pearl of great price came to mind. Sonje's insightful creativity quickly surfaced: what she was experiencing in the physical dimension with Michael was a picture of the heavenly. She had stepped through a new portal of light.

Interrupting her thoughts was the sound of someone knocking on her door. She looked at her watch. It was eight o'clock—she had slept in—it had to be Michael! Quickly putting on her robe and giving her hair a few strokes with a brush, she cracked the door six inches.

"Good morning, Miss Beautiful!"

"Oh, Michael, you know how to make my knees weak!"

With only her face showing through the crack of the door, Michael leaned over and kissed her, saying, "I will gladly make your knees weak every day of your life."

"You are a darling, my love, and I will be out in five minutes."

"A woman's five minutes is really ten," said Michael, "So Prince Charming will pick you up in his carriage in ten."

As he walked away, she closed the door and leaned back against it with a faraway look, saying to herself, yes Michael, I would throw all my wealth to the wind just to be with you for my lifetime.

Hans, Sheena, and her parents had already arrived at the dining room when Michael appeared.

"You folks should go ahead and order your breakfast because Sonje slept in and we'll be ten minutes late."

"I wish I could've slept in," said Mrs. Reznik. "My husband turns up the volume on his snoring at five in the morning and I forgot to put my earplugs in last night!"

Her husband, wanting to leave an intended pun, said dryly, "Momma, God has blessed you with wonderful hearing—nothing gets past those ears of yours."

His wife knew what he was really saying, but the way he framed his statement left her defenseless and mute. The others gave a slight smile over the interplay of words.

By the time Michael reached Sonje's room, she had finished with her makeup and was waiting. Unlike his earlier knock, the rap this time brought a wide-open door with the image of a beautiful woman in front of him.

"My, you look gorgeous!"

"You continue to weaken my knees."

"I'll try not to weaken your knees any further today."

"Maybe I like the sound of the music you play on the strings of my emotions."

"And that is always a two-way street," responded Michael. "Before we join the others for breakfast, I want to talk with you about my mission here in Israel before we fly out. It's a project that I need your help in solving." Michael closed the door and they sat down.

Back at the dining table, conversation was in full swing. Discussions were centered on the day's activities.

"Mom...Pop, your beautiful daughter and I are going to visit some ancient archaeological ruins and will be returning by one o'clock for lunch. Would you two like to visit the ruins with us as a morning outing?"

The old man and his wife looked at each other without saying a word. They had been together in life long enough that there were times when language wasn't needed to convey an answer. The old man answered for both of them.

"Yes, we're definitely interested. It will be a delightful, educational experience, and it'll enrich our understanding of biblical history."

By the time Michael and Sonje reached the dining room, others at the breakfast table were finishing up and were preparing to leave when Hans said, "Why don't the three of you get prepared for our excursion to the ruins while I talk with Michael about some technical issues."

"Michael, of the three sites we visited yesterday, which do you think is more viable for the plant we'll be moving in from South America?"

"Sonje tells me that this plant you want to move into Israel produces tractors, tractor parts, and farm implements that will be exported to dealerships around the world."

"That's correct. And the reason this plant is being looked at is because of the country's political instability."

"Before I can give my final opinion, I need to visit the plant site and inspect its physical layout. However, tractors and farm implements offer a kinder and gentler image than other forms of heavy industry, which means the plant could be closer to residential areas. Proximity to public transportation is important, and of the three sites we looked at, the second would be best suited for that. I might suggest that high-level secrecy be maintained until it's time to transfer everything to Israel. Having been in many countries of the world, especially communists-leaning countries, nationalization is their favorite sport."

"You raise some very interesting points," said Hans. "Next week, we'll send you unannounced to inspect the facility."

"Something else you may want to look at and consider is to duplicate here in Israel everything you have in the South American plant and expand the market so both plants are viable operations. Of course, this could only be done after careful evaluation of the country's stability."

"Another good suggestion," remarked Hans.

Family members came to see what was keeping Hans. Sheena had arranged transportation to the archaeological site and they were ready to go.

"Hans, the taxi's waiting for us," said Sheena. Turning to Sonje, she added, "Sonje, if you and Michael want to go, I'll get us another transport."

"Thank you Sheena, but Michael and I are doing a

special project this morning, and don't worry about us if we're not back for lunch."

Michael and Sonje spent breakfast alone. Later, when they boarded a taxi with three empty luggage cases, little did they know they would set in motion something that would shake Europe to the core. Their destination: the largest bank in Israel.

At the excavation site, the archaeologist in charge of the dig was giving Hans' party a personal tour. Invaluable relics had been recovered and stored temporarily in an enclosed building. The family was captivated and spellbound by the experience of seeing history come alive, except for Mrs. Reznik. She wished she had brought a book or stayed at their Villa. This was not her forte. In her opinion, when you've seen one excavation site, you've seen them all. It was when she saw her husband enjoying the experience that she took heart and tried to make the best of it. *She knew something else was going on that she was unwilling to admit: she didn't like being reminded of history in this manner because it always morphed into her own.*

She was being given a tour of seeing the history of a people and their culture unearthed, showing artifacts from the past, items used on their person, in the home, and even in business dealings. For Mrs. Reznik, history coming to her from the ground was ignoble and she didn't like seeing it unearthed in a forensic manner. She could handle the course of mortality in the flow of normal vicissitudes of life, but the articles she saw and touched today were too close to her own history. Seeing skeletal remains of those taken from the ground produced mental images of her people being sent off to death camps to be slaughtered and buried in open pits. Someday, these unknowns would be those who would face the sharp end of a digging tool by those seeking to explain the past. Unfortunately, the most puzzling question would never be answered: who were these non-people with nothing in the grave to tell the story of why they died in mass numbers? Covering her like a cold, billowing fog was the memory of her own history in the country of Romania, a country where family members lay buried in mass, unmarked graves. For the benefit of her living family at this site, she struggled to put forth an image of strength, found a shaded spot and sat down hoping for a closure of the day's history lesson.

Mrs. Reznik's lifeless spirit revived when their taxi pulled into the unloading area of their resort. Seen going through the front entrance were Michael, Sonje, and a bellhop, each carrying two pieces of luggage. *How strange, she thought, they left for a special project this morning, and now they're returning with six luggage pieces. Someone's been doing a lot of shopping.* She would have much rather gone with them shopping than to listen to a dry lecture about a piece of history where bad things happened to a culture.

Everyone arrived on time at their scheduled one o'clock luncheon. Hans requested the old man to give thanks. True to form, he spoke in Hebrew. Sheena was quick to order non-kosher and Mrs. Reznik had reclaimed her old self and was demonstrating it at the dining table.

"Michael, you and Sonje must have done a lot of shopping this morning by the number of cases you brought back."

Sonje was quiet and avoided joining in, but Michael could think and talk fast on his feet. "You know how women are, Mrs. Reznik, they love to shop. The woman I'm going to marry will have greater fulfillment in shopping because of having to buy for me. So what do you think I'll look like after she dresses me up?"

"Michael, there's method in your madness, and you're just trying to get me in trouble."

"Well, what do you think? Will I look like an Easter egg, a Philadelphia lawyer, or a lone hermit?"

"The real question here, Michael, is not what you'll look like after Sonje dresses you, but will you be comfortable and accept your new image."

"Mrs. Reznik, where do you get your incisive wit?"

"From reading and listening to people talk." Her husband who had been quiet up to this point leaned over the dining table and quipped, "My wife listens to everyone...except me." Then looking down at her, he gave a wink.

Sonje chose to wade into the waters, saying, "Roles can quickly change in a marriage. It just may be that Michael will buy or approve of what I wear...in fact, I believe he's already done that, and I love it!"

No one saw Sheena look at Hans with an adorable glance, followed by a quiet whisper: "That seems to run in the family by the evidence of my wardrobe!"

Mrs. Reznik had the need to know about those six pieces of luggage. By the manner they were handled and carried, some seemed to be heavy, others appeared light. She knew when she was impertinent—today it was borderline.

"Michael, Why all the luggage? You either did a lot of shopping or you have plans to do so." Her husband glanced down at her with an eagle-eyed stare that that spoke louder than words.

Intervention was provided when the waiter returned passing out the dessert menu. However, Michael was one who never left anything hanging, and it was in his nature to answer her question.

"Mrs. Reznik, in answer to your question, at this point it is confidential; however, I will gladly tell you tomorrow morning when we are in flight on our return trip."

"That sounds fair to me," answered Mrs. Reznik.

"Since that's been settled," said Hans, your afternoon and evening are free. My wife and I are going swimming and lounge in the ocean water. The rest of you can do what you wish."

"Sonje and I will join you," said Michael."

The old man's wife spoke up, "Papa and I will sit in lounge chairs and read."

It was early the next morning, and the plane was out of the hanger. The sun had yet to show its red face over the horizon, and everyone was helping load the luggage pieces from the two taxis used to reach the airport. Nothing passed Mrs. Reznik's eyes, and she took notice that Michael kept one luggage piece with him. Everything else went into the storage compartment of the belly of the plane.

"Fritz, did they deliver my special order of apple pie?" asked the old man.

"Yes, Sir, just about an hour ago."

"Dear," said his wife, "are we going over this pie business again?"

"Well, I ordered two so you won't have to bake this week."

"It seems to me, Mr. Reznik, you may not like my baking!

Hans moved close to the old man and whispered, "I see there's trouble in Paradise."

The old man was quick to respond. "Listen, son-in-law, you better be careful what you say, there's room for two in my doghouse."

The jest between the two continued until Hans added, "Just remember, you're the apple of her eye, and she'll not let another compete with her."

"Mr. Isler, you should've been a playwright with the plots you come up with!"

Sonje and Michael were the last of the family to board the plane, followed by one of the pilots who closed and locked the door. Hans placed his single case in an overhead baggage bin outside the captain's quarters, then turning to Hans, said, "Jacob, Sonje and I will join you in the captain's quarters after we get airborne. I have something important I need to share with everyone."

Given the look on both of their faces, Hans knew it portended to something unpleasant. When the pilot announced that the tower had given clearance and seatbelts should be fastened, Sheena saw concern on Hans' face and knew it wasn't from fear of flying. She could read her husband like a book. As the plane lifted off, she reached over and held his hand, saying, "Are you all right, dear?"

"I'll tell you later in flight."

As soon as the seat belt light was off, the door to the captain's quarters opened and in walked Sonje, followed by Michael carrying a luggage case. Mrs. Reznik's eyes widened when she saw the case.

"I have asked Fritz not to disturb us in this room until I have completed my mission. What you will be shown from this case is disturbing evidence of the Romanian Holocaust.

I have intentionally waited until now so your pleasant time in Israel would not be ruined. Some of the things you see here today may be too much for you to handle, and if that's the case, give it to Sonje and she will pass it to the next person in line. The first photo you see will show a Colonel Funar with his execution squad. Look at his photo carefully, and try to identify him in succeeding photos coming your way."

The room turned cold. Faces lost expression. Signs of fear surfaced at the mention of revisiting the horrors of the Holocaust. Everyone was speechless. Holocaust survivors were never immune to gut-wrenching photos. However, Michael continued while the curious Mrs. Reznik now abhorred the thought of wanting to know the contents of those cases.

Michael opened the case and placed it in an unoccupied seat. The first photo he took out was an eight-by-ten glossy print. Hans was first in line to be given a photo.

Michael continued to talk while Sonje facilitated the distribution and collection of the photos.

"When my friends, Bub and Moshe, came on board in our first-night operation off the coast of Romania, they brought with them what was found in Colonel Funar's residence. It was taken to Tel Aviv and stored in several bank deposit boxes. Yesterday, Sonje and I collected everything stored at the bank and have it on board in three luggage cases, one of which is with us in this room."

The first photos moved slowly through the group, but soon the tempo changed, some hardly looked at them before passing them on. Everything came to a stop when Mrs. Reznik interrupted.

"Michael, I don't know how others feel, but I have seen

146

all I want to see. Everything you have should be given to a Holocaust Museum so the world can remember."

"Let's hope the event will be better remembered," said Hans, "by the court reaching a guilty verdict. Sonje, would you please put everything back in the case while Michael and I step outside and discuss some matters."

The two stood outside the door of the captain's quarters. Hans led the conversation. "I will see to it that this man is brought to justice in a court of law and will spend whatever it takes to gather evidence to have him prosecuted. First, he must never know we're onto him, and in view that unskilled people will have to be used to identify him and his place of employment, professionals must lend them assistance. If he gets spooked he'll flee, and with the network the Nazis have, we'll lose him."

"I'll tell Bub and Moshe to pass on the word not to act on anything until they hear from me, that our people will meet with the necessary parties and work out a master plan."

"Can you communicate that to the ship Bub and Moshe are on in code form? If you can, I'll pull Fritz out of the radio room and you can get right on it."

"That'll be no problem; it's as good as done."

When Michael entered the radio room, Hans went into the captain's quarters and sat by Sheena. She looked at his face, and it told her that everything was all right.

Chapter 17

Assignments

When the corporate plane pulled in front of its hanger, two vehicles were waiting. The drivers stationed themselves at the foot of the exit ramp to lend assistance to the disembarking passengers. Michael and Sonje preceded the old man and his wife, followed by Hans and Sheena. With Michael supervising the drivers and Fritz, the luggage was soon unloaded with the three Colonel Funar cases going to the chairman's vehicle for storage in the company's safety vault.

Hans kissed Sheena, saying, "Pipse, I'll see you tonight. We have business to take care of at the office"

"You brighten my day using my special sobriquet!"

Sheena, her parents, and Fritz watched the chairman's vehicle pull away on the tarmac. *The old man who had the insight of an ancient seer, saw something peering at him through the thin veil of his tangible world. His lips moved without the sound of words. Unheard whispers carried a prophetic announcement: "Michael, you will have your day in court, and the world will be shaken by what it sees and hears from those documents."*

The old man continued to watch the chairman's vehicle fade in the distance. Sheena and Mrs. Reznik had boarded their waiting car, and the driver was still standing holding the door open for his last passenger.

"Papa, are you coming with us, or do you want to stay here at the airport?" asked his wife.

––––––––––––––––––––

Hans was on the phone arranging his afternoon schedule. "Freda, I'm now on my way from the airport, and I want you to have Max, our chief of security, there in your front office when we arrive."

"I'll get right on that Mr. Isler."

"There's a file in Sonje's office under Marku Albescu. Make a copy of that file and have it on my desk. Also, contact our records manager and tell her to meet me at the front security desk in fifteen minutes."

Hans looked at Sonje and Michael. "I'm requesting both of you to be with me in my meeting with Max because it concerns two important projects with which you'll be involved. I'm glad to have both of you on board to be part of an effort in creating an underground, modern-day railroad. Sonje, if a viable arrangement is reached with Albescu, I want you to coordinate the business and financial ends with our attorneys, something second nature to you, and Michael, you can help in the general management of procuring professionals experienced in tourism to lay out a master plan. In time, it may necessitate you visiting the field when the project gets underway. If that's the case, we'll provide you a new identity."

Hans continued. "When the Romanian government sees an indigenous national partnering with a European company to build and promote a tourism industry, it will be a positive thing. The country wants and needs foreign investment, and we'll gladly provide it, even with records showing a profit margin which will avert the government's eyes from the real reasons we're in the country."

The driver stopped in front of the central headquarters building and unloaded the three cases. Michael took the case he carried on board the plane that held Colonel Funar's photos, and the driver carried the other two.

The manager of the records department stood nervously at the security desk awaiting the arrival of the chairman, someone she'd never met personally. Her apprehension was whetted further when she saw him come through the front entrance with his executive secretary. Of all her years with the company, she had never been put in this situation, and what gave irony to her experience was the informality of it all. For the first time, she would personally meet the man people only talked about. The conversation between them began at the security desk by Hans extending his hand, saying, "I'm Hans Isler."

I'm Madge, the manager of the records department. I've been instructed to meet you here."

"We have with us some vital records that need to be kept in the safety vault in a room accessed only by approved people. We are leaving these two luggage pieces to be secured under your watchful eye. No one is to have access to these records except the three of us standing here. My driver will carry them to your office, and later, a third case will be delivered for safekeeping."

"You can be assured, Mr. Isler, they will be safely guarded."

"I'm sure they will, Madge. I've heard nothing but good reports about your management."

"Thank you, Sir."

They watched a security officer carry the two cases behind the manager to the records department until Sonje spoke.

"In view that it's lunchtime, I suggest we have a sandwich in the company coffee shop."

"A splendid idea," responded Hans.

It was not uncommon for the chairman to be let out in front of the four-story central office where he would use the main entrance, then take a private elevator that went straight to his office. Today would be different. Upon Sonje's suggestion, Hans and his party made their way down a wide corridor that led to the company's coffee shop that had an enclosed outside patio.

People pretended they didn't see the two powerful people walking by their offices with a stranger carrying a luggage case. Some remembered seeing the stranger with Miss Shuster on a previous occasion, and it was apparent they were now closer friends by their proximity and constant chatter.

Security protocol restricted where Hans could go for lunch, and with Sheena serving a full-course dinner every evening, he frequently ordered a lunch that was delivered to his office by the workers in the coffee shop.

The coffee shop was a place where the same people met every day at the same time, a dining room where friendly voices competed with the clatter of spoons, forks, and dishes. *When the chairman entered along with the company's second most powerful figure, silence fell over the room. The normal comfort zone was altered. Had Sonje been by herself, some would have greeted her. She was always approachable, but the chairman was an unknown—and what was with the stranger carrying the luggage case who seemed so chummy with Miss Shuster? This was interesting tabloid.*

The room atmosphere changed quickly when patrons saw the workers in the shop interacting with the chairman like they were family members. He was even calling them by their first names and asking about their families. The buzz in the luncheon room soon resumed. Unlike other days, today was a profitable experience for the patrons: they had material for conversation at the water coolers.

Hans led the way to his office on the fourth floor. Instead of using the front entrance, he chose his personal side entry. It was a spacious office with a small adjoining conference room used for such matters as the one scheduled today. After picking up the Albescu file on his desk, the three went right to the conference room.

"Michael, you and Sonje have a seat and I'll bring in Max."

They saw Hans sit at the head of the conference table and turn on his intercom. Waiting outside his office in the presence of Freda, who was filling in for Sonje, was big Max, the chief of security. When he came to see Hans, he always stood and walked the floor. It was his size that kept him standing—he needed a chair without arms and the waiting room had none. His pacing while waiting was another issue.

Max was a man few people crossed. He was a bulldog, and some thought he had no feelings. Behind his back, some called him the Enforcer. Everything had to be done by the book and was reflected in small details written into protocols. He had worked in the corporation for a number of years, having served in the military and the government's intelligence agency. He was bright and known to be a person who knew how to get things done. He had been an invaluable asset to Hans when he inherited everything and became chairman.

"Freda, is Max there in your office?"

"Yes, he's here in normal fashion."

"Please bring him to my conference room."

The secretary stood and walked away from her desk, saying to Max, "Please follow me, they're waiting for you in the conference room."

She opened the chairman's office door with Max following. *He wondered why the conference room, and why would others be a part of this meeting?*

Freda stood in the open doorway looking at a beautifully finished conference table around which sat three people, two of whom were her bosses. Protocol required acknowledgment of only the superior. "Will that be all, Mr. Isler?"

"Order some coffee from the coffee shop in thirty-minutes and supervise them getting it to this room."

Freda turned and walked away leaving big Max standing alone with his figure filling the open doorway. *What's this meeting about, thought Max. The chairman had come a long way since he took over, and today it appeared his growth in getting things done included others.*

"Come in, Max, there's a special chair for you there at the end of the table." Hans waited until Max got settled-in and unpacked his notepad and tape recorder.

"Do you want any of this recorded?" asked Max.

"There will be two topics discussed this afternoon. The first can be recorded, the second is highly confidential and forbidden. When we get there, you'll understand why."

Max never missed anything. His eyes saw a luggage piece in the corner of the room near the man who was the chairman's uncle, a man who was becoming a prominent player in the company, and from recent reports, someone of interest to the executive secretary.

"First," said Hans, "we need research done on a Romanian, Marku Albescu. Presently he works for our German Embassy, and our company may be going into partnership with him to create a front to get Jews out of the country for transport to Israel. We already know a lot about him, but it's imperative that he has a clean record with the government and local police. A pristine record will help build a respectable business. Sonje is in charge of this operation and Michael will be assisting her. You are to report everything to her. Any questions?"

"No questions, other than saying money in palms help expedite these matters. The country being what it is, the time-frame is not predictable."

"Do what you have to do," said Hans, "just push it so we can get this underway. In three weeks we have an appointment with Albescu, and it would help if the report is in by then."

"I'll get right on this the minute I leave this meeting."

"Good, then let's move on to a heavy topic. Michael is going to open a luggage case and show you some photos of a war criminal. Information has come to us that he slipped out of Romania at the close of the war and is now employed somewhere here in West Germany. A Romanian living here in this country claims to have seen him wearing a beard and knows where he works. Word has been sent to everyone concerned to step back, do nothing until our professional people come in with a master plan.

"Your assignment is to help set everything up. He must not be spooked or else we'll lose him. Our mission is to get close-up photos that will offer proof to the authorities so they can bring war-crime charges.

"Next, after viewing the gruesome photos here today, I want two sets of copies made of every picture, and when completed, stored in our vault in the basement. Then I want some time-progression prints of what an artist would conceive him looking like today with a beard."

Michael lifted the case, placed it on the table and was about to open it when someone knocked on the door.

"That's our coffee break," said Hans. "Leave everything as it is and we'll come back to it."

Freda was supervising the two coffee shop people pushing the food cart holding piping hot coffee, cream, sugar, cold drinks, and pastries. Everyone saw Max take three donuts, and before the group was served their drinks, he had eaten all three and took two more off the cart.

The attendants and Freda left after serving the four around the table, leaving the food cart inside the conference room. After Max finished off the last two donuts he took from the cart, he looked at Hans. "Dr. Hans, I may as well say it now, rather than later. What you are bringing to me with news of someone seeing a war criminal has happened before, and upon investigation, the reports have proved false. I hope with all that is in me that when we finish with our investigation that he's our man, but I add this only to keep reality in focus.

"I will assure you that the best people available, people who do this kind of thing for a living, will be used. What is your budget for this operation?"

Sonje waited for Hans to respond. "There are two parts to this: the first phase is proving he's Colonel Funar; the second is the prosecution stage. In both phases, we'll spend whatever is necessary to bring the man to justice." Had

Hans placed a ceiling on what the corporation would spend, Sonje was ready to carry the costs herself.

Those around the table saw Michael take charge. He lifted the case holding the Funar documents, placed it on the tabletop, opened it, and took out two sets of duplicate eight-by-ten photos.

"Sonje and I had these photos enlarged and printed the morning we took everything from the safe-deposit boxes. Inside the case are additional copies of these I hold in my hand. This matter of Colonel Funar will go nowhere unless we understand the importance of details. For me to illustrate this, I want to give Jacob and Max a test. Both of you will be given three photos of Colonel Funar. From these photos, you are to list any identifiable physical marks or traits you find. When you finish, we'll go over what you've found. Here are two magnifiers you can use."

"Michael, you're putting me back into a criminal justice class," said Max. "What qualifies you to be leading us in this exercise?"

Sonje saw Hans bristle at what Max said but knew Michael could handle himself.

"I'll answer your question, Max, after we see how well you do. Is that fair?" Max didn't reply, and Michael knew it was beneath him to do what he was asked. *It entered Max's mind that Michael was just getting even with him for the way he was kept from reaching the chairman after jumping ship. Yet, the chairman was given the same assignment.*

Michael poured Sonje another cup of coffee while the two worked on their assignments. Hans, being a doctor and knowing human anatomy, finished early and handed his answers to Michael, then got himself a cup of coffee.

After Max was done, he gave Michael his sheet of

paper, saying, "It's unfair to compete with a doctor in something like this."

"Sonje, will you please take the photos and grade their papers while I give them my last question?" Turning to the two men, he said, "Now that you've studied the other three photos, tell me what you see in this photo of Colonel Funar, and how it relates to the photos you examined?"

He held the picture in front of Max for thirty seconds, then in front of Hans, followed with the words, "This is conceptual. The question here is why is Funar wearing only one tight-skin glove? Now, write your answer down."

Hans saw everything coming down just as Michael planned, all to make a point. He and Sonje had organized this together. He wondered if Max would have any legs to stand on if he failed the test.

Michael took the papers Sonje had graded, looked them over while the two men finished their project. Instead of collecting their papers on the last assignment, he proceeded to go over what Sonje had graded.

"If you were using these photos to identify Colonel Funar and were able to identify all physical marks and traits in the photos, you would have come up with ten: five traits and five distinguishable marks, and there is a difference between the two terms. I see that Jacob has cited nine of the ten, and Max has four. So grading on a percentage, Jacob achieved ninety percent and Max scored forty. Because Jacob is a doctor, he could identify marks and traits that Max missed. I intentionally withheld the last photo until you had examined the first three.

"Max, will you read us your answer on why the colonel is wearing the glove on his left hand?"

Max stared straight at the wall in front of him showing

disdain for what Michael was putting him through, but forged on remembering that sometimes what goes around comes around. Perhaps this was his own comeuppance!

"My response to your question is that there's insufficient information to give a conclusive answer. Conjecture is all that can be offered."

"Before we go any further in this," said Michael, "Sonje will return to both of you the three photos you reviewed earlier, and we'll go over the ten traits and marks that are evident. First, we'll note the marks: a chickenpox scar on his nose, cauliflower right ear, a small scar on the left side of his neck, a mole just under his right ear and a very large Adam's apple. Max, you got two of these right and Jacob missed one—the mole.

"This leaves us with five identifiable traits, physical characteristics a person has because of certain dominant genes. In this man's case, he has more than usual which makes identification easier. They are a cleft chin, detached earlobes, widow's peak, a clubbed thumb, and a finger missing a joint that makes it shorter than the other digits. The physical marks and inherited traits come to the number of ten. Three of the inherited traits are found on his left hand.

"Now, let's hear what Jacob has written about the man who wore a glove on his left hand."

"The simple explanation is that the man was self-conscious about his deformity and wore a glove to cover it up."

"In my opinion," said Michael, "all we need is a good field photographer with high-tech cameras who can bring us clear prints of this man. This will do two things: it will expedite the matter and eliminate unnecessary overhead cost. The critical issue here is to have hands-on control until it reaches the authorities. The less-layered we make it, the greater the probability of success."

Max was in the doldrums, and it was written all over his face. He was now hanging out to dry after coming up short in what Michael put him through. He had done a number on him.

"Now, to answer your question, Max, as to 'What qualifies me to do this exercise.' It took me less than half the time to find all ten of these marks and traits than it did you and Jacob. For four years, I lived in the forest surviving on small intricate details. Life and death were always hanging by a thin thread, and if you couldn't see both sides of the thread at the same time, you would die. I'm alive today because my eyes developed a second sight. I have a photographic memory for details, and it was a tool that helped me survive in the wild. That's why other people died at my hands and I lived. And this man in these photos would have died at my hands had God not saved me with His message of life. Moreover, you want to know why I'm so intense about this, Max? It's because this man raped the girl I was going to marry causing her to commit suicide, and it's difficult to deal with!"

Michael had been standing. He reached over and placed his hand on Max's shoulder. "Max, I hold nothing against you and I want you to know that. It's just that you and I live in two different worlds: you see everything in terms of distance—I see a world made up of details. That's why you didn't see the minutiae in those photos; your eyes are made for big things." Max said nothing.

Quiet settled over the conference room. Hans showed no emotion, but inside he gave laudatory praise over

Michael's performance. Max's head hung down, his chin touching his massive chest. He looked as if he'd been sent into the Coliseum as a gladiator and was under the spear of the victor waiting for the crowd to give thumbs down. Sonje showed a controlled smile. She was proud of the man whom she would marry.

"I'll let all you get on with the meeting at hand," said Michael, "and Sonje, I'll be waiting for you in the coffee shop."

When Michael withdrew from the room, the silence was deafening. No one said anything, and the only response was a slight movement of Max trying to crawl out of the hole he fell into. "That man whipped me today like I've never been whipped."

"Max, you got whipped today because you needed it," said Hans, "not because you deserved it but because you needed it! Sometimes, we only learn from people who are our direct opposites, those who can hold a mirror in front of us and get our attention."

"He got my attention alright…like real good! If I had his intelligence, I'd go somewhere in life. He made me look like a child today, and my, was I humbled and embarrassed."

"You'll grow from it, and be a better person because of it. In fact, you two will become close friends because of what happened today."

"I hope you're not dreaming, Mr. Chairman, because he's on a tall mountain and that's a long way to climb."

"A day-at-a-time, Max, a day-at-a-time. Michael's suggestion is we minimize the layers of people we use in validating the identity of this man. I feel cool breezes coming from that recommendation."

Max showed contrition and bravery. "He survived four years living by his wits during the war and is better qualified than anyone I can recommend for the job. The Jewish agency we use that works in the shadows with specialized skills is always available."

"Right now," said Hans, "all he needs is a good cameraman with a high-powered, telescopic lens. I couldn't have said that had we not had our lesson today."

"You can add me to that list," muttered Max.

Sonje had been quiet up to this point but her concerns grew when this burden was being assigned to Michael alone, and that it could be over-taxing emotionally.

"I should apprise you that Michael may prefer to act as an advisor," said Sonje. However, I'm not speaking for him; I'm just giving you a heads-up."

"I believe it would be appropriate, Sonje, that we assign you the task of working with Michael in this matter."

"I will gladly do that, and before I leave, I want to tell Max that his response to everything today has shown character, and I respect him for that."

Big Max left the meeting with the sense that there was a competitor in his midst, someone who knew more than he did about how to stay alive. However, his job was not to stay alive but to keep others from harm. That's what he knew best. He had studied and practiced this in his military and professional training. When he went to military school he'd graduated at the top of his class, spent a lot of his military life leading special ops and learning survival techniques, but there was something about his competitor that gave him an advantage. Was it from being a predator in the wild? Necessity, the mother of invention, had driven him to nature to learn warfare. His cohabitation with the natural world had given him internal eyes and ears that could never be acquired in a military academy or on the field of battle.

Max remembered what Michael said, "You and I live in two different worlds: you see everything in terms of distance; I see a world made up of details. That's why you didn't see details in those photos—your eyes are made for the distant view." *He's right, Max thought, this man in the finer points of security in this organization could pick him apart because he saw details and knew how a predator thought. He wouldn't be surprised that Michael would be nipping at his heels in the finer details of how security was maintained.* He had two choices when that happened: welcome them, or complain to the chairman. He knew, for the good of the company, he should use Michael's talents and suggestions. However, asking for advice about security, his specialty, would go against the grain. He may be a large man, but he'd been made small today. Perhaps he could learn from this experience. He didn't need any more comeuppances.

Chapter 18

The Ring

Outside the steel gate of the walled Reznik compound was a company vehicle with darkened windows holding two lives that had been brought together by tragedy. The driver waited patiently while the guard gave approval for the heavy gate to be opened. Michael and Sonje had been back from Israel for three days and were entering the large Reznik compound where Sheena had lived before her marriage to Hans. The compound accommodated two homes, and it was the decision of Michael to live here in one of the homes until he and Sonje were married. When they pulled through the gate, they saw Fritz waiting for them at the front of the home.

"What's Fritz doing here?" asked Sonje.

"I requested him earlier today to come over and install a high-powered, teletype short-wave system for management of the Prince Henry operations.

The driver stopped in front of the home, stepped out to open the door for his passengers and found it locked, a signal they weren't ready to get out. He walked over where Fritz was standing and struck up a conversation. Inside the vehicle, the two passengers continued their dialogue.

"Hans seems to be leaning on you a lot," said Sonje. "Tomorrow, you're flying out to South America to inspect the plant there."

"It'll only be three days. You want to come along?"

"You know I want to go! I wish I could. I prefer being with you."

"After we're married," said Michael, "are you going to stop work, like Sheena did?"

"Only if I can be with you."

"With what the company pays me, I'll be able to support you quite well."

"I could live with you in poverty, Michael. You have taken the place of the thing I valued above all. Wealth meant everything to me, and now that you've come into my life, it means nothing. Hold me Michael and whisper in my ear the things you told me on the beach when you asked me to marry you."

Fritz and the driver saw the door of the company car slowly open with Michael emerging first.

"Good evening Fritz, did you get my project finished?"

"Good evening, Michael, Miss Sonje. I completed it a couple of hours ago and just returned from the Rezniks after having dinner with them. Mr. Reznik was generous— he gave me a piece of his apple pie.

"That means he likes you," said Sonje.

"Those people like everybody," responded Fritz. "I found that when Mr. Reznik isn't in Israel with his housing project, they help in a food and clothing distribution program through their shul. They're excited about you moving here."

"Let's go inside, Fritz, and check out the radio. I have an important call to make tonight."

Fritz was skilled in electronics and was employed at the central office as a radio operator handling the transmission of important data from around the world. After both checked out the system, the driver left to take Fritz home with the schedule to return and pick up Sonje.

Sonje was interested to know if the home were adequately furnished. While she made an inspection, Michael worked on a coded message for Bub and Moshe on a freighter somewhere on the Black Sea. First, he would write out the message before coding it:

Bub and Moshe,

I have been assigned to direct the colonel's case here in West Germany. Send me the name of the party who has identified him with either a phone number or address. If he wishes to remain anonymous, have him call me and leave a message at Katharina Enterprises.

Michael

Michael went to find Sonje to show her the rough draft he'd composed, and after looking in several rooms, he called her name.

"Sonje!"

"I'm back here."

He followed the voice to a room where she was making up a bed with sheets and blankets.

"I found these wrapped in plastic, and knowing they were clean I wanted to make your bed for the night."

"You are a doll," said Michael. "I have two questions for you: where did you learn to make beds, and are you going to be this domestic after we're married?"

She continued making the bed while answering the question. "I'll answer your last question first. Yes, I'll make our bed myself after we're married." She stopped and stood upright. "Regarding where I learned bed-making, it was after Katharina took me home with her upon being released from the camp. I made little Hans' bed many times and even learned how to cook and keep house. After I proved myself in Katharina Enterprises by doing her work so she could stay home with Hans, she gave me a million dollars worth of stock, and from that, I launched what became a fortune.

"You know some will say, 'I'm marrying you for your wealth.'"

"And before it's over," responded Sonje, "there'll be those who'll say that I married you for your notoriety as a hero during the Holocaust."

"We can make a prenuptial agreement," suggested Michael.

"Michael, did Hans make a prenuptial arrangement with Sheena? No! And I never want to hear this subject mentioned again."

"Okay, I'll never mention it again if you'll take this rough draft and look it over before I transpose it into code form."

Sonje read what was written. "It's clear and to the point. Are you sure you want to carry the burden of this mission?"

"If you're with me, I'll manage everything quite well."

He returned to the radio room and put the written words in code form, decipherable only by the parties who created it. The first step of his mission had been taken. Callback was scheduled in ninety-six hours, the day following his return from South America.

It was seven o'clock when the driver arrived to take

Sonje home, and to her surprise, Michael got in the vehicle with her. He had told the driver beforehand what was on his agenda, and that his night's work might be longer than usual. He was instructed to go to the upscale part of town where shops were open late.

"Michael, are you seeing me home?"

"Yes, but first I want to take you out for the evening." Sonje thought it strange since he was leaving for South America tomorrow, but she welcomed the opportunity to be with him. Then it got stranger still when he held her ring hand and kept feeling her ring finger. There was a prelude of silence, then came a soft whisper close to her ear: "I want to put something on this finger tonight."

Her heart leaped. Michael couldn't see in the darkness, and with the partition closed between them and the driver, they were in a private, sealed chamber. The lady who lived in the big corporate world found comfort and calm in her new small one that now enclosed her with the pledge of a ring, a symbol of her espousal, a promise of a future when two would become one. Size wouldn't matter...she had rings in her safe at home larger than anything Michael could buy. The ring he would give her would be from the heart. It was a new world she welcomed with just the two of them in it. She lifted her chin giving a proud look no one could see, and with a smile on her face, said, "I'll wear it with pride, and announce it on the rooftop." Then she turned and kissed Michael.

After letting the couple out at the mall, Luis, the evening driver, settled in the driver's seat to finish a book he'd been reading. Every turn-of-a-page he'd look up at the well-lighted entrance of the mall. For forty-five minutes he'd read a compelling drama, and when he finished the last page, he put the book

aside and watched another drama unfold. *Two people were coming toward the vehicle with such gusto and animation he didn't recognize them as his passengers. Locked arm-in-arm, they were acting like college kids, giggling, and laughing. Surely, this couldn't be them, he thought. How could a lady in such a prestigious position in the corporate world be acting like that?* The driver jumped out of the vehicle and opened the door, but before she stepped in, she held her hand up to his face, saying, "Look at this beautiful diamond, Luis. Now you can tell the gossipmongers that the rumor is true. I'm officially engaged to be married to this man."

"Congratulations Miss Shuster, and you too, Michael!"

What a night, thought the driver, and he'd seen it all. He adored this lady. She was the anonymous visitor at the bedside of his son when he was in the hospital and was the person who covered all the medical cost.

That night Sonje lay in her bed remembering the evening she had with the man she loved. She held the ring next to her cheek savoring the thoughts of Michael walking her to her home over the park-like path while nature serenaded them with blinking stars and moon-sparkling reflections from dew forming on grass and glistening tree leaves. Three days was a long time to wait before seeing him again. She had found love for the first time.

Chapter 19

Change

When Max went to work the next morning the word was out, and the whole building was rocking and reeling from the news about Miss Shuster. People would go out of their way to look at the ring on her finger, and when asked about it, she would proudly show it off.

Big Max found the news unsettling. He expected it but didn't want to believe it, and better put, he didn't want to accept it. It was like a dynasty being created from a family gene pool. This would not serve him well. Before Michael came along, the chairman was dependant on him for matters beyond the flow of normal business. Now others were grazing in his pastures, and he didn't have the fences to keep them out. However, if the grass weren't so green, maybe they'd stay out. This would require some creativity on his part, an area where he came up short. *If he knew how to give self-analysis, he thought, it might help in regaining his turf that seemed to be slipping away. Otherwise, inaction would push him adrift on a lonely, cold sheet of ice. Perhaps he would do the unthinkable when Michael returned from his overseas assignment.*

Changes had been made in the command structure at the top corporate level of Katharina Enterprises. Sonje was officially given the title of Vice Chairlady, a position that made the top administrative leadership and management of the company answerable to her. This freed up Hans to work at what he felt God had called him to do. Sonje would run the business enterprise and he would oversee the Consortium and clandestine operations of moving Jews to Israel.

Change in the administrative structure put a crimp in Max's style. Now, he had to report to Sonje who could be more meticulous and experienced than the chairman in matters of business. Then there was the unknown that would have to be factored in—her future husband!

Sunset was settling in with an orange glow marking the horizon when Sonje was dropped off at the airport. She was a public figure in the world of business being the vice chairlady of an international corporation. Newspapers in the business world carried the story of the celebrated woman who fought the status quo by reaching her place of prominence in a man's world. Though she got out of a company vehicle at the airport driven by a chauffeur, she intended this occasion to be private. The only thing she had on her person that reflected affluence was the engagement ring she wore. It was Michael's influence and acceptance of her that spawned a sense of self-worth that gave the freedom to dress casually.

She made her way through the crowds to the gate to meet a man who had changed her life. Being a first-class passenger, Michael was one of the first to exit the plane, and when she leaped into his arms, they went unnoticed by others. It was the place for reunions, tears, and joy. On their way to pick up his baggage, the conversation was about business.

"How did it go at the plant?"

"It was rough when attempting to communicate. I asked technical questions and they had difficulty answering. The plant was found to be highly inefficient and in need of revamping. The photos taken at the factory will help us select a site in Israel for another plant. Consultation with our industrial engineers will determine where we need to go in the project, and it might be altogether more feasible to go ahead and transfer the plant to Israel, and in the process upgrade everything."

"My expertise is in making management better," said Sonje. "Is improving management a viable option?"

"There's something systemic in the political culture that tells me that could be problematic."

"Perhaps, it's to our advantage," said Sonje, "to upgrade the plant in South America and then move it lock, stock, and barrel to Israel at one time. There will be lag time in production, but if efficiency is critical, in the long run, it'll prove productive."

"What can be factored into what you're saying," said Michael, "is that the government is following a far-left, ideology that in time could have a negative impact. Taking action on your suggestion could preempt that eventuality."

"Michael, while we've been talking, everyone has taken their bags, and yours are the only ones left. We'd better get them before they're taken to lost and found. Oh yes, I must tell you that an office has been carved out for you with a small back room where you can install a radio for your communication with Bub and Moshe. Also, a secretary is provided. We have to make you look legitimate."

"What's my title?"

"Over your door is written: Overseas Coordinator."

"Well, that's a good description of this assignment I just completed. What am I going to do with a secretary?"

"She'll write your letters, take calls, and do your gopher

work when you're not around. Michael, you have two weaknesses."

"Is that all, just two?"

"Yes, just two: number one is that you fell for me, which is a wonderful weakness that I appreciate, and the second one is that you want to do everything yourself."

"I'll accept only the latter point. In regards to your first point, both of us are afflicted with that condition."

"You are a doll, my love—let's get you home!"

"Not until we've had something to eat," said Michael.

"But what about the driver, it'll keep him out late."

"He has to eat too—he can join us at our table."

With squinted eyes and a sardonic look, Sonje said, "But that breaks Max's protocol, doesn't it?"

"I love breaking protocol—let's go!"

The next morning Michael stood in front of his newly assigned office looking up at the sign over his office door that read, Overseas Coordinator, when a lady came alongside him in her mid-thirties carrying a hefty, matronly look, asking, "Did you just install that new sign over this office door?"

"No, but why do you ask?"

"Well, you look like you're the maintenance person, and this being a new office with a new sign, I assumed you did the work. I've been assign to work here in this office. You're new around here, aren't you? My name's Birdie. Of course, that's not my real name—just my sobriquet. What's your name? If we're going to be working on the same floor, we should know each other's name."

"My name is Michael Pencovich."

172

The lady stiffened. Her animated, vivacious spirit caved to the will of her embarrassment. She wanted to flee, to escape to a dark corner, and hide. This man was her boss.

"I'm so sorry, Mr. Pencovich, I didn't know who you were and I'm so humiliated. Please forgive me."

Gossip had reached Birdie. This man she had been assigned to work for was engaged to the lady who was running the company, and whose nephew was the chairman and owner. *She had made herself look foolish assigning to him the role of a maintenance person. How could she do such a thing? Every male that worked here in an office at least wore a tie.* Then she saw that Michael was holding his hand out for a formal introduction.

"Birdie, you can call me a maintenance person if you like, but I'd rather be called Michael."

"Oh, you embarrass me further, Sir, you are most kind."

"Well, since we've been introduced, Birdie, let's get the office sorted out."

The office had three sections to it and was located on the top floor. The front section was the secretary's space, the middle, Michael's, and the small back room would be supplied with essential communication equipment to keep in touch with those working on freighters in Operation Henry.

"Birdie, I have worked up a written statement of responsibility above and beyond the normal perfunctory secretarial tasks. There are things a secretary can be written up about, and it takes several of those violations before action can be taken. However, this secretarial position carries the responsibility of secrecy. Any information leaving this office, tangible or intangible, makes subject to immediate dismissal, and in the light of this statement, it would serve you not to try to find out anything beyond your secretarial responsibilities.

"Now, Birdie, I want you to think about what I just said. We all have had issues of talking out of turn, and you may want to work in another office if this is too much pressure on you. I'm leaving this written statement with you, and you can look it over and think about it while I'm gone. I have to see someone about a piece of equipment that goes in my office."

Michael handed her the written statement and left. What she was told was sobering. She sat at what was to be her desk and began reading the statement. She read it once and was reading it again when a large figure opened the door. It was big Max, the chief of security, whose nature matched his size. People considered him pushy and could be dogmatic when he thought security was involved, and some thought he acted like a general and treated others as low-ranking privates. Without speaking, he glanced over at the secretary and moved on to the door that led to Michael's office. He placed his hand on the door handle, was about to enter Michael's office when he was startled with a yell from the secretary, "Stop!"

Max stopped in his tracks, turned slowly and looked at the woman seated at the desk.

"It's forbidden for anyone to go into that room," said the secretary. She had just read what Michael gave her, and it stated that no one was allowed to enter his office, and it was to be kept locked at all times when he was out.

"I beg your pardon, Miss, is this order coming from you or someone else? I happen to know that Mr. Pencovich is not in his office and I want to leave him something."

"I'm the one who gives the orders about that room. If

you have something you want to leave him, you can leave it with me and I'll see that he gets it."

Max thought the new man on the block had not only done a number on him, he did one on his secretary. No one had ever dared to speak to him like this. This doesn't bode well for him, and the envelope he was leaving Michael may only make the grass greener when it was intended otherwise.

The sternness of the secretary had positive results with the big man. His attitude softened. "Please leave this envelope with Mr. Pencovich." Her eyes showed firmness as they followed him to the door, and when he left, she took a deep breath and slowly exhaled hardly believing what she'd done. Today, her boss had forced her to grow to match the challenge.

Michael returned to his office, followed by Fritz and another technician who was pushing a cart with several boxes of communication equipment. They were led to the back room where Fritz took charge installing a teletype system. Upon its completion, he would have two sites where he could access the activities on board freighters plying the waters of the Black Sea. Michael came out of his office and shut his door.

"Birdie, have you looked over the paper I left you?"

"Yes, and I want to tell you that I had an experience here in the office after you left that made me realize that I am capable of doing this job to the standard you require."

"Why your sudden confidence?"

"It was Max, chief of security. He came barreling in here like a barroom brawler without saying anything and started to go right into your office until I yelled at him. He stopped, turned around, and acknowledged me. To be honest, it gave me great satisfaction to see him take an order from just a secretary. He thinks he's the only one around that can lay out demands."

"What did Max want?"

"After I stopped him, he said, 'he knew that you weren't in and wanted to leave something for you.' It was then I told him to 'leave it with me, and I'd see that you got it.'"

She handed the envelope to Michael, then asked, "Did I do the right thing?"

"Yes, you did the right thing, and remember your experience stays inside this room and is not to be discussed elsewhere.

"Birdie, if someone comes to see me and I don't answer the intercom, it means I'm in my communications room and I must never be disturbed."

"Yes, Sir, I understand. On the matter of something else, Sir, I was told that I would be making your travel arrangements by first class. Do you have a carrier preference?"

"Who requested my flights be first class?"

"Oh…the chairman himself, Sir."

"Any major carrier will do."

Michael was still holding Max's envelope in his hand when Fritz and his assistant came out of the back room.

"Well, Michael, it's ready to go."

"That didn't take long."

"That's because it had already been wired for a teletype system."

"Thanks, fellows, it will be put to good use." Michael went into his office, shut the door, and after seating himself, opened Max's envelope.

Michael,

It is not in my nature to admit my shortcomings, but in the showing of your strengths, it uncovered my weaknesses. You spoke truth when you said how opposite we are, that I see distance, whereas you find details. It is my intent to do my job to the highest level possible, but to do so I need help finding weaknesses in the security system that only people like you can find.

It is humbling for me to ask, but what suggestions can you make that will improve the level of security in this company?

After thinking this matter through, please meet with me, or respond in writing.

Max

Michael considered responding to Max in letterform. He was gifted in linguistics. As a child, he had learned to read and write Hebrew, Romanian, and Yiddish. When he worked aboard freighters moving cargo to and from ports in Europe and Russia, he learned to speak German and some of the Slavic dialects in the Black Sea region. After finding his nephew in West Germany, he intensified his efforts in learning the written language. Therefore, it was easy for him to respond to Max in writing.

Max, your letter comes as a surprise! I would rather be saying to you in person what I'm writing. You not only have a distant vision, you have long arms that keep your people at a distance from you. What you're asking me should have been asked of those near you, those who receive your orders. They are the ones who should be your eyes for details. Leadership is knowing and using others that are better than you. I suggest you create a committee from your security people who would meet weekly without you being present and allow them to offer suggestions.

My last statement is that you should make an effort to shorten the length of your arms. Let people get close to you, have coffee breaks, and don't make everything about business. You're not in the military. Max, having said these things, I want you to know that there's no one who can match your skill in getting big things done, and that is your great talent.

Michael

The handwritten reply was folded, placed in an envelope, and sealed.

"Birdie, please come to my office."

"I'll be right there, Sir."

While the secretary stood in front of his desk, she saw him write on an envelope the name, Max.

"It seems, Birdie, that today I'm making you a quasi-harbinger. I have an important call to make soon, and I would like you to take this to Max's mailbox. You aren't afraid to do this are you?"

"Sir, after today's experience, I have no fear."

Chapter 20

The Room with Two Faces

Dark memory sparked pain inside Michael as he sent his teletype message to his two friends waiting somewhere on a freighter in the Black Sea. They had bonded like brothers when they were children and survived together in the pit of fire during the Holocaust while taking avengement on the guilty. Their lives had now come to the point of releasing those energies for another kind of justice: that of seeing a war criminal brought to justice on a world stage. Their efforts were aimed at shining light on the darkest corner of unthinkable horror.

The initial wording over the teletype from Michael was customary, ending with the statement: I await your information. *The response came within minutes and was in code form consisting of only a phone number and a secret identifying password. His heart lurched. Bingo! Michael thought, now we'll put this in motion. He was on the phone with Sonje.*

"Sonje, I have just received the phone number of the man who asserts that he has information on the whereabouts of the colonel. I need you or Jacob to give the order for the vault to be opened so I can collect some photos to take with me to meet this person."

"Go to records on the bottom floor, and by the time you arrive you'll have your clearance. This is good news, Michael."

Michael stood at a long, tall counter alongside two secretaries, one requisitioning a file, the other submitting one for storage. Each had a clerk assisting them. Behind the counter were several desks where clerks were busy with their work. Files submitted for storage were reviewed, and those that carried legal criteria were sent to a lawyer in a nearby private office where they were microfilmed and stored in the company's fireproof vault. All other records were indexed, cataloged, and filed in a large, open storeroom. What Michael had come to pick up was in the fireproof vault.

One of the clerks seated at a desk behind the counter saw Michael waiting to be assisted. He was different than other men who came to this department. He wore no tie and presented himself in a very informal manner. "Can I help you, Sir?"

"I am Michael Pencovich, and someone has called your office approving the pickup of some items in the vault."

The name Pencovich reverberated throughout the room. Every head turned to look at the man at the counter. The office was put on pause. Sonje had called the manager of the department, gave the name of the person who was approved to enter the vault, and word quickly got around. Others in the office looked envious of the lady who had gone to the counter to help the man dressed in informal clothes. Now she would have the bragging rights of helping the person everyone knew was engaged to the lady that ran much of the corporation.

"I'm sorry, Sir, that we didn't recognize you when you first arrived."

Remembering the introduction to his secretary, he

played the jester with a bit of satire. "Is that because I'm dressed like a maintenance person?"

"Oh no, Sir, it's just that people in administration usually come with a formal look. We are required to keep a record of everyone entering the vault, so please come to the end of the counter where you can register."

Everyone in the office watched them walk toward the vault, and when out of view, the manager made a loud tapping sound with a paperweight that carried the signal to stop staring and get back to work. The large vault was a fireproof library that contained thousands of microfilmed documents, all cataloged, and indexed. He was led to the end of the cavernous room where the attendant stopped in front of a closed door.

"This room is accessed only by approved people," said the attendant. "Only the manager of our department has a key, and it was opened just before your arrival. If you need any help, I'll be outside at my desk."

He waited until the woman walked away, then paused to consider what he was about to do. Behind the door he would open was evidence that would be used in a court of law, a legal system foreign to him. It was a court where others would determine guilt or innocence.

He couldn't escape his history. Memory was ponderous. He had used the only court available to him, one that enacted personal justice against those who took everyone and everything from him. Had not God come into his life, his own hands would have already judged and condemned Colonel Funar, using a method of justice that was always quick and efficient. What he was now embarking upon was neither. If the man proved to be the colonel, it would be a long journey of litigation, but the process would put everything on a global stage for the world to see.

The handle turned easily as Michael pulled the door open. The room was dark, the essence of that was inside the three pieces of luggage. Another picture was showing itself. People frequented this vault daily but would never come to know what was behind this door. Footsteps would be heard in front of it, shoulders brushed near it, and some would even attempt to open it. Somewhere out there in society was another kind of door that hid the face of a man, behind which were kept dark, evil secrets that went unnoticed by the passersby.

Michael reached over to switch on the light, saying to himself, the evidence inside this room would be the real light switch that would inform the world of an evil unknown to modern man.

The manager of the records department was standing outside the vault when Michael exited with several folders in his hands.

"If you are through, Mr. Pencovich, I'll see to it that the room is locked!" She noticed his countenance was different, and when he spoke, his voice carried authority.

"See to it that no one opens or enters that room without my approval."

"Yes, Sir, I understand. My staff will be informed of your request."

Chapter 21

The Informant

Michael was back at his desk dialing the phone number received from Moshe and Bub. The man was expecting his call, and knowing he could speak Romanian, he would use the language common to both. The phone rang and rang, and when the party at the end of the line lifted the receiver there was silence...then came a subdued, "Yes." It was spoken in German. Michael responded in Romanian.

"This is MP, and the password is, 'Remember Jerusalem.'"

The man's voice turned vibrant, responding in Romanian, "I have a lot of information for you. Do you wish to meet halfway or in your city? Everything should be discussed away from where the man works and lives. "

"Come my way, and when you reach Munich, give me a call and I'll send a driver to pick you up. Try to wear a disguise so if someone snaps a picture of you around our place, you will remain anonymous."

"I'll be there tomorrow morning and will call you when I get into town. I'm bringing something that will be very telling about the man as well as detailed maps where he works and lives."

"The number I'm leaving with you," said Michael, "is my secretary's. Don't talk to anyone but her, and she will identify herself as Birdie."

After leaving the man his office number, he went to his

communications room, sent a message to Bub and Moshe, then called Sonje's private line. She picked up immediately.

"Hello, Michael!"

"Everything's go! I'm to meet tomorrow with the man after he calls."

"Shall we go out and celebrate by discussing our wedding plans?" said Sonje.

"By all means. However, in view that you turned everything over to Sheena to act as organizer and promoter of the event, there'll be little for us to discuss.

"All the better, Michael. The evening will be about us."

It was midmorning when a large vehicle with darkened windows pulled alongside the curb where a man stood dressed casually wearing a hat, sunglasses, and holding a briefcase. The heavy vehicle's rear door facing the sidewalk swung open, and a voice was heard coming from inside, saying, "Get in!"

The man climbed aboard and sat in a vehicle he'd only read about and seen in pictures. It was spacious with a glass window sealing off the driver's front seat, over which was a drawn curtain. The man who sat across from him didn't match the vehicle he had boarded. Where was the business suit with polished shoes, white shirt, and cufflinks? The stranger who had just boarded the vehicle became concerned. He had in his possession vital information that could prove fatal if compromised in the wrong hands. Fear evaporated when the man spoke in Romanian.

"I'm Michael Pencovich, the person who called you

yesterday and made this arrangement with you. Much of our preliminary business will be done in this vehicle. We are both Jews, and I'm assuming you also experienced the horrors of the Holocaust in Romania."

Michael watched the man remove his sunglasses and hat. His head showed a broad face with deep-set, dark eyes crowned with a healthy body of dark hair.

"I'm Herman Fine, and yes, I went through the Holocaust in Romania and was the only survivor of my family. I'm married, have no children, and live in Stuttgart where I have a small jewelry shop near the bank where Colonel Funar works."

"How did you arrive at such an early hour?"

"Took an early flight and rented a car."

"And where is your vehicle parked?"

"In a garage nearby."

"Does your wife know what's going on?"

"She knows everything. In fact, she's the one encouraging me to push this thing."

"How positive are you that this person is the colonel?"

"I will never forget his face. It has tormented me with nightmares ever since my family and I were forced to stand in line where he supervised his death squads in choosing those who would be shot and those who would be sent off to the slave labor camps. I was singled out for forced labor, and my mother, father, and two sisters were shot at open pits."

Cold messages riveted through Michael. Temptation lurked in the background. He had a skill few people knew anything about and had he not found God and Sonje, that skill might have now been called into action. *This man's story was one of thousands, Michael thought. But he didn't*

185

arrange this meeting to get bogged down with the emotions of the event. His success had always been in his use of emotional detachment and reason. It was necessary that these qualities surface and take command again—but for a different kind of justice.

"How did it come about that you saw and recognized the colonel?"

"It was noontime when someone came into my shop asking my employee if we sized rings. I was helping another customer in another area of the shop but could hear someone speaking with a Romanian accent. It was a man who had a beard and was dressed in a professional manner. After the patron I was helping selected what she wanted, I requested her to go to the cash register and I would ring the item up for purchase. She said she would be there shortly but wanted to look at something else.

"I went and stood by the register waiting for my customer. My employee is a trained gemologist, and the patron he was assisting was told it would take twenty-four hours before he could pick up his order of a resized ring. It was an expensive ring holding a large diamond, and it's our policy at the shop to issue a deposit receipt to the customer showing the owner's address, his signature, and the balance owing. These receipts are made with carbon copies. The original stays with the shop and the copy is given to the customer. The man requested that all inscriptions on the ring's underside be removed. While waiting for my customer to come to the register, I saw and heard everything and said nothing. It's my policy in my shop to avoid personal conversation. It's not good business etiquette for those listening in, and I said nothing to the man even though I knew he had a Romanian accent.

"After the man and lady customer left the shop, my employee gave me the work order explaining the man's request.

"I always personally examine an expensive work order with a cursory inspection to determine if special handling is required. In following through with this order, and remembering his request about the inscription, I found a script on the underside of the ring that hit me like a bomb. Alongside a small Star of David were the written words: To my Love, Aaron, 1940.

"Everything came together at once. First, the inscription, then the memory. The memory undressed the man. I saw him without a beard clothed in his military uniform, an evil creature possessed by the darkest shadows of the underworld. He had erased the life of the owner of that ring and now was trying to destroy the evidence of him having ever lived.

"I was so disturbed I gave the project to my assistant but had enough sense to safeguard the form he'd filled out showing his signature. I left for the afternoon realizing the significance of the inscription. It was evidence and had to be preserved. I returned and finished the project myself using a soft alloy to fill in the inscription knowing that if the ring were retrieved, the inscription could be restored."

"And how did you find his place of employment?"

"I didn't sleep much that night, and it came to me that if this man were the person I believed him to be, he should be followed. The next day after picking up the ring, a friend of mine trailed him to the bank where he worked. After work, he followed him home to the address he gave us at the shop."

"When he was in your shop, do you remember seeing

any identifiable marks that stood out?"

"He was right-handed, but there was something about his left hand. He kept it fisted and off the counter, even when signing the deposit receipt form."

Michael said nothing. He didn't want the man to be influenced by suggestions that could alter or interfere with his fluid memory. His questions were broad and specific.

"Was the man bald?" It was a question of yes or no, with opportunity to qualify his answer.

"No, he wasn't bald; in fact, he had a healthy head of hair that came to a point at the top of his forehead."

"Did the man have any unusual features about his neck?"

"Now that you mentioned the neck, he did have a prominent Adam's Apple."

"From what you said, he never heard you speak?"

"That's correct."

"Is your assistant Romanian?"

"No, he's an indigenous German."

"My concern," said Michael, "is that we do not give him any reason to be suspicious until our net is woven, and when we reach that stage, it'll be too late for him to flee."

The stranger in the vehicle thought Michael's apprehensions were unwarranted and attempted to give him the bigger picture. "Stuttgart is a city of commerce with foreign workers and businesses from every corner of the globe, and to hear a Romanian accent among other foreign elements would be a common event. Besides, he appeared to be comfortably hidden in his role of having a respectable job living among people in a middle-class community."

A thought flashed through Michael's mind: the door, the locked door inside the vault that kept hidden an evil record from those who daily brushed up against it. The man seated next to him couldn't have described it better. Up to this point, the colonel had succeeded in concealing what was behind that door. But that was about to change.

"Allow me to lay out for you an overview of our plans. First, it is important that you talk to no one about our meeting today, and that you tell those with whom you've spoken that this man is not the man you thought he was. We want to calm the waters so we can get close to him.

"From your cursory description of the man, it appears this is Colonel Funar, but to convince the authorities to take legal action, we must gather irrefutable evidence and it all starts with taking the initial step of getting close-up photos to confirm this is our man."

The vehicle had come to a stop in front of the Reznik compound, and the driver was waiting for the guard to open the automatic steel gate. The man seated beside Michael was overwhelmed by the security and structured formalities just to gain access to a walled compound.

"Why all the fanfare of security?" asked the man seated beside Michael.

"The same reason I gave you the instructions about dispelling the validity of your statements concerning Colonel Funar to your friends. There's an underground Nazi movement here in this country and they stop at nothing to achieve their ends. I work for a company committed to supporting Israel, and the underground has already made attempts on the life of the company's owner.

"Sir, you have entered the enemy's territory, and it's best you show your valor by being quiet about matters until you're called upon, which will be an inevitable event."

"I have no family, Mr. Pencovich, because of this man,

and stand ready to be called upon when needed. It will never match the bravery and courage you demonstrated in Romania during the Holocaust. Oh yes, the moment you gave me your name, I knew who you were. You are a legend to many who know the horrors of those times."

Michael said nothing in response to the man's words. When the vehicle came to a stop, he turned and faced the man beside him. "This is where I live, and it will be our first planning site for the creation of a net to ensnare an enemy for the world to see. In ancient times, enemy captives were herded down public streets to be shown off as trophies of war. We're in a war, Mr. Fine, and it'll not be public streets that expose the defeated but rather a world stage through mass media. Come, let's go inside and look at the evidence."

Both men carried a briefcase, and when they reached the front door, it swung open before Michael touched the handle. Standing in front of them was an elderly man with striking blue eyes. His face showed his years, but when he spoke, the wrinkles faded.

"Welcome Michael. I see you brought a guest."

"Glad you could make it, Mr. Reznik. Yes, this is Herman Fine, a vital witness who has brought all of us together. Please get acquainted while I go to the kitchen and lay everything out on the table."

———————————

The manager of the records department had a small, glass-enclosed office with a view of the entire workspace. She had just returned from lunch and was seated at her desk looking over some files that were to be microfilmed when she heard a voice being raised at the counter. Her eyes required reading glasses, and looking up at the distant scene through her prescription lenses, she could see fuzzy outlines of three of her people assisting several at the counter, but her attention was drawn to one of the figures at the counter that was three times the size of her svelte workers. Her head slowly tilted down allowing her glasses to shift to the end of her nose making her look like a middle-age schoolteacher. Now, she had clear vision, and the owner of the raised voice was none other than Max, chief of security.

She never interfered with settling problems unless a situation warranted it. She removed her glasses, stood to her feet, and waited. She knew Max well. Both had worked for the company for several years and had had run-ins in the past. Her concerns were for her workers, who were young for the most part, and she didn't want them intimidated. Max was persistent in what he wanted, and knowing that the only thing he yielded to was authority, it was time for her to look into the matter.

"Do we have a problem here?" asked the manager. The presence of the manager immediately brought change in the big guy. He lowered his voice expressing his issue.

"I am in charge of a special project that includes the materials stored in the vault, and now I'm being told that I don't have access to it. Can you explain this change? The chairman himself requested this and I would like to know who has superseded him?"

"Max, Mr. Pencovich gave me an order when he was here that no one enters that room without his approval, and we're carrying out his request."

Those around Max saw a cold pallor settle over his face. Some who used sound and gesticulation in carrying out authority can sometimes experience a measurable inversion of those traits when suddenly threatened or embarrassed. Max became quiet, asking, "May I use the phone in your office?"

Everyone saw Max walk slowly to the manager's glass office. Realizing he'd be in a fishbowl, he turned around and headed for his own office. He would do battle on his own turf.

It was a long walk to his office and was made longer with the soliloquy going on inside. His lips weren't moving, and sound wasn't heard, but he was in a rage inside. He was so consumed and immersed in thought that passersby who greeted him got no response. He had come to believe that he was in a crucible of metamorphic change over which he had no control, and things weren't going well for him. Events were forcing him to become something he'd never been or wanted to be. Unlike the organism in nature that gallantly accepts its metamorphic change to something higher and more noble, he had neither the desire for change nor the will to accept any forced upon him.

The Letter, why did he write that letter to Michael? It did nothing but set himself up for the touchy, feely domain, a place he avoided visiting. It wasn't his nature to get close to people—he needed distance. That was who he was. Perhaps he should call the chairman, but that would make everything look petty and not bode well for him. He knew where the chairman would lean, even though he was the one who commissioned him to make copies of everything in those luggage cases. He would be told that the contents of those cases didn't belong to the company. They were the private property of Michael, and he alone had the final authority over them. If he went to the Lady now on the throne, she would throw him to the wolves.

Max finally reached his office and sat in his oversized chair at his desk. His turf was narrowing. He used to own the place, people jumped at his command, and they called him, Sir, at every turn. He opened the drawer to take Michael's letter out to read it again. His eyes fell on a small plaque he intended to hang on his office wall. It read:

And we know that all things work together for good to them that love God, to them who are the called according to his purpose.

Max held Michael's letter in his hand thinking that there was a lot of working going on with him, but the good was hidden somewhere out of sight.

Everything taken from the storeroom inside the vault had been laid out on Michael's kitchen table. The articles consisted of Colonel Funar's photographs and documents bearing handwritten letters and signatures. Michael and the old man were observing Mr. Fine laying out the materials he'd brought with him when a knock came at the door.

"If you gentlemen will excuse me, I'll get the door," Michael said.

Michael opened the door and found it to be his driver. "Sir, there's a call for you on the car phone!"

"Who is calling?"

"It's Max."

"Tell him I'm in a meeting and I'll call him later."

When he returned to the kitchen, both men were using magnifying glasses to observe the photos. Michael's interest was in comparing the colonel's signatures on the documents he'd brought along with the handwriting Mr. Fine had in his possession.

Without suggesting a writing comparison, Mr. Fine took the signed receipt form showing the man's cursive written address and signature and placed it next to Funar's signature on a signed document. Stark quietness filled the room. What they saw gripped them with such reality that they knew destiny awaited them with open arms: the signed name he went by in West Germany, Moritz Altenbach, and the accompanying written address showed precise similarities.

"I have carefully examined the photos you brought," said Mr. Fine, "and I find them very disturbing but remarkably clear, and the images are as I remember him. Also, you were wise in asking me for physical characteristics before viewing the prints. I see from the photos I did quite well."

"Mr. Reznik has been working with me on finalizing our mission. He is in contact with special agents who have the responsibility of obtaining close-up photos of our infamous subject."

"I might add," said the old man interrupting Michael, "they are scheduled to arrive in a couple of days for consultation.

Michael continued. "When we finish with this project, information gathering will be launched to find survivors who have witnessed firsthand the colonel's killings and brutality. We have scores of documents detailing his orders for mass murder, but we need compelling live people to tell their stories to give life to the documents."

"I think we should take a break and go to lunch," said the old man. "My wife won't be pleased if we're late."

Chapter 22

The Man in White

Mr. Fine and the old man left Michael with his driver to make a call while they took a stroll through the beautifully kept compound. The man who carried the look of age moved with almost youthful vigor alongside his guest as he ushered him through paths of designed splendor made up of exotic plants and flowers. The guest thought he was a botanist describing everything with technical terms and descriptions. It was as if he were reading from a botanical text book.

The further they strolled, the younger the old man appeared. His aged, deep-wrinkled look was being dwarfed by the strength of the person he was inside. He had morphed in front of his eyes. The visitor then remembered that the first look of the human eye always showed an upside-down picture and that it required the second action of the brain to correct the image. Today, the guest saw a picture of an old man's wrinkled mortality up-righted by the strength of the person he was on the inside.

Max was seated at his desk when his secretary gave the message over the intercom that Mr. Pencovich was on the line. He felt uneasy about this call, but he was the one who initiated it and would follow through with it.

"Hello, this is Max."

"This is Michael. I'm returning your call."

There was lingering pause. Max felt he had nothing to hold onto when dealing with this man's robust self-confidence. Did this self-confidence come from what he was, or because his nephew owned everything both of them walked on?

"Yes, Michael, I just wanted a clarification on the stored cases in the vault. The chairman requested that I make copies of everything and I find that you've put a hold on that order so I haven't the authority to access the materials. Can you give me an explanation of what's to be done."

"The materials are not to leave the vault for any reason. You may bring in photographers to capture on film everything inside the cases but only in my presence."

"That being the case," said Max, "I'll keep in touch when everything is arranged."

"To give you a heads up on the matter of Colonel Funar, the man being identified as the colonel has been confirmed with physical evidentiary proof. Everything will be completed soon with photography, and we'll need your expertise to hire the right people to follow and keep tabs on him."

"The issue of surveillance will be no problem," responded Max with the sound of a raised spirit.

Michael showed a grasp of the big picture. "We'll seek out lawyers who specialize in war crimes when it comes time to turn everything over to the State for prosecution."

When Max hung up he felt good about the conversation. He managed to control himself and show respect but was it out of genuine deference or because of who the man was. Why was the man so well liked? Even his own people bowed down before him. Perhaps he would study him closely and try to find that answer. *He took Michael's letter out of the drawer to read it once more…it was tormenting him like a musical tune that wouldn't leave his mind—it was those words, the words telling him that he needed shorter arms to touch people up close—this was what bothered him.*

The old man had finished giving his guest a tour of his botanical gardens, and the two were moving in the direction of his residence when the compound gate opened allowing two vehicles to enter. The wrinkled face of the tour guide showed a sudden spirited lift. Grabbing the guest by his arm, he exclaimed, "Mr. Fine, I want you to meet the apple of my eye, and the rest of the family too."

Two women and a man got out of one vehicle, and the younger of the two women ran over where the old man stood and embraced him, saying, "Papa, you're looking good."

"Dear, I want you to meet my new friend. Mr. Fine, this is Sheena, my daughter, the joy of my life."

The stranger among them was busy doing the customary exchanges with the old man's daughter unaware that the man who had arrived with the two ladies was now standing nearby.

"Mr. Fine, you've been introduced to my daughter, now I'd like you to meet my son-in-law, Hans Isler, formerly Hans Baughman."

Everything went blank inside the guest. He knew he was among wealthy people when he entered the compound earlier today but when the names Baughman and Isler were given, he was about knocked off his feet. He stood in disbelief that people of their wealth were a part of this operation.

"Where's Sonje?" asked Sheena, "I want her to meet our special guest."

"Where do you think she's gone?" said Mrs. Reznik who was nearing them. "She's looking for the missing party, the one she's going to marry in a few months."

"Now my friend," said the old man, "I want you to meet the love of my life."

Mrs. Reznik lost no time getting what information she could from the guest standing among them.

While everyone was interacting together, no one paid attention to the second vehicle from which emerged three men who were assigned to set up picnic tables under the well-shaded oak trees, whose long-reaching limbs held hanging clusters of colorful, potted flowers. Everything that would be served was carried from the vehicles into Mrs. Reznik's kitchen and kept warm.

"I say let's eat," said the old man. "All of us have to get back to our work."

"What's the hurry Papa," said his wife, "they haven't seen each other for twenty-four hours, and they need time alone."

"I say let's gather at the table and they can come later," replied the old man. He led the way to the park-like setting and upon reaching the beautifully prepared garnished table, they saw Sonje and Michael already seated sipping a tropical drink.

"Mr. Fine!" Michael yelled out, "come, sit by me. I want you to meet someone special!"

When everyone was

seated, the old man took charge of the group, not because the luncheon was at his residence, but because he carried the burden of being a shepherd to his family. When he spoke to Jews of his Messianic faith, he always used the Hebrew text Jesus used.

He stood to his feet and took from his pocket the Hebrew Bible and read Isaiah fifty-three. It was a chapter for the special guest among them. After reading it in Hebrew, he read it in German, a language everyone understood, then shared his experience when fleeing from the Nazi Iron Guard.

"All of us here today, except my lovely daughter, carry the bitter experiences and memories of the greatest tragedy in modern times. We try to forget our experiences of the horrors of what happened and what we went through, but there is one experience I don't want to ever forget.

"We had been hiding in the forest from the Romanian Nazi Iron Guard who was rounding up Jews, taking their valuables and marching them off to be shot or put in forced labor camps. They were making a sweep in our area and we could hear commotion off in the distance. My wife and I, wrapped in each other's arms, were hidden in the brush praying to God. The sounds of soldiers yelling and the wailing screams from those they were herding to their deaths pierced us like a sword. Everything got louder and louder. Then we heard nothing, and when we opened our eyes in our kneeling position, we saw two bare feet with ugly, deep wounds. Raising our faces up, we saw a man in white showing us his hands also bearing wounds. Like a vapor, He vanished. Later, we came to know that He was the Suffering-One in the Scriptures I just read."

Seven people sat in front of empty plates waiting to be

filled with gourmet delights prepared by the best chef to be found, but after the old prophet's testimony interest in food faded. Even the stranger among them was showing tears and the old man knew they were in the throes of mystery, and something providential was in the making.

Mr. Fine raised his head and looked at the old man who was still standing. Everyone was startled by what followed. "Mr. Reznik, you have told my story. My mother and father, along with my two sisters, were shot in open pits, and I was forced to be a slave laborer. After four months of living on starvation rations, I was willing to take the chance of escaping, risking my life to be free of the horrors in the camp. I knew that certain guards slept on duty at the midnight hour, and one night when these guards were on duty, I climbed the fence and dropped to the other side. The sound of hitting the ground alerted the dogs that awakened the guards. I fled into the woods using all the strength I had in my weakened state. I ran and ran until I collapsed on the forest floor. The sound of barking dogs penetrated the evening air, and the cover of darkness offered little help as they neared with flashing lights and snarling dogs. I knew the guards would find me, and I would soon be shot or carried back to the camp and beaten unconscious. With all the strength I had, I pulled myself into a fetal position and prayed, waiting for the end to come.

"The sound of barking dogs lessened, and a quiet calm settled over me. I thought that perhaps I'd died. That was the only explanation for the quiet peace I felt. But when I looked up, there was a glow around a man in white, and he had wounds on his feet and in the palms of his hands. Through the years, I thought I had hallucinated, but that never explained why I wasn't found by those pursuing me.

"Only now, after these many years has the identity of the man in white been revealed to me."

The old prophet left his place at the table where he was still standing, went and stood behind his guest, laid his hands on his shoulders, saying, "Mr. Fine, the man in white who saved us in the forest from the Nazis was Jesus, the Jewish Messiah, the Suffering-One who died for our sins, the Lamb of the Passover. He saved us for a reason and you will know that reason in time."

Quiet settled over the group around the table. Everyone heard what followed: "I see the truth of what you're telling me. I see it! I see it! Only now, after a lifetime, do I see the truth!"

The man covered his face with his hands and wept.

Chapter 23

Photos That Don't Lie

Hans, Sheena, and Sonje had left the Reznik compound after inspecting everything Michael had laid out on the table. The team of three was left to organize the events in front of them. They were sitting drinking coffee and looking at the maps Herman Fine had brought with him when the phone rang.

"This is security at the front gate. May I speak to Mr. Reznik."

"Yes, this is Reznik."

"I have two men here at the gate saying they have an appointment with you and their vehicle shows a lot of boxes in the back seat."

"Ask them for the password."

There was a pause, then the guard came back to the phone, saying, "They say it's Isaiah fifty-three."

"They have arrived two days early, but this works out even better with Michael and Mr. Fine already here. Bring them up to Michael's place."

The old man had the responsibility of recruiting special surveillance photographers, people who were assigned to do classified work with the Israeli intelligence. It was understood that upon the completion of their project all film and negative materials were to be left in the possession of those ordering their services.

Mr. Reznik met them at the door. Both men carried a serious look, and initial indications showed they were comfortable with being in charge of operations.

"Formalities aren't necessary," said the one who seemed to be in charge. You will never know our real names, so just call me Aleph, and my colleague here will go by the name, Tov."

This was a strange operation for these men and their team. The project was simple and straightforward, yet it was turf never walked on before. They were a special breed of people and their services and skills had been requisitioned by their superiors and were told specifically that the locals had the final word in matters that concerned them.

"We requested a space for a dark room to develop our film," said the man who went by the name of Tov. "Everything in the vehicle needs to be unloaded so we can get our planning session underway."

"We have arranged a room in the guard house that will serve you well," added the old man. "It also has sleeping quarters if you need to stay the night."

"We'll see what our project is before deciding our overnight stay. First, let's unpack the vehicle."

In short time everything had been unpacked and they were all in Michael's kitchen going over the photos and maps laid out on the table.

Aleph, the leader of the two photographers, took charge, saying, "First, I want us to address each other by a first name. Herman, Tov and I need to know a lot about the area of the bank where the man works and the layout of the neighborhood where he lives. This means we'll spend several days preparing for when, where, and how the photos will be taken.

Michael interrupted the man with an authoritative tone. "I want you gentlemen to know that whatever photos you get of the colonel, none will serve to our advantage unless you can show certain definable physical traits."

Taken aback by what Michael said, the two men looked at each other. Here was someone telling them how to do their job.

Aleph responded, saying, "I believe we know what we're doing, Michael...I think you said your name was Michael."

"Let's be clear about something, gentlemen," said Michael. "You are under our command in this operation, and we are using your expertise in photography, and you are to use our experience in the forensics of details, the kind of details that will cause the government to take action on a legal matter involving a war criminal."

The three men around the table saw Aleph give his colleague a laser-eyed stare. It was a message that moved Michael to challenge their expertise.

"On the table here in front of us are photos of Colonel Funar. If you are confident in your work, then I want both of you to find the physical traits and markings that are unique to his person, the kind of markings that will cause authorities to take action. You may use the magnifying glasses to do so."

The command Michael showed sobered the two. What he was asking them to do was a hard turn to make, but they knew a very influential person at the highest level had approved this project, and it wasn't to their advantage to get crossways in an inconsequential matter.

When they finished examining the photos, Michael asked, "How many identifiable marks and traits did you find, Aleph?"

"I found four."

"And you, Tov, how many did you come up with?"

"Five," replied Tov.

They saw the man who had given them a visual test take a paper from off the table. "Tov, you scored fifty percent, and Aleph, your score was forty. There are ten measurable markings, and here is a list identifying them. Some are probably too small to show up in your photographic work, but others are prominent: the cauliflower right ear, Adam's apple, cleft chin, detached earlobes, widow's peak, and the most significant of all, the left hand. If you look at the left hand closely in one of the photos, it shows a clubbed thumb and a finger missing a joint that makes it shorter than the other digits.

"You are to take these photos, study them carefully so you can find them in your telescopic lenses. We're looking for details in the images you capture that will connect him to these here on this table. If you can't, you'll be of no service to us."

The old man was showing his approval of Michael by the grin and look of admiration on his face. Herman Fine had sat through everything without saying a word but inside he knew he was with someone who was a leader of men.

Aleph, the one directing the operation, had been challenged. He saw the grasp Michael had of the project, and with the command he exerted over its intended outcome, he realized he was a man of experience; today, he had humbled him by demonstrating his knowledge of details. Character revealed itself with Aleph's response.

"You are correct, Michael. You have taken us to the woodshed about details, and upon your advice, we'll study these photos carefully and do our very best to capture the major identifiable traits. We'll go back to Stuttgart with Herman today and work with him in laying out plans, and when we complete our project there, we'll return here to develop the film."

Herman Fine and the two photographers drove away, and Michael and the old man walked down to the Reznik home where they joined Mrs. Reznik, and their special guest, Sonje, who had just pulled into the compound. They would enjoy the leftovers of the outdoor luncheon and discuss their wedding plans with the old prophet, an event that would involve him.

Chapter 24

Setting the Stage

Herman Fine had gotten up at dawn in Stuttgart to meet with Aleph and Tov, the two photographers assigned to capture close-up images of Colonel Funar. Herman had been the key figure in identifying Funar when he came into his shop. His role now was to point out the place where he worked and the neighborhood where he lived. The downtown streets were empty of pedestrians and vehicles, a perfect situation to measure the distance from the roadway to the front door of the bank and examine the exteriors of adjoining businesses and restaurants.

By the time they reached the neighborhood where the colonel lived, life had not begun to stir, school buses were not seen, and cars hadn't left their garages. Inside the vehicle with Herman Fine were the two men experienced in taking photographs of subjects without their knowledge.

Tov was the driver, and Aleph sat in the passenger seat. Aleph turned around and faced Mr. Fine.
"Herman, I want to lay out what we're going to do and what your role will be in our operation. You are key in identifying the man we'll be photographing. The two of us are not the only people involved in this mission, and it is not for you to know anything more than what you see and hear. Your role is to identify for us the man that goes by the name of Moritz

208

Altenbach. This will be done with you in the back seat. Once we get a good look at him, your work with us is done, and everything will be on our shoulders. You can tell Michael that what he taught us about details won't be forgotten.

"Do you know who Michael is?" asked Herman.

"I only know him as Michael," responded Aleph.

"His surname is Pencovich, the uncle of Hans Isler."

Everything became dead quiet in the car. Silence told the story. "Oh my," said Aleph, "I was kept in the dark. He's the one bringing in all those new immigrants to Israel, and his wealthy nephew is providing hundreds of housing units for them."

"And you forgot to add that the old man who brought you into this operation is the administrator of the funds going to that project, and is Isler's father-in-law."

"I hope I can recover enough from what you told me to do my job. This is earth-shattering, knowing that these people are part of this project."

"You only know half the story of Michael, and I leave it for history to tell you the other half."

"Herman, I'm breaking protocol! They need an eyewitness of what we're doing, and you'll be the eyes to tell the story. You're going with us the whole distance. This is the way things will roll.

"First, employees usually arrive thirty minutes early before the bank opens, and Tov and I will be on the street near the front, not together but within viewing distance. When you see him, you will send us a signal with an electronic device apprising us of his arrival, and because you say, 'he sports a beard,' that will make everything easier. When we accomplish this, we'll move to bigger things.

"Everything moves a step at a time, and our first step is to get to the bank, secure an early parking site, and rehearse our actions."

Michael was sometimes late getting into his office because of his supervision of the Prince Henry operation in the Black Sea. Communication with Bub and Moshe onboard freighters was done at his residence during the early hours between six and ten, putting him at his office an hour before noon. After spending time on the radio with Moshe and Bub, he arrived late at his office and found Max waiting like a patient to see his doctor. His secretary sat behind her desk carrying on an animated conversation with Max. But upon Michael's sudden appearance, conversation ceased.

"Good morning, Max...morning Birdie!" Michael noticed that the big man had a briefcase at his feet where he sat.

"I want to leave you with some reports, Michael. They just came in from those doing footwork for us in Romania."

"Come into my office, Max. Birdie, has anything come in for me?"

"Yes. A Mr. Fine called to give you a report and I told him I'd give you the message."

"Next time when a call comes in from outside this complex and I'm not in the office, be sure I'm contacted at home or on the mobile in my vehicle."

"Yes, Sir, I'll make sure to do that."

"Come on in Max," Michael said as he opened his

office door and led the way.

Max didn't si t down, and Michael remained standing while the big man opened his case and lifted out a file, saying, "The requested police reports on Marku Albescu have come in from Romania, and I'm delivering copies to the chairman and Miss Shuster. You'll find the originals in this folder showing the man has a clean record, and that an in-depth search was made at several agency levels."

"Thank you, Max. You've done a good job and I'm sure when the project takes on tangible form, Miss Shuster will require your expertise."

Max left and closed the office door. Michael sat down and opened the folder to review the reports, all written in Romanian. *His office was soundproof for normal conversation outside his door, but today he heard Max's garbled talk with the secretary, and he wondered why the sudden change given their confrontational history.*

When silence resumed, there was a light knock.

"Come in," answered Michael. He knew it was Birdie.

"Because Max was here in the office, I was unable to place on your desk the phone number where Mr. Fine is to be reached."

He took the paper holding the number, and as she walked toward the door, he asked, "Did you and Max settle your differences? It seems he and you are on speaking terms now."

Birdie appeared almost embarrassed. "You might say that. I never knew there was a soft nature to him, and neither did anyone else. But he has shown me a side that I didn't expect."

"I am told Max carries a lot of pain. What I'm telling you goes with the confidence and secrecy of your job, and the only reason I'm telling you is because of your run-in with him. Max lost his wife in a tragic way several years ago and you might consider this in the future when dealing with him."

Compassion was evident in the secretary's eyes. "That may explain a lot of things," said Birdie. "However, in the office today he demonstrated a kinder and gentler side, something I've never seen before."

"Well, perhaps he needs more of your confrontation," said Michael.

"Oh, I'll not wish for that, Sir, but it did make me a stronger and better person, and apparently it did some good for him too—he gave me respect."

———————————

Herman Fine was in his shop in a back room he used as an office after being dropped off by the two photographers. He sat reflecting on his early-morning drama of identifying Colonel Funar when his phone rang. He had been waiting for the call.

"Hello."

"Is this Herman Fine?"

"Yes."

"This is Michael, and I'm returning your call."

"I'm glad you did. I want to give you a report. Things here are moving fast. This morning, the colonel was identified by both photographers up close after I alerted them with an electronic device. One stood on the street holding a city map looking like he was lost, and when the man walked by he asked for directions. The other photographer was near the bank entrance."

"It sounds like a good beginning."

"I'm on call as a ride-along eyewitness, so I assume I'll have a front-row seat. At this point, I have no information on the time-frame, but I'll keep you informed."

"It will be good if you keep Mr. Reznik informed as well, he's a key player in this critical stage of ensnaring this person."

"You're so right. I'll call him when we hang up."

Hans was on board his company plane returning from England after meeting with the Consortium's executive members when Fritz knocked on the door of his compartment. He opened the door and was handed a teletype message from Sonje. He quickly read what was sent: *Albescu will be with us in four days. The police report is positive, and I'm requesting you to be in the interview along with Michael. He is more capable than either of us in handling any cultural nuances.*

"Fritz, send these two words to Sonje: 'I agree.'"

Hans returned to his seat reflecting on how his adoptive mother seemed to have had a premonition of how his life would turn out. Because of her, he could carry this burden. God had blessed him with a wonderful, devoted wife, an uncle with unusual abilities who had come to know Jesus, the Messiah. Then there was Sheena's mother, father, and Sonje who was now engaged to be married to Michael. These people were far more important to him than all the wealth he controlled. God had been good to him.

Chapter 25

The Net

A smartly dressed lady stood in a queue waiting to be assisted by a bank teller whose eyes kept darting in her direction. Her willowy frame and fashionable dress with high heels gave her a commanding appearance. The lady carried a fashion-model look with a profile showing a tilted-up chin and nose, giving the aura of affluence and importance, all matching the elegance of her diamond-clustered fingers and large Louis Vuitton handbag hanging from her shoulder.

When she reached the front of the line, she heard the teller say, "May I help you, Miss?" Eyes of the bank's customers turned toward her as she strode to the teller's window. The unheard conversation between the teller and lady-of-fashion only enhanced the mystery of the woman.

"I want to talk with someone here who was recommended to me regarding long-term investments. His name is Mr. Moritz Altenbach, and is an investment counselor."

"Certainly," answered the teller. "If you will have a seat in the lounge area someone will be there to assist you."

The lady no sooner reached the lounge section of the bank when a bank attendant arrived, saying, "If you will come with me, I'll take you to Mr. Altenbach's office."

The elegant-looking woman was led to an office where

a man dressed in a dark suit stood and introduced himself.

"Please to meet you, I'm Moritz Altenbach, and I understand you are interested in long-term investments?"

"Yes, I'm an American and would like to diversify my investments here in Europe, and I know that this country has a sound economy with good returns."

The man noticed the lady spoke German with an American accent. "Please be seated, and I'll go over some of our bank's investment plans."

The lady removed her large purse, placing it on the man's desk, and for fifteen minutes they dialogued about the various investment schemes the bank offered. During this time, she took from her large handbag at different intervals a pen, a small writing tablet, and a Kleenex tissue. It went unnoticed that each time an item was removed, it was accompanied by a slight adjustment of her handbag on the table.

The lady could tell the man was more interested in her and the jewelry she wore than the commission he would make in the sale of his bank's product.

When her session was over, she gathered the different forms for investment considerations. Holding the forms in her left hand, she took her expensive handbag from the man's desk and carefully hung the dangling straps over her left shoulder, then stood to her feet. Her standing obliged the man behind the desk to comply with the customary respect of standing also.

The lady's elegant, diamond-laden right hand was extended toward him across the desk with the gesture to shake his hand, followed by the words, "Thank you, Mr. Altenbach. I'm sure you'll be hearing from me in the near future."

When the man extended his hand toward her to bid farewell, the bundle of forms she held in her left hand fell onto the desk.

"Oh, I'm terribly sorry, that's so clumsy of me!"

The man's instinctual reaction was to use both hands to gather the loosely fallen forms, and after grouping them together, he handed them to her with his right hand.

The man still standing, watched the smartly dressed lady turn and walk from his office, unaware this event would haunt him the rest of his life.

Herman Fine found it difficult to focus on attending to the business of his shop. Everything was in a state of flux. He had been the central figure around which everything was swirling, and he could be called at any time to join the crew to put the final closure on a project that appeared to be somewhat simple. Unknown to Herman, the team of people who came for this mission were highly qualified and most respected in their fields and were preparing for the outcome that would stage an international drama.

The team of people chosen to engage in this mission prepared everything for predictable results. The agents Herman Fine saw moving the operation along were just visible figures on top of a floating iceberg driven by the current of human events. The affair that brought them here might be considered small and insignificant at this point. It was only a Holocaust survivor remembering a face, the face of a man responsible for the deaths of thousands. However, life always came from two opposite microscopic cells. On another level, another form of life would be created from two opposites: photographs of a war criminal and Herman

Fine's living memory. Both would serve to give life to a justice system on a world stage.

It had been almost two full days since Herman helped identify the colonel in front of the bank and was preparing to close shop when he received a call from Aleph.

"Herman give us your address, and we'll pick you up at eight in the morning. We'll be in a van with darkened windows."

He thought once he reached this point anxiety would subside but it had an opposite effect—he hardly slept. His wife prepared breakfast and sent him out wishing him success.

The vicissitudes of life had chosen him to be the center of an event that would shock the world, and when he boarded the van for a well-planned mission, an eerie feeling gripped him. Nothing was said as he took his seat. His attention was drawn to the van's interior with its array of surveillance equipment, cameras, and an overhead turret reaching through the roof allowing a 360-degree sweep. Everything showed that it was a vehicle used for undercover operations. Aleph sat across the seat from him in the back, both in jump seats, with Tov and a woman driver in the front.

No one spoke, and Herman Fine had questions but knew it wasn't the right time to ask. He was brought along as a pair of eyes appointed to tell the story.

Unknown to Herman, the colonel's car had a bugging device attached to it so it could be monitored in its movement giving the crew a constant feed on the location of the colonel's vehicle. The bank opened later than most other businesses, and foot traffic from patrons and employees going to work clogged the streets with pedestrians. The lady driving the van stopped at the corner near the bank. Tov got out carrying what looked like a knapsack attached to his chest. Two people, a man and a woman, met him and together they started a slow walk toward the bank. The lady held what appeared to be several office folders.

The atmosphere inside the van became tense. "The vehicle is about two blocks from our site," said the woman who was driving. An electronic signal was sent to the three walking together. The team's experience was evident by the smooth operation of the mission. A change of pace was seen with those on the street as they moved to position themselves for what was about to go down. From having done dry runs, they knew how long it would take to park a vehicle and walk to the spot on the street near the bank where the filming would start.

The man in charge of the operation inside the van had chosen to be silent up to this point. Now, that was reversed, and he began to chatter like he had too much to drink. When things got tense, he had the need to talk.

"If things don't sync, we'll be back later today or tomorrow. If it comes off today, it'll be because we've put enough practice and planning into it. Absolute stillness and quiet are required. We have only fifteen seconds to focus our cameras and shoot the subject, and you, Herman, have a free ticket to the performance."

"Here comes our subject," said the driver.

Aleph became quiet again as he positioned himself on his knees behind the camera that was permanently fixed to the inside wall of the van. The colonel's stride was matched by another male about fifteen feet behind. Tov and the lady had moved to some other point. The driver crept slowly matching the pace of the subject while the photographer snapped photos with his telescopic lens.

Herman's eyes were glued to the infamous man who had come to his shop bearing the ring of someone he'd murdered. Now, in real time, he was watching another kind of history at play, one filled with Western jurisprudence. Anger rose to the surface of Herman's emotions. *Men like him who'd committed genocide didn't deserve to die without physical torture first, and if volunteers were needed to put him on the torture rack, he'd be first in line. However, many would never bring themselves to believe that this well-dressed, sophisticated banker killed helpless thousands. Rushing through Herman's mind was a question that kept him awake at night: What dies inside a person to cause the conscience to be over-ruled by such darkness from hell?*

He disciplined his thoughts away from morbidity to the scene on the street. A smartly dressed lady in high heels holding office folders was seen walking briskly toward the colonel, followed by a man with a knapsack. As the lady neared the colonel, a heel on one of her shoes collapsed causing her to lose balance, fall against the well-dressed banker, then onto the hard cement sidewalk. Papers from folders were scattered everywhere on the ground. The man was lost in a confused, disoriented world, unaware there were three cameras pointed at him. In fifteen seconds, the three photographers had snapped a total of twenty-four close-up shots with state of the art cameras using the highest fine-grain film available in the commercial

219

marketplace. The van drove away, and the two men on the street walked in opposite directions. Bystanders were assisting the lady to her feet who was now apologizing profusely to the man. Others helped gather her folders and scattered papers, then she walked to a parked taxi and drove away.

Chapter 26

Measuring Success

Inside the surveillance van, the driver and Aleph acted like everything that went down was a normal workday. The mission at Stuttgart was completed by ten o'clock in the morning, and Herman Fine, the eyewitness, was on his way to being dropped off at his residence.

Relief was written on Aleph's face as he took the film from the mounted camera. Looking at the guest onboard who had seen an event that should've happened years ago, he saw a face withdrawn and pensive. In deep thought, Herman, the central figure who pushed the first domino to cause the successful operation today, now realized his place in history. All he had left after the holocaust were painful memories, and tucked down inside that pain was a face that was brought to life at the sight of a ring. It was only a small spark, but now it was poised to ignite a flame across the globe.

"Herman!" yelled Aleph from the back of the van. "Are you still with us?"

"I'm lost in the maze of history," responded Herman.

"We don't live in history," said the photographer, "We only visit the past for the purpose of making the future better. What we did today was for tomorrow, for our children who will follow us."

"The truth you speak is sublime, my dear friend," said Herman.

The leader of the operation moved over and sat near Herman. "Herman, the operation here in Stuttgart went down in two phases. You only saw the second phase, and I'm leaving with you the negatives and some prints that came from our first effort, which was remarkably successful, thanks to one of our ladies. You can look at them carefully before you deliver them, and tell Michael we have three rolls to develop at his place tomorrow which will show greater detail than those you'll be given today."

"My wife and I are driving down this afternoon and will deliver your message. When shall I tell him you'll be arriving?"

"Tomorrow morning."

"How many will be in your party?"

"All seven of us. We'll be flying out of Munich tomorrow night."

"I'm sure Michael and Mr. Reznik will want to meet you and your team."

"That will be a pleasurable experience for us. In fact, it will be a great honor."

After Herman Fine was dropped off at his residence, he carried a large, sealed office envelope with him, greeted his wife, and went to a small room he used as an office in his home. *The envelope was opened, and he couldn't believe what he saw: there were eight, five-by-seven black-and-white photos of Colonel Funar showing in great clarity his face, widow's peak, cauliflower ear, and his deformed left hand. The thoughts surging through him were electrifying. The photos he held in his hands weighed*

*hardly an ounce, but in a court of law, they would weigh a
ton. He immediately dialed Michael.*

Mrs. Fine wanted to support her husband in every way
she could, but going to Munich and associating with people
of their standing and importance was beyond her reach.

"Herman, you know this is very difficult for me.
However, I'm going to be strong because it's the right thing
to do."

"My dear, you'll find that the people are very different
than you think they are."

"After you told me their names, I went to the library
and researched who they were. The gentleman you've been
working with is engaged to a very important celebrity in the
women's business world."

"Dear, this is a truism and it will be true as long as we
live: Holocaust survival victims are all on the same level
and share a common experience that transcends everything
that divides and stratifies."

Their car pulled in front of the Reznik compound,
stopped in front of the massive gate and saw a large, burly-
looking guard move in the direction of the driver's side.

"This looks like a fortress," said the wife.

"I thought the same thing when I first saw it, then I
was told the reason why these people live behind walls and
use guards for security."

The guard leaned low enough to peer inside the vehicle
that was now waiting to be cleared to enter the compound.

"Mr. Pencovich is expecting us," said Herman.

"Yes, I know. I just wanted to see who your passenger
is. When the gate opens, you'll have to park in the parking

lot and walk up to his place."

The gate and fortified wall reminded Mrs. Fine of some of the English novels she'd read with all the pomp and ceremony at the nobleman's castle. As of yet, she hadn't seen a castle, but the Edenic look of foliage-filled trees hovering over flowers effusing lusty, deep colors gave the tranquil feeling that there must be a castle hidden somewhere in this scenic wonder. It was a world she'd prefer to be a part of than the one she would be joining that included people beyond her reach.

After pulling into the parking site designated for visitors, they saw two people coming toward them from two different directions. Mrs. Reznik had been watching and waiting for the arrival of the Fine couple. Guests at her home were rare and when they did show up, they were always treated like family.

"Do you know these people who are coming our way?" asked Mrs. Fine.

"Certainly, the man is Michael, and the lady is Mrs. Reznik.

Mrs. Fine found her host animated and engaging as she was led off to the Reznik home.

"Mrs. Fine, let's address each other by our given names. I was given the name of Ruth, but I wasn't a Moabite, though some in my family thought I was a bit strange."

"What a coincidence," said Mrs. Fine. "I'm almost embarrassed to tell you. I'm Naomi, your mother-in-law. We must've gotten switched in some kind of time warp." The ice between them had been broken with a little jest and humor, and by the time Mrs. Fine reached her host's home, she thought she'd walked through Butchart Gardens.

The moment Herman got out of his vehicle, he handed Michael the packet of photos given him by Aleph.

"You'll find these amazingly detailed, and tomorrow there'll be three more rolls to develop and print, approximately twenty-four additional prints. We've hit the jackpot, Michael, and we didn't have to go to Monte Carlo to do it."

Michael said nothing. Today he held Colonel Funar photos in his hands. Had not God change his life, his hands would not be holding photographs but the man's life itself.

"We'll let Mr. Reznik be the judge of how useful these photos are. He's the wise one among us."

They stepped through the door expecting to see the old man waiting breathlessly to view the prints but found him asleep in the overstuffed chair. Herman and Michael looked at each other.

Michael looked over at the old man and smiled. "He's gone to sleep on the job."

"I'm not asleep," came the voice from somewhere under a wrinkled face. "I've been sharpening my saw."

"Here," said Michael, dropping the packet of photos on his lap. "Look at these and tell us what you think."

The packet wasn't sealed, and it was easy for the old man to pull out the eight photos. He slowly and carefully looked at each one before moving to the next. When he finished, his visage was fixed. Looking at Herman, he asked, "How many still photos are left to be developed?"

"Approximately twenty-four," responded Herman.

The old man looked up at Michael. "It's good you're getting more photos, but you really don't need them. These eight prints show everything the authorities need to see, especially the left hand...it's a dead ringer!"

Michael wanted to see the old man's initial reaction before he viewed the photos. He took the packet and looked over the prints. "If the other photos are on par with these, it'll be a double barrel shot across the bow of the legal system."

Michael knew the significance of what they had in their possession, and turning to the old man, he said, "Mr. Reznik, this is because you pulled the right strings."

"No, not really, it's because of the reputation Hans' company has for its support for Israel that they sent the best and brightest. And I believe you had something to do with this by your demand for details."

"I concur with him on that," said Herman.

The old man stood to his feet. "My wife loves to cook, and when she has help things move along rapidly, so we better get down there for dinner. And you, Mr. Fine, will have the choice of staying here with Michael in his extra room or with us."

"Oh, we came prepared to stay in a hotel and wouldn't want to put you out."

"Nonsense, you'll stay with us!"

Phone lines were buzzing between the chairman, vice chairlady, and Michael. All were anxious to see the prints, and when Hans heard the team would be at Michael's place the next day to finish up, he placed some calls for special arrangements to fit the occasion.

At eight o'clock, Michael and the Fines were having breakfast at the Reznik home preparing for their big day. Michael had already talked with Bub and Moshe who were among the first to be told about his upcoming marriage and were now making arrangements in their schedules to be in attendance.

The old man checked in several times a week with his contact person in Israel and rarely made many notes. He oversaw the administration of funds going to the housing project and would sometimes leave the accountants shaking their heads when he discussed from memory a detailed list of figures and major orders requisitioned for the project. Every two weeks he and his wife flew to Israel and inspected the progress. Mrs. Fine, who had reservations about coming, had quickly adjusted by their acceptance of her.

At nine o'clock, Michael was back on the radio talking to Bub and Moshe listening to a report of their recent pick-ups. The information received would be forwarded to the government absorption center in Israel who would then work with the housing authority for temporary settlement. He had just signed off when his intercom buzzer was activated.

"What is it?" asked Michael.

"This is the front gate, Sir. We have a van here with seven people, and they tell me you're expecting them."

"Yes, we're expecting them. Take them to the guard house and tell them I'll be there shortly."

"Yes, Sir."

By the time Michael arrived at the guardhouse, the team was busy unpacking the chemicals and setting up the equipment. Aleph came over to where Michael stood.

"Mr. Pencovich, I hope you're pleased with the initial prints we sent you! The ones we print today should be even better since we got shots from three different angles."

"I'm well satisfied with what I saw, and from what Herman told me, the performance on the street was a class act."

We had two class acts there in Stuttgart, but Herman saw just one. We used another agent the day before at the bank where Funar works. Her camera took the photos we left with you."

"Tell your crew my place is open to relax in with cold drinks in the fridge and coffee in the cupboard. Some very important people will be here at one o'clock to look at all the photos. You will have them completed by then— won't you?"

"We should be through in a couple of hours."

"Only you and Tov are here...where are the others?"

"Mrs. Reznik took them inside for breakfast."

"What about you two?"

"We'll get this underway and take a break later."

"Don't overdo the late breakfast because there'll be a ton of food brought in this afternoon."

Michael's driver pulled his vehicle near where he was talking to Aleph, stopped, got out, opened the door, and waited for him.

Michael boarded his vehicle and wondered where the old man was. It was unlike him not to be present upon the arrival of the guests, but when the driver neared the front gate, his concerns abated. He was sitting with Mr. Fine off the roadway under the shade of a large oak tree holding his opened Hebrew Bible talking to a man who was making the same journey he'd made that changed his life.

Chapter 27

Celebration

Max, chief of security, had an office on the bottom floor near the garage. When Michael's driver pulled into the parking garage, he chose to drop by the big man's office on his way to his floor. Outside his office in the hallway hung a bulletin board where relevant announcements and notices were posted. He took time to look over what had been posted and found a printed notice showing the scheduled dates and times of a newly formed recommendation committee. Michael smiled as he turned to go to Max's office. He found his secretary seated at her desk.

"Is Max in his office?"

"Yes, but someone is with him."

"I'll contact him later," said Michael.

"Oh, wait Mr. Pencovich! I believe he'd want to see you since you're here."

"How is it you know my name?"

"It goes without saying, many people know who you are. Have a seat please."

Michael saw her buzz Max, and he quickly came into the waiting room to greet Michael.

"Welcome to my quarters, Michael. Please come in. I want you to meet my understudy." Michael followed Max into his office whose walls were covered with his meritorious military awards and memorabilia. The theme was past tense and Max's visitor thought it a bit ostentatious and out of place. Michael was relieved when he was spared an official tour of Max's military history. Though his military service was honorable in the new Germany, the formality of his memorabilia hanging on the walls left Michael with a bitter taste. It reminded him of his own history when he resisted repressive, genocidal armies. Max had the need to remember his past; Michael strove to forget his. Max's honor was visible on the walls of his office; Michael's was hidden in the hearts of those he saved in the Holocaust.

"Michael, I want you to meet Helmet. He's my Lieutenant who is filling a new position created upon your advice of decentralizing our security system. He's heading up an advisory committee."

"I'm pleased to meet you, Mr. Pencovich. All of us in security know of you, and now I can proudly say that I've met you."

"The name is Michael if you don't mind. Max, You do an excellent job with your team managing the security of the chairman's family. I know this is a small part of what you do, but his family appreciates it."

"It's our job," said Max.

Michael's presence had brought closure to any discussions going on between Max and Helmet, and Helmet knew it was opportune for him to show deference by dismissing himself. When the door closed, Max looked at Michael.

"Would you care for a cup of coffee?"

"No thanks, I'm just passing through to my office and wanted to see you for a minute. We have finalized our photography operation with predictable results, and the executive officers are meeting with the agents at the Reznik place at one o'clock to view the prints. I think it's important for you to be there as my guest. The chairman is celebrating with a lot of fanfare, and I think you know what that means."

"That's kind of you to invite me. I'll clear my schedule and be there."

When Michael left, Max felt like his feet grew in size to support the frame he carried around with him, that he belonged to this organization once again.

Michael's driver stopped in front of the large steel gate. It swung open. The guard came to the driver's side, saying, "They've asked me to give you the message that everyone is waiting at Mr. Pencovich's place."

The driver pulled onto the compound and Michael could see the food purveyors out in full force. Tables covered with linen had been set up in the beautiful, shaded floral garden. He rolled down the window where he sat in the vehicle to smell the chicken, beef, and lamb being cooked over the open grills brought in for this special event. After Michael was dropped off at the front of his house, he saw other vehicles pulling through the iron gate. The old man came out and stood with Michael in front of the home to greet those arriving. First arrivals were Hans, Sheena, and Sonje. They had come together in one vehicle, followed by Max. Michael took charge of the event at this point. He requested Aleph to come outside.

"I want everyone here to meet Aleph, the one who directed this operation and who will lead us inside for the viewing of the photographs."

After introductions, Aleph spoke. "I would like to say something to everyone. This was not a dangerous operation, but it required a lot of planning, rehearsing, and expertise. You will find on the table in the kitchen and on the countertops thirty-two photos of our subject. With Michael's emphasis on detail, we did our best to capture the markings that would readily identify him. We will be leaving with you the negatives and three copies of each print"

Aleph led the way through the front door with Michael, Sonje, and the rest of the group following. The photography team and Mr. Fine stood to their feet as they entered.

Hans soon felt Sonje's hand grasp his with a whisper close to his ear, "Michael, I know this is difficult for you, and I want you to know I will always be at your side."

"Sonje, you are one of the reasons I am today viewing Funar's photos instead of sending him to Mr. Hyde's courtroom." Michael felt a tight squeeze on his hand.

Sheena saw that her mother was absent from the group. Moving closer to her father, she asked, "Papa, where's Momma?"

"Your mother has seen all the photos she wants to see and is home with Mrs. Fine."

"I understand, Papa, but I miss her not being with us."

"Just don't you worry, she'll be there with bells on for the big luncheon and will probably grab all the attention."

"I'm sure of that—it's her style!"

Everyone behind Michael saw him pay close attention to the finer details of certain prints. Those who followed wondered why special attention was given to some while other prints were passed over, but the old man knew. He'd been a diamond cutter in life and possessed the skill to sort out the industrial diamonds from those that would be used to adorn expensive jewelry. Michael was exercising that skill by examining details that would embellish another kind of ring, a ring of truth that jurors would hear and see loud and clear.

Thirty-two photos were viewed by those whose families and relatives died in the Holocaust. Tragic emotional scars were written on every face. No one spoke. They had the need to escape the physical site of photos that were giving life to an evil man from the darkness of hell. They moved quickly to the living room and found the team that took the photos still standing giving respect to the event.

Hans was first to shake the dirge-like quietness from the group. "Friends, the solemn atmosphere created here isn't due to the pictures of the monster we saw, but it's from the memories we carry of those we loved that he took from us. Because of Michael, we will be the victors in a court of law, and the Lawyers who handle the legal work of hunting down Nazi criminals will have a field day with all the vital evidence we have on hand. Soon, the free world will be shaken with the news of a war criminal being tried for his crimes. As this goes forward, it will do so because of your help.

"We say to Aleph and his team, 'Thank you for your success in getting these excellent photos.' It all warrants a celebration, but before we enjoy that celebration, a man who is a spiritual father to us all will give us a Scripture and a prayer."

The old prophet took out his well-worn Hebrew

Bible. Wrinkled hands showed his age, and though deeply furrowed, they had the look of stillness, like the hands of a marble statue found in a museum. Standing straight and tall, his smooth, deep voice matched the person he was as he read from Zechariah.

> *For whoever touches you touches the apple of His eye...Shout and be glad, O daughter of Zion. For I am coming, and will live among you," declares the Lord. "Many nations will be joined with the Lord in that day and will become my people. I will live among you and you will know the Lord Almighty has sent me to you.*

Chapter 28

More Photography

The following day Max and Michael stood at the counter of the Records Department along with three of the team members enlisted to photograph Colonel Funar. Michael requested they stay over and photocopy the contents of the three cases of evidence inside the vault.

The manager of the department had been apprised of the need to access the vault, and that it would be off-limits until their project was completed. When she came to the desk, she only acknowledged Michael.

"Good morning, Mr. Pencovich."

"Morning…I'm leaving Max in charge of supervising our project in the vault. No one is to enter the room until everything is done, and when it's locked up, the same restrictions I gave you the last time are still in force."

"I'll see that your wishes are carried out as you requested. If you gentlemen will sign in, I'll take you to the vault."

"This is a big project," said Michael, "and I've ordered two folding tables to be brought in, so when maintenance arrives, you'll know what to do with them."

"Are these four gentlemen the only ones authorized to be here?"

"Yes, only these four."

Michael walked to the vault along with the others in

his group and stayed until the tables were brought in and set up. Before leaving, he gave instructions to Max.

"Max, I have told the team here that we need two copies of every document, photograph, and letter. Copies of the 16 mm movie film can be done at a later date. If there are any complications, let my secretary know. The sooner we have these copies in our hands, the sooner the case can be processed by the authorities. I'm scheduled for an important meeting shortly, and I leave it with you to see that the work gets done."

"It appears they've brought in everything needed to do the job, and they're professionals, so we'll be out of here by noon and I'll see that they stay with the project until it's done."

"Please do that, Max, and you can also get your surveillance people on Funar anytime now that we have the photos. If he jumps and runs, we'll know where he is."

"I've already made these connections, and it'll only take a call to get them on it."

"It's like I said, Max, no one is better than you when it comes to acting on big projects."

Max gave a slight grin, saying, "I am trying to explore the new world of small things."

"I know you are, Max….It shows."

Behind closed doors, Hans, Sonje, and Michael were in the chairman's conference room discussing off-the-books operations while waiting to interview Marku Albescu, the Romanian Hans had recruited for a business partnership as a cover to move Jews to Michael's freighters.

Michael had just submitted his quarterly report on the Prince Henry successes in the Black Sea and the projection of expanding the pickups in other Soviet Bloc countries by adding another freighter.

Hans was leaning more and more on Michael's skills in public relations and his insightful decisions in technical matters. His recommendations coming from his South American trip would put the company on the right track for a long-term favorable bottom line and provide employment for new immigrants. He commanded respect from everyone and it didn't come from Sonje's position in the company. He was a natural born leader.

"Michael, because you are talented in dealing with people and know how to get things done, it would be easy to overburden you with our private agenda, and I must be careful not to do this. What I want to do is officially delineate our responsibilities on two major issues before us: Colonel Funar's prosecution and our proposed offer to Marku Albescu, who is scheduled to be with us shortly.

"Being a doctor, I sense that it will serve you well to continue with the Funar case until it goes to court. Your personal emotional growth in this matter is exceptional in the way it has made you a different person. Also, you have established yourself among us as an independent thinker outside the box, and it would help me to know your thoughts on steps that might be taken to optimize a successful prosecution."

Sonje sat looking at two men, uncle, and nephew, who, if they were near the same age, would pass as look-alike brothers. However, they displayed more than physical characteristics—both carried an inner energy of acting on the good they found in others. Hans displayed that quality when he first found Michael in his fallen state of seeking justice for people who would never be prosecuted for their crimes. Michael could have thrown Max overboard but chose to see his positive side, befriended him, and was now experiencing inner growth because of Michael's acceptance.

"In answer to your question, Jacob, apart from presenting the photos and documents to the government to initiate the case, I would appoint Herman Fine to be the point man to search out survivors of the Romanian Holocaust, people who personally witnessed the atrocities caused by this man. We need voices and faces to accompany the documentation on hand.

"Next, I would attempt to apprise the authorities before his arrest that they seize the rings he wears, and all jewelry in his possession. It was a ring brought to Mr. Fine to be resized that started all this. Funar requested the script on the underside be polished off, which bore the evidence it was taken from a Jew. The inscription showed a Star of David, a name, and the year 1940. Mr. Fine knew the significance of the inscription and filled the engraving with a soft metallic substance that could be removed without damage to the ring and the inscription. Any evidence of Holocaust jewelry in his possession will only augment the weight of guilt."

"As usual, your incisive thinking potentiates the opportunities available to us," said Hans. "I think if Mr. Fine is willing to take on this responsibility it would serve to expedite everything, and we will certainly cover any expense he incurs."

Hans saw Sonje looking down at some notes she had placed on the conference table and knew they had nothing to do with the subject under discussion. She was avoiding participation because the conversation centered on Michael.

"Sonje, you've said nothing about this subject. Would you like to add something?"

Hans and Michael saw her lay her pen down on the table. "At this point, my concerns are on the periphery of what you two have discussed. Historically, Max has been a good facilitator in issues like the ones we're discussing, but I don't want Michael to be over-stressed. Is it possible to incorporate Max in this somewhere so Michael's burden will be lighter?"

"I have no objections to Max's involvement," said Hans, "and I think that should be left with the two of you to make that decision."

In response to Max's involvement, Michael gave an update: "As a matter of information, Max is overseeing the photographic copying of the materials in the three luggage cases as we speak. When these are processed, we'll give copies of everything to the lawyers our Israeli friends have recommended. When that time comes, I'll make sure Mr. Fine is present with the lawyers when we present evidence. He's our prime witness."

Sonje saw Hans give a meditative look, then staring off into space, said, "Michael...my mother, your beautiful sister, would be proud of what you've become: a gallant hero to our people and a partner with her son in moving Jews to Israel."

Tears came to Sonje's eyes.

Chapter 29

Loyalty to a Greater Cause

There was nothing flamboyant about the well-dressed man getting out of a taxi in front of the Katharina Enterprises building. His appearance blended well with others coming and going. Steps taken were slow and deliberate as they moved him down the walkway lined with exotic plants and flowers imported from around the world. When he reached the halfway point, he stopped at a large water fountain filled with expensive koi fish. It was the centerpiece that complimented the pristine, manicured landscape. Peaceful sounds of trickling water surrounded by floral beauty gave rise to introspection.

The man was remembering his first visit to this site, a time when he never took notice of the beauty that surrounded the mammoth Katharina central headquarters. That day he had come for business, the collection of his final payment for a project he was hired to do. However, today was a different matter. He took a few steps toward the entrance and stopped again to look at the enormity of the building covering a city block that was the nerve center for investments and corporate operations around the world. He had been singled out by the man who owned it all. It was an unbelievable strange world he was entering.

Security at the front door of the central office of

Katharina Enterprises permitted only employees with company badges to enter. Those who were not employees were required to be approved at a security desk where they would be given a visitor's badge. The attending female security officer at the counter saw a man approaching who was well dressed holding a briefcase exhibiting a show of tension. She was trained in the skill of profiling people who came to the counter, and with someone displaying these signs, special precautions were taken to clear them for further admission.

"May I help you, Sir?"

"Yes, I am Marku Albescu and have an appointment with Sonje Shuster."

The security person had signals going off in her head. *Here was a man showing a nervous look saying he had an appointment with the vice chairlady. If the man checked out, thought the officer, he would have good reason to show anxiety. The woman he was to see was a powerful person in the company...anyone would be nervous under those conditions.*

"One moment please," said the officer.

The man saw the officer dial another party.

"Is this the office of the vice chairlady? I have someone here by the name of Marku Albescu who says he has an appointment."

The man saw the officer wait for a few moments before she hung up.

"One of our security people will escort you to her office, but first you'll have to sign in and be cleared by security in our side room with proof of identification. Your briefcase will also be searched."

The front office secretary who handled the traffic

for the chairman and vice chairlady was at her desk when a well-dressed man accompanied by a security officer entered the large front waiting room. The security person stayed near the door until the man he escorted introduced himself to the secretary.

"I am Marku Albescu and have made an appointment with the vice chairlady, Miss Shuster."

"Please have a seat, and I'll tell them you're here."

Hans, Sonje, and Michael were in the chairman's private boardroom when the expected call came from Freda at the front desk. The flashing light on the intercom was answered by Sonje.

"What is it, Freda?"

"Mr. Albescu is waiting here for his appointment."

"Would you bring him in please?"

The Romanian, now having entered the chairman's plush office, looked across the room at a desk where he had sat with Dr. Isler several weeks before with fear and trembling. Memory had a way of pushing through one's mind, in a split moment, events that defied the elements of real time. His experience with Dr. Isler, who had hired him through intermediaries to research his family's records in Romania, was an event that brought him to an agonizing point of fear for his family and himself. He had a file telling the story of his Jewish heritage and involvement in helping Jews get out of the country. The man who could have destroyed him offered life of a different kind, an opportunity for partnership in helping Jews get to Israel. Today he was nervous but for a different reason. He had explored everything he could about the chairman and his company and found that he was a person who used his great wealth to support Israel, and his proposal to him was part of that effort. This second visit to his office took on a different aura. Even the expensive paintings that hung on the wall gave a new aesthetic luster he never saw before. The flash of memory faded quickly when the lady said, "This way please." After taking a few steps down a short hallway, they stood in front of a door that read: Conference Room.

A knock on the door brought an immediate response. It swung open, and standing in the doorway was the chairman himself. Freda was first to speak.

"Dr. Hans, this is Mr. Albescu."

"We have already met, and it's a pleasure to see you again, Mr. Albescu...Freda, please have the coffee shop send up some coffee, sandwiches, and water."

"Mr. Albescu, I'd like you to meet Miss Shuster, our company's vice chairlady, someone you met on your previous visit, and Mr. Pencovich, our overseas coordinator."

Both were seated at the conference table. They stood, shook hands without speaking as Hans took charge of opening the business session. "Everyone be seated please."

The man was nervous. He hoped his eyes didn't show it. Here were people of power and money. The lady across from him was tall, lissome, and beautiful. She and the chairman looked too young to be in such responsible positions. The third member of the group resembled the young chairman, and experience was written all over him.

"Sir," said Hans, "each of us here in this room is aware of our previous conversation when we first met. In our first meeting, after you were thoroughly investigated, I put a proposal to you that involved a business

243

arrangement between our company and you with the understanding that it would be a front to smuggle Jews out of Romania into Israel. I requested you to contact Miss Shuster if you were interested, and you have done this, which leaves us the message that it is in your interest to pursue this course of action. Can you give us a statement of your intent in this matter?"

The man shuffled his feet under the desk as a signal to himself that he needed poise to continue what he'd started after extended thought and discussions with his wife on this topic.

"Let me go on record to say that my wife and I have discussed this matter and are unified in our decision knowing it will change us in every way. I am already in danger of having helped Jews get out of the country and now remain stealth but out of reach because of the loyalty of others, which now includes the three of you. My concerns are for the safety of my family, but Dr. Isler has assuaged that issue with the arrangements for them to live out of the country. We feel obliged to help my people in a greater way. My organizational and public relations skills qualify me to carry out the proposed objectives of the mission, and my fluency in German can do nothing but help in this area."

Sonje interrupted the man, asking, "How do others view you in the community where you live?"

"My, that's an open-ended question, so let me just say our friends look upon us as an average family."

"In the country of Romania," asked Sonje, "Is there such a thing as an average family?"

"Let me put it this way: because I work for the embassy, I am viewed by others in a respectable way, and probably make a higher salary than those who are not part of the corrupt political establishment."

"What I'm leading up to, Mr. Albescu, is what will the people say when they see you suddenly becoming involved in a large entrepreneurial project."

"They will say, 'A European company is just using a Romanian to further their foreign investment.' It happens all the time."

Sonje continued. "What is your level of business expertise?"

"I understood this part of the project would be handled by trained people from outside and wasn't part of my portfolio."

"That is true, but you will be the party reporting to the government about finances…the profits, losses, and taxes, not that you would prepare the reports, but you must be able to explain them to authorities."

"I've never been a person who lacked ability in learning new skills. My position in the embassy would support this statement.

"Mr. Albescu, the chairman has given me and Mr. Pencovich the responsibility of overseeing this project. I will handle the business end of it, and he will supervise the engineers and consultants in the physical development. He will also be your contact person when the smuggling operation begins."

Sonje continued. "All matters that are personal, such things as finances, travel, lodging, and college tuition will be arranged and handled by the chairman. The first action to be taken is that you will meet with professionals who survey and evaluate potential tourism sites. You will be the figurehead in the country to answer their questions and work with them in obtaining suitable investment sites. It is important that when offers are made on suitable properties that they see you as the investor and not a European company. As the chairman informed you in your first meeting, you will take out a sizeable loan making yourself a partner with a legal dummy corporation in Europe. This will hide from the Romanian government and the public who the real financial sponsors are. Our lawyers will start on this right away, and it will be up to you to determine when and how you leave your employment with the West German Embassy."

Up to this point, Michael had said nothing, but when he did he spoke Romanian. "Mr. Albescu, can you tell me how long you've worked for the embassy?"

Albescu was shocked hearing Michael use his mother tongue and others took notice of the man's slow response in choosing which language to use.

Instead of answering directly, he looked at Hans and Sonje, saying, "Mr. Pencovich has asked me my length of employment with the embassy. Then turning to Michael, he spoke in Romanian. "I have been with them for twenty years."

Michael continued speaking in Romanian. "Do you have access to the archive records of those who were issued visas?"

Again, he brought Hans and Sonje into the conversation, saying, "I'm being asked, 'If I have access to the archive records?'"

"Yes," he replied in Romanian, nodding his head in affirmation.

Michael then spoke in German. "It is the small things that can sometimes measure one's greater self.

When you chose to include those who couldn't speak Romanian in our conversation, it showed your grasp of adaptability and inclusiveness. My suggestion is that you say nothing to the embassy officials about leaving until we've gone through some names in the visa archives."

"That's a wise suggestion," said the man, "and if you have access to those names, I'll get right on them."

"My name is Michael, and one of the first things you'll have to do is memorize a secret code with which I use to communicate."

The man expanded his summary impressions of the person named Michael: he had the look of experience and carried persuasive charisma that would make him a leader of men.

A knock was heard at the door. "That's Freda with our coffee," Hans said. Acting like he was one of the help, he went to the door and assisted those bringing in the cart of hot coffee, sandwiches, and pastries. Freda followed behind with a file in her arms, laying it on the desk in front of Michael.

"This is from your secretary, Michael." He quickly read a handwritten note from Birdie: "Max has passed on the information that everything is photographed and two copies of each item will be delivered tomorrow morning."

Everyone was being served sandwiches, coffee, and pastries. Michael stepped out of the boardroom to make a call. With six people in the room with a large cart, only Sonje saw Michael leave. Five minutes later, she left the room to check on him and found him just getting off the phone at Hans desk.

"What was that about?" asked Sonje.

"A meeting with Max this afternoon."

With a sardonic, eye-squinting look, Sonje said to Michael, "You two are becoming friends, aren't you?"

"The friendship you speak of," responded Michael, "is helped along by the secretary you provided me."

Everything stopped that was moving with Sonje. A thousand thoughts lurked from the corners of her mind. Like a zombie, she turned and faced Michael showing a slight smile.

"Are you telling me what I'm thinking?"

"Yes, I'm telling you what you're thinking."

Sonje's hands went to her face to conceal her expression of surprise. Michael remained stoic.

"Wow! That's earth-shaking!" said Sonje.

"It's your contribution to our friendship," said Michael, with a grin now showing on his face.

Again, Sonje broke into a controlled chortle. It was a pleasant scene for Michael to watch Sonje almost giggle over the thought that Max was taken to Birdie. It showed health and even happiness, and he would like to think he had something to do with it.

Chapter 30

The Evidence

The long-awaited day had arrived. Michael walked alone with a briefcase in hand toward the company's boardroom where men of wealth and power met and made decisions that touched people's lives around the world. Today, it was not about wealth and finance but justice for a people who perished in the Romanian Holocaust. An epic event was in the making, and what would happen today in that room would exceed anything the walls had ever witnessed.

Michael knew ships, had earned his captain's license and navigated waters around the world, but today he would become the captain of another kind of ship, one that would be inaugurated and christened, not with a bottle of champagne across its bow, but by the photos and documents he carried in his briefcase.

He stopped outside the room—looked at the door that kept hidden what went on inside. Today, it would be closed again, but it would never silence what was about to be revealed. The story he carried inside his case had been gestating in the womb of a dormant time capsule, and its delivery was about to be made to the world.

He pushed the door open and stepped inside. The room was empty of people, silent, except for the swish of the door closing, followed by the sound of a click. If only his memory had the silence of this room with a door that could lock out unwanted voices from his past.

How strange, he thought, the mind was mysterious in the way it shaped the memory of human experiences. It seemed to act independently of the will by imposing its own theatrical stage props for best effects. Yet, there was competition between mind and will. The will sometimes blocked unwanted memory scenes coming from one's history, but he was never afforded that luxury—his memory was a burden he had to bear—o*h, that the prop scenes coming his way that gave vivid stage performances could be removed! But he knew healing of the memory was more about what he added to it than what was taken from it. He remembered reading the account of his ancient people calling upon Moses to heal the community's water supply. The polluted, undrinkable water was purified when the prophet cut down a tree and added it to the water. It would be what he added to his memory that would quell the dark voices of his past. He could only weaken the darkness of his history by yielding to the light of the future.*

The room in front of him seemed to have staring eyes, leaving a sense of imposing destiny. What went on between these walls changed people's lives around the world for good and bad. He was one of them. He'd visited this room once before, and it left him changed forever. It was in this room a dead person started coming back to life, and it all began when his only surviving relative opened his arms and put him on a new path. He embraced the memory of the new change going on in his life, which had its beginning in this room. Some of the physical props were remembered: the smell of leather covering each luxurious chair; the large conference table that glistened with a surface almost reflecting one's image; the exquisite paintings creating an atmosphere of elegance. All these were part of a sensory support system that gave life to the memory of finding a surviving relative who reached out to him. This room might be cold and formal to some, but for him, it was a portal that opened to a new life.

Michael placed his briefcase on the conference table, then heard the sound of a click. It was the door. No one was expected until later. Turning around, he saw a woman with outstretched arms wanting to be embraced.

"Michael, I've come early to be first to board this special ship on which you're making a maiden voyage. Come and give me the assurance that you're up to this today."

"I'll do more than that; I'll install you permanently as my first mate."

"Does that position come with a special hat?"

"No," said Michael, "it comes with a special ring on our wedding day." Holding Sonje in his arms, he reflected on how this experience went with his history in this room, and that it would serve to crowd out the unwanted painful memories of his past.

Max had security out in full force for the arrival of special attorneys representing an organization known to be Nazi hunters. They had offices established in major countries whose work it was to fight anti-Semitism and expose those guilty of war crimes. They were the sleuths combing through the archives of history ferreting out those who had gone into hiding and used what they found to persuade governments to prosecute them to the full extent of the law. The organization had been contacted by the chairman, and Michael was prepared to lay before them the most extensive and detailed evidence they'd ever seen.

Max had sent a company vehicle to the airport to pick up the lawyers the organization sent to investigate and examine documentary evidence. One of the prerequisites from the chairman was that they would bring along someone fluent in Romanian, a person who could act as translator.

Max met the two lawyers at the entrance, assisted them with signing in at the security office, and led them to the conference room where everyone waited. Hans sat at the head of the table, and on his right were Sonje, Mr. Fine, and Michael. Laid out on the table were photos of Funar, the ones Michael had taken from his home showing him in military dress near open pits of murdered Jews. Alongside these photos were those recently taken by the special-agent photographers. Each Romanian document bearing Funar's signature had stapled to it a German-translated copy.

The conference door opened, and Max led the two lawyers to the table. Everyone noticed the look the two men gave the room as they neared. Hans stood to his feet.

"Gentlemen, we welcome you to Katharina Enterprises. I'm Hans Isler, to my right are Miss Shuster, Mr. Fine, Michael Pencovich, and you've already met Max, our chief of security."

Both men carried a small attaché case, stood at about the same height, but defined themselves quite differently in dress: they bore no resemblance to corporate lawyers. Their work followed trails that took them away from plush offices and opulent lifestyles. Today was different—it defied their normal paradigm: the office was plush and they were among wealth.

"Please be seated," said Hans.

The one with the more rumpled look appeared to be in charge. He spoke first.

"Before we're seated, I'd like to introduce the two of us. To my left is my colleague, Ivan Berkman, and I'm Eugen Tace.

After being seated, the lawyer continued. "Your case was given to us because the person of interest is Romanian and resides in West Germany. I am fluent in Romanian and can speak German but not with the fluency of Ivan. Now that our introductions are over, let us get down to business. Can someone at this table give us an overview of what we're about to review?"

Michael stood to his feet. "We have not spoken to your organization with specifics, as you well know. All you know is that a Romanian is living and working in West Germany who has been identified as a war criminal and that we have photos and documents to support this accusation.

"In front of you on the table are copies of documents I personally took from Colonel Funar's home, our subject under investigation. The originals are secured in storage. Alongside the documents are photos of him standing with his killing squad near the open pits of the dead. Next to these photos are current ones just taken with markings showing the two to be the same person. Translations have been made of the documents for those who don't read Romanian."

After Michael sat, both lawyers turned and looked at each other, giving the message that they'd never been in a meeting like this with the preponderance of documents purporting to be evidence against a war criminal. They were taken aback by the command, control, and confidence the man exuded. Eugen, the lawyer in charge, took half the documents off the top and handed them to his colleague to look over.

On top of the stack of documents in front of the man overseeing the project, was an order from Colonel Funar that would shake his world. An eerie silence blanketed the room as those at the table watched the two experienced investigative lawyers examine the documents. Everyone around the table noticed the startled look that came over the face of the spokesperson. In his hands, he held a document that was riveting him. The judicious, professional in-control-image the man had cast about the room when he arrived, slowly faded as he looked over the document. Those in the room witnessed twitching hands, large sweat beads forming on his brow, and a stalwart-looking frame bending to an outline of fear.

Michael saw more than others that sat with him at the table. The document the man held in front of him was forcing open a door of personal tragedy. Memory carried with it the pleasantries of the human experience but could be a cruel nemesis to the soul. That enemy had emerged from the dark underworld, awakened by the tangible evidence the lawyer held in his hands.

Everyone watched the man close his eyes like he was honoring something from his past. Tears showing pain he couldn't hide forced from his lips words spoken in soliloquy.

"I lost my family because of this order I hold in my hands. Three thousand Jews were ordered to be taken by train to labor camps. My mother, father, sister, and I were all forced into one of the boxcars along with others with standing room only, and for three days we were locked in a death chamber without food or water, some even drinking their own urine. Ninety percent of the people inside that car died by the time the steel door was opened at the camp. I was the only survivor of my family."

The man stood to his feet, looked over at Max now seated alongside Michael. "Max, show me the men's room."

No one at the conference table spoke until the door shut. Ivan sat stunned. He reached for the document Eugen had been reading giving the order for the transfer of three-thousand Jews to labor camps.

Hans said to Ivan, "I can see this is very difficult, we'll take a break and return in thirty minutes."

Sonje saw that Michael was doing well and chose to return to her office for work that demanded her attention. The others picked up Max in the hall and all four walked together without speaking to the empty coffee shop where they ordered coffee. No one said anything until Herman Fine took a folded paper from his vest pocket. "I know they'll be asking for this, so I came prepared. This is a single-page description on how Funar's identity became known to me in my shop. I leave it with you, Michael." Michael took the paper, and silence continued to hang over the group.

When they returned to the conference room, they found both men going through the photos and documents. After everyone sat, Eugen addressed the group.

"Never in my experience have I seen so much solid evidence to indict a war criminal. The recent photos are dead ringers. They prove without a doubt that the two men are the same.

"The country of West Germany was a perfect place for a Romanian war criminal to change his identity and go undetected. Romanian Holocaust deaths exceeded all European countries, except Nazi Germany, and they managed to keep it covered up with only a few being brought to trial. In the post-war years, the courts in Western Europe sought mostly German Nazi war criminals, and for this man from Romania to be exposed with this documentation is a miracle.

"Now, I have a question for you, Michael. How did it come about that you found this treasure trove inside the home of our subject?"

Max sat on the right side of Michael, the others to his left. No one looked at him when he answered.

"In our attempt to locate Funar, his estate had been under my surveillance for several days. It was at the time of the war when the Americans were making bombing raids in the region, and he never came around. Then one night, everyone in the home carried boxes to waiting vehicles and vacated the premises. That's when we entered the home and found the originals packed in boxes."

"So you have the originals of these copies here on the table?"

"Yes, and a great deal more. We just brought the weightier ones."

"Come court time, we'll need the originals. By the way, Michael, what was your motive in trailing the subject?"

"He was to be executed."

"You mean assassinated?"

"No, I mean executed! Four men raped the girl I was going to marry, causing her to commit suicide. I had already executed three, and Funar was the last, but he slipped into hiding."

"I'm sorry you didn't find the subject at home that night. The world would've been better off."

"But the world would never come to know what it's going to know when this trial is over," said Michael.

The man's eyes fell back on the stack of documents in front of him on the table, then darted back at Michael.

"You're telling me this...and I'm the one who's supposed to be the lawyer! Sometimes the light of Western jurisprudence dims when you experience personal tragedy. The idealism of our justice system is reserved only for those who can see the future. Michael, were you ever tempted to take this person out like the others after you found out who he was?"

Those who knew Michael were apprised of his quick-witted response in conversation, and when he paused to answer the question posed to him, they paid special attention.

"Yes, it entered my mind, and I struggled with it. But God has changed me, and I now live for Him and the special lady who has come into my life."

Eugen was almost doing a soliloquy again, looking off into space, his face smothered with pain remembering the horrors of the death train where his family perished.

Speaking to no one, he said aloud, "Not everyone who has been through the Holocaust can make that step of finding God after what's happened to the Jews, the people who are supposed to be God's Chosen-Ones."

"Eugen, you and I need to have a long talk. I once asked the same question, and a wise person told me that we only lost a major battle, but we'll win the war because the Messiah is coming to live among us."

Hans, having overheard the conversation, closed his eyes and thanked God for the miracle of a changed life.

"What you've given us, Michael, is enough evidence to lay the groundwork for the authorities to act. When everything reaches the indictment point, we'll pick up the rest of what you have in storage. These matters sometimes have political overtones, and because this man is an imported Nazi war criminal, events could move fast."

Michael put everything he had laid out on the table back in his case, including the single page Herman Fine had given him detailing how Funar's identity became known, then handed it to Eugen.

"The decision to give these to you absolves me of the heavy responsibility they carry, and having done so, I will become a better person."

The man knew what Michael said carried a cryptic message. His statement held hidden meaning, a personal history that was part of the man's complex, mysterious past.

The lawyer took the case, looked away, gave a deep sigh, and reflected on how life had made Michael what he was. With a tinge of regret, he said, "Perhaps, had I been more like you, Michael, if I'd resisted like you resisted, I would have something to offer to make me a better person. Your noble acts of resistance for a just cause are measured by what I will carry from this room."

"And you, Sir," said Michael, "will show nobility every time you shine light on the dark shadows of evil. Perhaps that's why God doesn't take those dark memories from us. He wants us to be reminded that light is the only cure."

"You have well-spoken, Michael. You carry a mystery inside that compels others to want to know what it is. We must get together sometime and share common experiences."

The man turned and faced the group at the table. "Now, for my final word. Each of us today will swear to an oath of silence. You'll hear from me when the government takes action on these documents, so until then we'll hope for the best. Before we leave, I have further final remarks to make.

"We must know the game plan. After the court acts upon this evidence, anyone connected with this case, and this includes each of you in this room, will avoid talking to anyone about it and must never give an interview or talk to a reporter. When this reaches the press, it will be the biggest news event of the decade, and only after the trial will you be free to speak your mind.

"I can see your security is already at a high level here around your plant, which is good, but if the media find out that this trial came about because of this company, or someone connected to it, it will attract those who have a history of terrorism. We have a big fish on our line, and we don't want it to get away."

"Before you leave," said the chairman, "we want to thank both of you for coming, and if we can give further help, let us know. Max will give you an envelope to cover your initial expense in this mission, and future payments will be made to your central office. Katharina Enterprises already supports your organization and payments going to your efforts in this endeavor will be above what we already contribute."

Everyone watched Max escort the two from the conference room, and when Michael heard the click of the door closing, it reminded him that another session had been conducted in this room, but it wasn't about money, stocks, and dividends. It was all about justice in a free society that held people responsible for acts of genocide.

Chapter 31

Reports

Hans was back in the air on his way to Brussels for a quarterly meeting with people of wealth who had pledged support to Israel for the coming Messiah. The Consortium his adoptive mother founded had elected him to its chairmanship. Of the fifteen members, he was the youngest and the only one who was born of a Jewish mother. The members considered it their calling to use wealth to support Israeli nationalism, that geography and a people were required to be in place for the Messiah to return.

Today, Hans had brought Michael to give a report on the Prince Henry operation that was moving ahead of schedule because of his efforts. Combined with his report, would be a filmstrip presentation showing immigrants now living in new housing units.

When the plane taxied in and parked, a company car and driver were waiting for them. The driver had opened the door, and his passengers were about to enter the vehicle when they saw Fritz coming from the plane carrying a folder.

"Michael, this just came in from your secretary."

It was a coded message from Bub and Moshe. Michael quickly read the message to himself.

"Fritz, teletype Birdie and tell her to send Bub and Moshe the message that I'm working on the matter and I'll call them later today."

"I'll get right on it."

When the driver pulled out, Michael closed the window separating the front seat from the back, held the message in his hands. "This is a coded letter from Bub and Moshe, who are telling me that in a couple of days they'll be picking up three scientists from Odessa, an area further north of the coastal shores of Romania. They are important to Israel's research, and once picked up, should be moved to another freighter further out to sea away from the coastline.

"How will you do this?" asked Hans.

"We carry speedboats hidden inside the ship that can be launched for these emergency situations. Normal people have no high alerts put on them when they go missing, but scientists are watched closely, which requires immediate removal from the area. When the speedboat reaches the distant freighter and the transfer is made, it is taken on board and stored out of sight."

"And this problem will be solved in what way?" asked Hans.

"We'll do it by moving one of our freighters in the Black Sea within a hundred miles of the pick-up ship. We have two days to get a ship in place, and on our return flight, I'll get on the radio and set everything up for that event. A freighter can travel up to six-hundred miles in a twenty-four hour period leaving the ship plenty of time to settle in for the transfer."

Hans was amazed at Michael's control of every movement going on in the Black Sea. His management of details on the wide-open seas was learned from his experience of surviving in the wild during the war. His grasp of seeing the whole with all the integral parts made him a very unusual person.

"How do you do it, Michael? It is amazing what you've done with this project on the Black Sea. It's put together like a Swiss watch."

"It was my years of living from day-to-day, moment-by-moment in the mountains during the war. Under those conditions, one learned his environment inside-and-out…your life and others depended on it. It was a microcosm of the bigger state I now live in, and though I am a reader, I couldn't have learned it in books, or in a classroom. It was the American philosopher, John Dewey, who said, 'One learns best by doing.' The principles one learns in the darkest of times are what makes the paths straight in the light of day."

"Now you're becoming the philosopher," said Michael.

"Not a philosopher, Jacob but a complete person. My regeneration is like the life coming from two conjoined opposite cells. I was one cell, opposite and far from God, but he joined Himself to me making what was dead inside alive. I have been birthed into a living organism with a growth pattern determined by transcendent DNA."

Hans had been fascinated with Michael's management of the Prince Henry operation on the Black Sea. Now, he was left speechless by his insightful understanding of Messianic rule over the human heart.

———————————————

The vehicle carrying Michael and Hans turned onto the property of an old, empty, metal warehouse building on the industrial side of Brussels. The driver drove through a large rolled-up metal door and parked alongside the vehicles that had carried other members of the Consortium to the site. Stationed near the entrance were two security people waiting for the signal to close the large metal door and secure the area. Members of the Consortium had already arrived and were waiting inside a non-descript room located over three small offices.

Before getting out, Hans turned to Michael, saying, "Max arranges the security coverage for these events."

"That's his specialty! He's to be commended. By the way, big Max is taken to my secretary, Birdie."

By this time, the driver had opened the door for his passengers, and upon the news of Max and Birdie, Hans froze while the driver continued to stand alongside the open door.

Response was slow coming, much like Sonje when Michael released the news to her. He processed what he heard with a slight chuckle, then a hearty laugh erupted, followed with the statement, "I hope I can focus on our meeting in there today—you've thrown me a curve."

Both saw the large, steel, roll-up door close, sending cold, hollow, reverberating sounds of clanging and grinding throughout the old structure. *The building spoke of a picture Hans had seen in lives of patients when he worked as a doctor: the emptier a life was inside, the louder the clanging and grinding. Had this building been packed with goods and merchandise, the closing of the door would go unheard.*

The two walked toward a two-story office on one side of the interior that at one time bustled with employees and truck drivers coming and going. Creaky and un-swept wooden stairs led them up an old staircase where two security men stood on a platform bordered by a wooden oak rail encrusted with grime, nicks, and dirt. It told the story of the kinds of hands that touched the rail through the years. When Michael took hold of the wooden rail and touched its ugly surface, he knew that underneath beauty existed as it did when it was first installed and that a skilled cabinetmaker could remove the years of dirt, grime, nicks, and restore it with a look of newness. That's what God did to him, and he had to be brought to a place like this to see its truth. *It was a picture of his life. The beauty of his soul and spirit that God created in His image had become soiled by the touch and handling of this world, and the great Cabinetmaker was at work in his life restoring what had been damaged.*

One of the security guards opened the door and Michael followed Hans into a room where fifteen men were standing, clustered in groups, talking. When they saw Hans, the room became silent, and each member politely greeted both of them with a handshake.

Michael thought the scene was the height of irony: wealthy men who lived in luxury meeting in an old warehouse in the worst of blighted conditions. Yet, they were doing what he had learned during his days of survival during the war—using tactics to confuse the enemy. Rich men didn't go to these kinds of neighborhoods, but it was a venue of security for those who supported biblical Zionism.

Hans called the meeting to order and after the secretary read the minutes of the previous meeting, the treasurer gave an extensive report on the vast outlay of funds going to different groups and agencies that supported Israel.

It was Hans' intent that the members of the Consortium not know that Michael was related to him. This would give him the credit he deserved and wouldn't appear to be contrived because of family connections.

"Friends, we are honored to have with us today a person who came onboard to direct our Prince Henry operation. The executive committee has been kept informed of its progress, and today, the whole body of our Consortium will get a first-hand account by the person who has made it a success. Michael Pencovich came to us as a bona fide sea captain having sailed ships around the world. He alone was responsible for developing a highly sophisticated operation of moving Jews from countries that don't permit emigration. I will let him give the current status and success of this mission."

When Michael completed his report and filmstrip presentation, the group was in awe. Upon seeing the pictures of those who braved the hazardous waters to reach the ships in makeshift boats, and the new housing units going up in Israel, moved some of the Consortium members to tears.

Before the meeting was officially closed, Hans had Michael give a Scripture reading. He read Isaiah fifty-three and closed the book, saying, "Of all the Scriptures in the Bible, God used these to show me the truth of the Jewish Passover." Then Michael remembered the grimy, top rail on the staircase just outside the room where he was speaking.

On board the return flight, Fritz was having lunch with Hans in the kitchen, and Michael was busy adjusting the movement of ships on the Black Sea. Unknown to others, Michael was teaching Sonje a secret code known only by Moshe and Bub. After tweaking the schedules of a couple of freighters, he sent Sonje a message in code: *Love, tonight I want to take you out to the restaurant where we went on our first date, but I leave it with you to decide where we spend our honeymoon.*

Before the plane landed in Munich, Fritz gave Michael a message that came in over the teletype. He knew its source, and that only he would understand the contents: *Across the table tonight, I'll hold your hand longer than I did that first night, and where we spend our honeymoon will be in Israel where we walked the beach barefoot, and you held me in your arms and proposed marriage.*

Chapter 32

The Witnesses

Herman Fine sat in the business-class section of a jumbo jet welcoming the high-shrill sound and jostling movements coming from the plane's struggle to get airborne for its flight to Munich. He needed something external of himself to compete with the morbid thoughts racing through his mind. He had been on a mission in Israel searching for survivors who'd been victims of a Holocaust war criminal, found them, and recorded their stories on tape. Though locked in a sealed case and stored overhead where carry-on luggage was kept, he could still hear their stories ringing like clarion calls, voices pounding inside his head, voices that carried names with faces marked by pain. He had visited their homes, seen photos of vanished family members who'd been whisked off to their deaths, leaving only bitter memories as a memorial where they knelt to place flowers of love.

When the aircraft was airborne, the man pushed his seat back, placed his head on a clean pillow provided by the flight attendant. His eyes couldn't escape the view of the overhead compartment where he had stored tape recordings and photos of survivors he'd interviewed in Israel. When he accepted the assignment of finding witnesses who would be willing to give testimony against a Holocaust war criminal in court, he wasn't aware of the emotional trauma that would accompany his efforts. He was in the throes of a personal labyrinth trying to keep himself afloat as part of a construction crew in building a legal stage to prosecute someone guilty of genocide.

He needed the strength of a Michael Pencovich. Some people were strong, while others were willing—Michael was both. He knew he didn't lack the will, else he wouldn't be where he was, but it would take more than willingness. What he was and what he would become were in the crucible. He was being measured in a cloud of mystery. Some would call it fate, others would use the term Providence. He preferred the latter.

He had been chosen for two major events in life. One had already happened when he escaped the death camp and was found and protected by the Man in white. The second event was when he became the central figure in identifying an infamous war criminal. He now carried the burden of bringing to life voices of the past, each telling the gut-wrenching story of horrors suffered because of a man who now lived incognito in a country that gave rise to Nazism. Herman Fine was chosen to be thrust into the center of what would become a global stage, selected when the law of mathematical probability was overruled. What were the chances of a Nazi war criminal using the services of a Holocaust survivor to repair jewelry he'd taken from Jews twenty-five years earlier? The odds were infinitesimal. The law of probability reached even further contravention—the owner of the shop where the Nazi brought the jewelry for repair had stood in line with hundreds of Jews watching him give orders on who would die and who would be sent to forced labor camps.

Herman's eyes went from the overhead storage bin to his feet where he'd placed a briefcase that held photographs of the man responsible for killing thousands of women, men, and children. To honor the survivors, he took care to segregate the two sets of photos, the ones belonging to Funar at his feet on the floor, the others in overhead baggage. It was his job to make the overhead photos come to life with real faces showing the pain inflicted upon them by the evil villain confined to the briefcase at his feet.

Herman remembered the time-worn proverb: *a picture was worth a thousand words.* That axiom was iron-clad, a truism, whether on an ancient painting of a cave wall or a glossy, modern-day print. A picture throughout time always spoke a thousand words. It was a fixed law, and the man now trying to compartmentalize his life couldn't escape the burden of his commission—he had to reverse that proverb by making a thousand horrifying words tell the story with one picture. God would have to give him strength to match his willingness.

Calm came over the brave survivor as he closed his eyes and remembered his visits to the homes of the victims he had interviewed in Israel.

The kibbutz Herman Fine's taxi came upon looked like something he'd seen back in West Germany. On the right side of the road were three-hundred Holstein cows lined up for milking outside a barn that operated with the most advanced electronic milking machines on the market. To the left were acres and acres of tower-reaching, green corn lining the private roadway. Then diversity rushed at him with the change of scenery of a hundred acres of pink grapefruit. Herman thought this must have been what the ten spies saw when they were sent out by Moses. Then homes began to appear. In front of him was the hub of what looked like a small village, self-contained with a large central dining center used as a multi-purpose room. Nearby were school buildings and a clinic. What couldn't be missed was a large, raised mound of earth under which was a cement bunker used during turbulent times of conflict. The kibbutz consisted of twelve hundred acres of farmland with manufacturing as part of its enterprise. It was here that Herman Fine met and interviewed Fane Tarbarta, a Romanian Holocaust survivor. He was the manager of the small plastics factory on site.

The taxi pulled into a parking place near a sign attached to a building marked, office. Privately owned vehicles were sparse because of the availability of public bus transportation and Kibbutz vans.

Herman opened the door and saw that everything carried the look of a typical office. Two ladies seated at desks in front of him were engaged in paperwork in an open front room, and behind was a private office. When they saw Herman, one of them addressed him without getting up.

"May we help you, Sir?"

"Yes, I am here to see Mr. Tarbarta."

The lady was dressed in a typical informal manner and was perfunctory in response. She stood up, went to the office door behind her, and without knocking opened the door, saying to someone inside, "A gentleman is here to see you," then returned to her desk and continued her work. Immediately, a man from inside appeared in the doorway. He was tall, probably forty-five years of age and carried a stoic, smooth, rugged face. His hair was dark, full, and coarse. The demeanor on his face showed a dread of what he had been called upon to do. He was first to speak while still standing in the doorway.

"And you are Mr. Fine?"

"Yes," answered the visitor.

The man moved toward the front where Herman was still standing, stopped, looked at the two women. "I don't want to be disturbed at home today for any reason."

They hardly looked at him as he moved toward the visitor with an outstretched hand to welcome him.

"Welcome to Israel, Mr. Fine! We'll go to my residence to discuss the matter you broached me about."

After leaving the office, the man continued speaking as they walked along.

"Here on the kibbutz, everyone works at some kind of job. My wife teaches in our school, and except for the highly technical positions, people are moved around to different posts so different skills are learned."

Conversation between the two men seemed to be a way of putting off the inevitable. It was like someone with claustrophobia being pushed into an MRI machine whose past experience didn't go well, a time when more concern was over entering the chamber than what the outcome might be. The story to be told and recorded was the dreaded, tight chamber the man would put himself in, reliving that narrow space of time when unbelievable horror happened. However, the difference between an actual MRI experience and the kind he would be putting himself through today was that he already knew the test results.

Fane Tarbarta had been chosen to be interviewed because he was a survivor of a massacre ordered by Colonel Funar. Quietness punctuated the atmosphere when they entered the man's front room. Photos usually kept in another room had been brought out and placed in plain view. He had prepared himself for the event.

"As I discussed with you on the phone," said Herman, "it's necessary for me to record our conversation so the legal team will have something to work with in laying out the approach they take."

"I have no problem with that."

The man saw his guest take from his briefcase a tape recorder and a packet containing several photos. After turning on the recorder, he took out several pictures of Colonel Funar showing him in army uniform, handed them to Mr. Tarbarta, saying, "Do you recognize the person in these photos?"

Saying nothing, he looked at each one slowly, then went through the group again. No answer was forthcoming. His eyes turned to one of the family photos he'd placed in the front room and proceeded to engage in a quasi-soliloquy.

"My grandfather migrated from Russia to northern Romania in the late nineteenth century because of pogroms against the Jews. He was among thousands who fled to the region of northern Romania. Systemic anti-Semitism in Romania grew, and certain people used it for political and material gain. Jews have survived under the best and worst of times throughout the centuries, and when Nazism gained control under Hitler, it became the worst of times on an unbelievable scale.

"The army and gendarmes went through towns, villages, and rural country-sides collecting Jewish men, women, and children. All were marched to holding centers, some destined for labor camps, others for mass slaughter. I was eighteen years old at the time and was at my friend's home when the soldiers came through and herded us out with hundreds of others. I wondered where my mother, father, and sister were. I wanted to be with them but was forced at gunpoint to march wherever they were taking us. Snarling dogs and the butts of rifles were used to push and beat the masses along until we ended up in a large police courtyard enclosed with a seven-foot wall. I was standing with my friend. Death and fear were written on the faces of his family, and I wondered about my own—where were they? Could they be among the thousands being herded and compacted together like animals inside this walled courtyard? Fright tormented weeping mothers holding crying children. Thousands were forced together and others kept coming, all were Jews.

"For eight hours we were in the hot sun without food or water. Little children were in agony, mothers begging for water for the little ones while the gendarmes and soldiers walked the perimeter driving them back with clubs and dogs."

The man telling his story stopped talking, glared at the colonel's photos he still held in his hands, a glare that told a story in itself. Then looking away like he was seeing the event in real time, said, "There was an army truck near where I stood with an officer standing up in the back scanning the people with field glasses, selecting certain young women to be separated from the group and taken to a building outside the enclosed compound. I knew one of the girls, she was about my age."

Then turning and looking at Herman with his face showing the agony of his personal pain of history, he continued. "Soldiers and dogs moved the masses away from the truck as it drove outside the compound. Once outside, hidden machine guns were uncovered and the officer who was still standing in the truck gave the order for the slaughter to begin.

"Bullets were zinging all around me. Children were screaming, bodies lay on the open ground, some still alive moaning with pain. Those still standing were falling everywhere. I lost sight of my friend and his family. Hell had opened its mouth and its evil was measured by the glee on the executioners' faces.

"My only hope was to scale the wall. Others had the same idea and had fallen dead, only to have others behind them experience the same fate. Bodies at the base of the wall were stacked three and four high in places, and being a good athlete, I knew if my footing were correctly placed on top of the dead, I could quickly clear the wall. My eyes scanned the closest gunner, and a miracle happened in front of me. A brave man in his wounded state wrestled from a guard his weapon, turned it on other Nazi soldiers nearby. It was my chance. I stood up, ran toward the wall, and leaped to my freedom. After landing on the other side, others quickly followed. From where I was outside the wall, I could see scores streaming through the front entrance, some barely able to walk, others running at full gait. The officer in charge who had given the order to open fire was still standing in the back of the army truck and was now firing his sidearm weapon at those running out the only exit. I knew unplanned chaos was going on inside, and was later told that several brave men had taken the weapons of killed soldiers and used them briefly against the Nazis.

"My hands and clothes were covered with blood and I was in need of a place to hide until dark. Nearby, was a large army truck that I crawled under and found a cavity on its underside where I remained until dark."

The man's eyes, frozen to a time in history, turned toward the pictures of his family. A Long silence hung in the air—the kind that could be cut with a knife. Herman Fine said nothing. He was an audience of one measuring how this survivor's compelling story would move the world.

Without looking at Herman, the man who had bared his soul spoke words that carried finality. "Mr. Fine, over three thousand Jews died that day, and included among them were my mother, father, and sister."

With photos still in his hands and eyes riveted with a laser stare, he gave closure to the dark passage he'd made. "The man who stood in the back of that army truck and gave the order to kill the Jews in that courtyard was Colonel Funar, the person in these photos I hold. Today, I go on record that I will make myself available to be a witness in any court of law to see that justice is done to a modern-day Haman."

The man aboard the commercial flight to Munich had dropped off to sleep and was awakened by air turbulence. He found that rest helped sort out troubling issues.

The voices coming from those he interviewed were quieter. He was going through a growth experience. He had been a Holocaust survivor himself, and until now, everything had been measured in terms of his own experience. He must allow the creative part of his psyche to bend to the will of his mission. To deal with all the horror and pain, he would use the coping mechanism of compartmentalizing everything—file it away inside so the good, the bad, and the ugly would surface independently. However, this would be problematic. There was little good to be found.

He remembered the others he'd interviewed, those who suffered two kinds of pain: the pain of memory and the pain of the experience. He recalled the elderly, elegant-looking lady who carried a warm smile when she opened the door for his interview appointment at her flat in Tel Aviv. After switching on the recorder, he heard her description of the conditions in the forced-labor camp where the sick and those who moved too slow were shot.

Then there was the horrifying eyewitness account of Ionel Abaza, who was sixteen years of age, was separated from his family in a forced march with hundreds of other Jews to a region set up as a site for mass genocide. When the section of his column reached the forest, he bolted. *With rifles firing, he kept running and when reaching heavy growth, gunshots went unheard.* Now he was free, but he didn't know the extent of that freedom until early the next morning when he heard incessant gunfire. When he crawled to the edge of the forest, he saw rows and rows of freshly dug deep ditches.

It was a killing field. The Romanian killing squads had become more efficient. He saw soldiers take ten victims at a time, line them up at the edge of the pit where they were shot, followed by another group of ten. This went on the whole day. He knew he couldn't hide or stay in the area. Nights became his friend, and under the evening glow of overhead stars, he managed to reach a region where he found relatives in hiding.

Herman Fine, the man on a mission seeking stories of Holocaust survivors that would move people in a court of law, now found himself making a personal journey on his return flight to Munich. He was a survivor of the Holocaust, and up to this point, the Holocaust was about his experience. However, walking with others through their dark chasms of evil made him a different person: the Holocaust wasn't about him alone—it was about six-million other Jews.

For Herman Fine, Romania was but a memory of a trail of tears. Perhaps his work in collecting some of those voices will serve to bring guilty verdicts in a court of law.

Chapter 33

The Arraignment

It was Saturday morning and Michael was at home at the Reznik compound waiting f or Sonje to arrive to spend the day with him when his phone rang.

"Hello, Michael, this is Max. Something big is going down. My man who has Funar under surveillance just got off the phone with me and says authorities have picked him up and taken him downtown to the police station. It appears your efforts in providing all those documents with the photos are bringing results."

"Where was the subject when they took him in?"

"Three plainclothesmen were at his front door this morning at eight o'clock, loaded him up in the rear seat of an unmarked vehicle and drove him straight to central headquarters.

"Do you want to report this to the chairman or do you wish me to do so?"

"That's your call, Max. You did the work and it falls under your purview. I'll touch base with Jacob later. You may want to call Mr. Reznik and Herman Fine and keep them abreast of this development. Both have put time and effort into this project."

"I might also add," said Max, "that it appeared they had a search warrant and called in another team who went through the house and carried out several boxes that may contain jewelry from the war years."

"It looks like the Nazi hunters, Ivan and Eugen, are working closely with the authorities," responded Michael. "It would be the height of poetic justice if what they carried from the home included the ring Funar took to Herman's shop to be re-sized."

"I'm sure Mr. Fine will soon know," replied Max. "For your information, Funar had a common-law wife who lived with him, and whether she knew anything about his background, it remains to be seen."

"At this point," added Michael, "Funar will declare innocence with a high level of confidence, but when the evidence we took from his home is presented, he'll have to be put under a twenty-four-hour suicide watch. He must be kept alive for the world to see the evil that happened in Romania during the war. It will be a trial on a world stage showing the guilt of two entities, one being the man, the other, the country itself."

Max wondered how it was possible that the man he was talking with could have the record of executions he was purported to have in his old life. However, he was in no position to judge a person who lived where laws that existed were created for his people's destruction. The man had no judicial recourse, no protection under the law. Two things had changed his life: he had come into God's court of forgiveness through His Son, the Messiah, and was now finding a new life with a woman who never looked at a man seriously until Michael. *Max was smitten with an aura of guilt. He had been in war, a combatant, killed those who were not guilty of war crimes. Perhaps he carried more guilt than Michael, the Avenger. Each bore his own pain in his own way, and God gave grace and forgiveness accordingly.*

Max quickly came back to the conversation at hand. "Michael, allow me to address a subject that portends to a negative aspect of this trial. With reference to a suicide watch, some may try to slip him a rope, or a deadly, quick-acting pill to expedite this. Others may want personal revenge."

"I leave that part of it with you, Max. It's interesting how a case of this notoriety had its beginnings with just one small ring. It reminds me of the Scripture I recently read in Zechariah, "Who dares to despise the day of small things."

When Max hung up the phone, he kept hearing Michael's words about small things. *Was this his own conscience speaking or just well-placed words from Michael to remind him he needed shorter arms to touch people up close? Reducing the length of his arms to build close relationships was a high bar for him, and it would be a slow, painful process.*

Sonje sat in front of her bedroom mirror applying makeup. She was filled with excitement. All week long she had looked forward to this day, a day that would be spent with the man she would live with the rest of her life. She had everything a woman would want, but now it meant nothing. She had entered a great awakening, something she'd never seen before. Sermons had come her way, and materials had passed her eyes, all bearing the theme of Christ and the church, His espoused. But the depth of that truth was never realized until Michael entered her life. She now saw that the union of marriage was a picture of another order of transcendent love.

Before Michael came into her life, she needed wealth and material things to satisfy the demands of her ego. Now, her newfound love had assuaged those desires. She could walk away from it all, as long as Michael was at the center of her life. The painful memory of her abuse in the concentration camp had faded because of his acceptance of her as a complete, chaste woman. *The preponderance of biblical truth came to her: Jesus did the same when He made her a complete person through His death and resurrection. She had crossed a threshold into a room filled with the light of another world, another dimension, and having experienced this enlightenment, her union in marriage would have greater meaning.*

Chapter 34

Wedding Bells

Sonje had assigned to Sheena the responsibility of organizing and directing her upcoming wedding. The picture it would carry had already been determined: it would be a small wedding attended only by close friends and family and performed by a Messianic Rabbi. However, for public consumption outside the inner circle of those in attendance of the wedding, Sheena had hired a publicist who would promote the story of Sonje's rise to success after having suffered in a concentration camp because of hiding a Jewish family from the Gestapo. The hired publicist would be circumspect in showing the triumphant success of a woman in a man's world of business and finance. Sonje approved of the concept providing Michael concurred.

The intent of promoting the public image was to get ahead of the curve, thwarting social muckrakers' efforts to sensationalize and tarnish the reputation of someone known to be part of an international corporation that supported Israel. Underground Nazis always had tentacles reaching into areas they could influence. They had learned propaganda shaping well under Goebbels and it continued with Nazi sympathizers.

Sheena arranged, with Sonje's approval, professionals to do all the invitations, food catering, and promotion. Bub and Moshe would arrive two days before the wedding date and stay as guests of the Rizniks. Though only family and friends would be invited to the wedding ceremony, a large community center would be used to celebrate the event afterward with a full-course dinner and the formal cake-cutting exercise. Unlike most wedding celebrations, the bride and groom would appear only briefly for the traditional cake cutting exercise before departure to an unknown honeymoon location.

The wedding day for Michael and Sonje came without great fanfare. Both parties had handlers arranging the details of the event, a professional team under Sheena's supervision. Michael gave his spiritual father, Mr. Reznik, the task of structuring the formal ceremony. The traditional Jewish Kiddushin marriage rite would be assigned to the old man's Messianic Rabbi at the shul, but he would be responsible for opening the formal ceremony by reading Scripture and addressing the guests on the theme of marriage.

The day of the grand event came and Herman Fine and his wife pulled into the shul parking lot already packed with vehicles. He saw big Max with his shiny baldhead talking to several of his security people stationed around the area. Herman and his wife had been given personal invitations by Michael, and his wife had joined him knowing that a crowd of people would hide her lack of social skills. After parking, Herman saw increased anxiety in his wife.

"Are you up to this, dear?"

"I'll be fine as long as I'm in a crowd...you will see to that, won't you, love?"

"I'll do my best."

They were still in the car when Herman saw his wife's eyes look down at her nervous hands, then they turned toward him.

"My husband has been placed in the limelight with important people because of the ring incident at his shop and has become part of the cast on a public stage. When the curtain rises for the next act, he will have a leading role. Though I don't want the notoriety, I'm in support of you, regardless of how it turns out. God will give us strength, and perhaps I will grow from it—my, how proud I am of you!"

"My dear, let's go inside and watch an event that will cheer us up and give us a sense of what life should be about."

Standing at the front door of the shul, a well-dressed security person in a pin-stripe suit stood almost blocking the entrance collecting admission cards sent out with the personal invitations. A wedding attendant ushered the Fines to the middle section of the sanctuary. Mrs. Fine was artistically inclined, and when she saw and heard the small orchestra stationed at one side of the auditorium playing classical love-songs, her anxieties yielded to calm reflections in a musical world that belonged to her.

Big Max was carefully monitoring the site waiting for the arrival of the people he was paid to protect. First on the scene was a large limo carrying the bridegroom and his groomsmen, Bub and Moshe. Max had arranged a canvas-covered walkway that jutted out from the building so that when wedding party members arrived, they could exit the vehicle and enter the building unrecognized.

Next to arrive were the vehicles carrying Hans and Mr. and Mrs. Reznik. The elderly Rezniks were escorted to their reserved seating in the family section at the front of the shul, and Hans waited with the bridegroom and groomsmen in the side room. Everything had been meticulously planned and carried out with one last eventful stroke remaining: the arrival of the beautiful bride. At this point, big Max went inside to join the invited guests.

Seated in the sanctuary, the guests waited patiently and acted like most groups do at a wedding when there is a pause for the main event. On occasions like this, when lips weren't moving and ears weren't listening, the creative, introspective genius of the mind was at its height. Mrs. Fine was one of those caught up with the freedom to wander over twisting trails without restraints. She noticed that women around her were dressed quite ordinary. Her issue was about herself, as was the case with most people who felt uncomfortable about themselves in a given situation. In an effort to compensate for her lack of self-confidence, she had bought special clothing for this occasion, and now her wandering thoughts told her she was overdressed. But the focus on her dress suddenly changed when a large, bald man sat in front of her alongside a woman that appeared to welcome his accompaniment. To her surprise, her husband leaned forward and spoke to him, then turned to her, saying, "That's Max, the chief of security for Katharina Enterprises."

While everyone was becoming restless inside the sanctuary waiting for the main event to happen, outside a large limo with darkened windows was pulling onto the shul's property. Word was passed to Michael, who then proceeded to walk ceremoniously down the center aisle, followed by Moshe and Bub, his groomsmen. After taking their places and leaving a space for Hans who would later stand with them, they were joined by the Rabbi and Mr. Reznik. Hans waited at the side entrance for the bride's arrival.

Anxiety hung over the crowd. The bride would make her debut at any time, and it wasn't proper to turn and look back at her entry until the orchestra gave the signal. The live music now took center stage. The wedding was all about the bride, and those standing up front were of little interest until the arrival of the lady in white.

The limo that held the bride and her wedding party came to a stop under the covered canopy. The driver, dressed for the occasion, opened the rear door, and the first to step out was the matron of honor, the beautiful Sheena. She, in turn, assisted the adorned bride who was covered with a veil, followed by the bridesmaids holding her formal train. Inside, Hans took her arm and the traditional wedding march was underway. At the first sight of the bride, the nine-piece orchestra that had been playing throughout the waiting period announced her arrival with the traditional, resounding, wedding-march song. The guests stood and faced the bride now being escorted down the aisle dressed in her white, flowing, formal gown and train.

Everyone's attention was on the lady in white. The wedding party under the Chuppah saw Han's lips moving, but the guests he passed going down the aisle heard nothing from his whispers.

"Is my beautiful sister nervous?" asked Hans.

"Nervous no, but tense with you talking to me like this."

"Mother always told me I was impertinent at times."

"You were that then and still are by talking to me."

"I can't tell you how pleased I am that you'll be my big sister and aunt at the same time."

"Those words make my wedding day special even though spoken on my way to the altar."

Everyone watched the bride and the one giving her away stop in front of the Rabbi and Mr. Reznik, followed by a brief pause as the bridesmaids took their positions, turned and faced the bride. At Michael's request, adjustments in the traditional Jewish rite had been made to include the old prophet who was his spiritual benefactor. The guests were still standing when the old man opened the ceremony.

"You may be seated," he said to the company of people in the sanctuary.

A solemn quietness blanketed the room. A sudden baritone voice with authority was heard reverberating throughout the auditorium, "Who gives this lady to be married to this man?"

"Her brother, Hans Isler," spoke the man standing at her side.

When Sonje heard those words, a covering of warmth settled over her. Hans moved alongside Michael as his best man while Sonje smiled inside because of his acceptance of her as a sister. In a flash moment, though standing at the altar, she reflected on how her best friend in life would be pleased with the way things had turned out between her and Hans. Michael stepped next to Sonje, took her hand, and faced the old Prophet.

The people in attendance of this special event saw an aged man whose frame had been fitted with a formal suit selected by his fastidious wife. He stood tall and straight, unlike peers of his age and had overpowered his articulate dress by the person he was. His silver hair and face carried markings of wisdom and kindness, arms that hung at his side were like flying buttresses that held up ancient, church-towering walls, though now frail, had embraced people in life leaving them stronger by his touch. The sacred, well-studied book that had been passed down to him by his ancestors was in the firm grip of wrinkled hands that neither shook nor wavered. When he spoke, everyone hung onto every word.

"Friends, today we have gathered here to celebrate an ancient social function that pictures a story that reaches into another world. God was more than a Creator when He made man. He was the first teacher who used the method of show-and-tell. It was the first marriage in Eden that God showed a picture that He would talk about throughout the rest of His sacred writings, and the telling part of that picture continues to be told in the marriage of Michael and Sonje. It speaks of God seeking the creation of a woman for a mystical marriage to His Messianic Son."

The old man opened his Hebrew Bible and read passages from the Song of Solomon, followed by reading them in German. He then closed by looking at the couple, saying, "The picture you're showing us today in becoming one in a marriage union is an object lesson that tells the story of the Messiah joining the human race to become one with His elect."

When the old man finished, he went and sat beside his wife who took his hand with a proud smile on her face. She'd spent a lifetime with a man who'd been faithful and honorable throughout their married lives, one who gave her a beautiful daughter, the sunshine of their lives. The man beside her had today demonstrated a special talent of touching people with a message from God.

The wedding ceremony had followed the request of Sonje: small, only family and friends in attendance. However, she did want the public to see the person she was proud of marrying and agreed to what would follow.

Herman Fine saw Max slip out immediately at the closure of the wedding ceremony. The heavy responsibility of security was at the next big event—the reception. Max rehearsed in his mind what he thought was a nightmare awaiting him. Keeping his army of people organized and on their toes for the reception event was his challenge. The safety of the chairman and his family was utmost. He was reminded of Michael taking him to the woodshed about small details in the photos he was forced to review. The chairman paid him well, and today would prove his worth. It was the biggest public relations event the company had ever planned where so many of the chairman's family would be present.

The weight of security on Max's shoulders required him to know every detail of how the event would go down from the beginning to the end. The late-afternoon format at the reception would be simple. The bride and groom would appear on stage. The chairman would welcome the hundreds of guests and introduce the newly married couple, followed by the traditional cake-cutting. With everyone standing, the orchestra would play the traditional nuptial exit march as they moved between two lines of formally dressed schoolchildren throwing flower petals, followed by the wedding party. Outside, a limo would await their arrival and proceed according to Michael's directions.

Max had security attendants at every door. The same rule enforced at the Shul would be applied at the conference center: admittance permitted only with an approved invitation card.

The building was filling up with people finding their way to large, round, linen-covered tables with pitchers of water and soft drinks. In front of them was a menu with the choice of three main entrees.

Max was at the front of the auditorium watching everything come together as planned. His team of people was carrying out their duties like a well-oiled machine, and the professionals Dr. Sheena used to organize and put together the massive dinner and formalities were performing on schedule. A special section of tables was reserved for those who had attended the ceremony at the Shul and they were now beginning to arrive. The stage was empty except for the orchestra that was performing for the audience. Max knew a fortune had been spent on this event, but whoever was paying for it would never miss it. What he did know was that it didn't come from the bridegroom's pocket. This was where he and Michael had something in common—both had empty pockets.

Like clockwork, everything had come together, and Max stood at the front of the auditorium watching the nuptial couple leave the stage moving in rhythm with the orchestral music, followed by the wedding party. The standing crowd watched the bride and groom move between two lines of beautifully dressed children, kids of families Sonje knew. At one point, everyone saw the bride stop to give a little boy a kiss before moving on with the groom at her side. His parents, standing at a nearby table, knew what it was about—the bride had provided funds for a special surgery so their son could live a normal life.

Max followed behind Moshe and Bub through the large front doors and down the stairs to the front of the building. The bride and groom were standing alongside the limo being hugged and given congratulations and best wishes from all the family members. Max watched the group after the limo drove away: the women were weeping, the men were quiet, and the old prophet had his arms on the shoulders of Bub and Moshe telling them about the Messiah of Isaiah fifty-three. Interrupting it all was the chairman's command, "Let's all get back to the stage. The food servers are waiting to take our orders." Then Max was surprised and almost embarrassed when Hans yelled over to him, "Max, you and Birdie can join us on the stage if you wish!"

Everyone in the wedding party wondered where the newly married couple would spend their honeymoon, and throughout the whole event, the one who had the need to know everyone else's business had held her tongue until they were all settled in at their tables.

"Hans," said Mrs. Reznik, "is it a secret, or can you tell us where the couple is going on their honeymoon?" Everyone stopped what they were doing.

Those farther from the chairman bent their heads forward to listen.

"In thirty minutes, they'll be on the company plane on their way to Israel for a week, then from there they'll take an Israeli cruise ship for a week's cruise on the Mediterranean."

Moshe was sitting near Hans when he took from his pocket a sealed envelope and handed it to the chairman, saying, "Michael asked me to give this to you."

The envelope showed his birth name: Jacob. He opened it immediately. As he read the letter, Sheena saw a face turn paradoxical—an image bearing an infectious smile with tears coursing down his cheeks. He stood to his feet, walked to where she sat and handed her what he'd been reading. "I'll be back shortly," he added.

The wedding party was busy talking, eating, and making comments about the event. Even Max was wielding stories about the paparazzi trying to get in to find a story for their papers. While Hans was away from the table, Sheena read what Michael had left his nephew:

My Dearest Nephew:

There's not enough stationary in the world for me to express what I feel about someone as noble, loving, and caring as you. When we found each other, I was dead, but now I'm alive and joined in a union of marriage with someone I love.

You are my lovely sister's son God chose to save in the Holocaust by the acts of a gracious saint who became your mother. She not only saved you, she saved me through you, and her labor of love in giving continues in others.

Life gives birth to itself and its trail of origin leads back to God.

I will forever be grateful to you for the meaningful life I have today. Upon our return, Sonje and I will resume our efforts in moving Jews to the land of their ancestry. I leave it with you to take any action necessary with the Funar documents that are stored in the vault.

Michael

Soft, warm, velvety breezes were ruffling the hair of a beautiful woman entwined in the arms of a man who was whispering in her ear what she'd heard months before at the same site. The sand beneath their bare feet at the water's edge reminded them of the historic event, a time when they were two, discussing the matter of becoming one. Now, they were reliving that first experience, not as two but one. The man embracing her heard her say, "Emotion that kindles love is like a living healthy organism that grows and shapes itself into many beautiful patterns. It is mysterious and carries life for those who bond with it. Michael, you have made me a complete person, and our marriage is a state of happiness I never dreamed was possible."

Michael never said anything, knowing she had the need to be held and heard. This was their third day of retracing their steps to the exact site where Sonje first heard Michael's marriage proposal.

That evening they went to their favorite beachside restaurant where Michael had reserved an outside table under the vast, starry evening sky, where sounds of swishing waves could be heard from the nearby beach. He was at the front desk requesting their table when Sonje's eyes caught the headline on the front page of a daily newspaper. Michael took her hand and led her to their table, and before they were seated, he asked, "What is bothering my beautiful one?"

"You notice everything, don't you, Michael? You stay here, and I'll be right back!"

Two minutes later, Sonje walked up to Michael who was standing at their table waiting for her to return.

"Michael please sit down." After he sat, Sonje moved behind him placing a newspaper on the table in front of him. It was a widely circulated daily paper showing a full, front-page picture of Colonel Funar in uniform. At the top of the newspaper were the words written in large bold print: *NAZI WAR CRIMINAL ARRESTED IN MUNICH.*

From behind, Sonje leaned over Michael embracing him with both arms, saying, as she nuzzled her face close to his ear, "As we speak, this photo is being seen on front pages of newspapers by millions in the West—all because of you. It must give you a great feeling of satisfaction."

Under nature's theater of dazzling, radiant stars and intermittent sounds of ocean water swirling over ancient sand that numbered Abraham's posterity, Michael took her ring hand with both of his, pulled it to his lips, then melted her heart with the words, "Sonje, you are the dearest and most wonderful person in my life, and no one but you can give me a feeling of satisfaction."

"Michael felt Sonje's arms around him give a tight embrace, followed by the words, "Michael, you are a gem...my beautiful gem."

www.ingramcontent.com/pod-product-compliance
Lightning Source LLC
Chambersburg PA
CBHW071251170626
46809CB00001B/166